MY GRANDPARENTS ARE
SECRET AGENTS

CREATED AND WRITTEN BY SCOTT CHRISTIAN SAVA
WITH ART BY
JUAN SAAVEDRA MOURGUES AND INVASOR CREATIVE ART STUDIO

"In Memory of my Godfather, Nicholas Anthony Trama."

Scott Christian Sava, 2009

www.IDWpublishing.com

ISBN: 978-1-60010-314-8

11 10 09 08   1 2 3 4

Layout by Neil Uyetake • Edited by Justin Eisinger and Amy Betz

Operations: Moshe Berger, Chairman • Ted Adams, Chief Executive Officer • Greg Goldstein, Chief Operating Officer • Matthew Ruzicka, CPA, Chief Financial Officer • Alan Payne, VP of Sales • Lorelei Bunjes, Dir. of Digital Services • Marci Hubbard, Executive Assistant • Alonzo Simon, Shipping Manager • **Editorial:** Chris Ryall, Publisher/Editor-in-Chief • Scott Dunbier, Editor, Special Projects • Andy Schmidt, Senior Editor • Justin Eisinger, Editor • Kris Oprisko, Editor/Foreign Lic. • Denton J. Tipton, Editor • Tom Waltz, Editor • Mariah Huehner, Assistant Editor • **Design:** Robbie Robbins, EVP/Sr. Graphic Artist • Ben Templesmith, Artist/Designer • Neil Uyetake, Art Director • Chris Mowry, Graphic Artist • Amauri Osorio, Graphic Artist

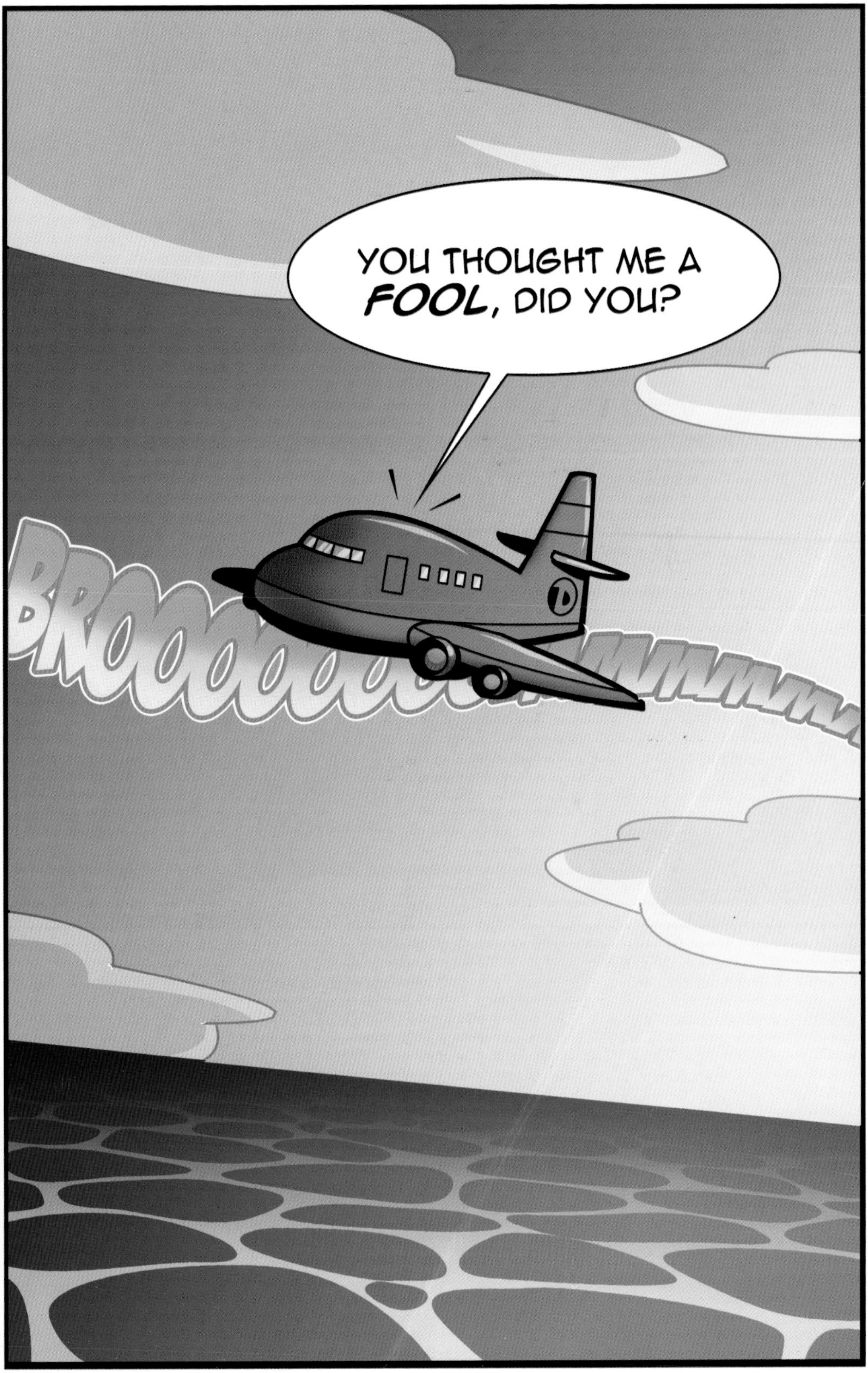
YOU THOUGHT ME A *FOOL*, DID YOU?
BROOOOOOOMMMMMM

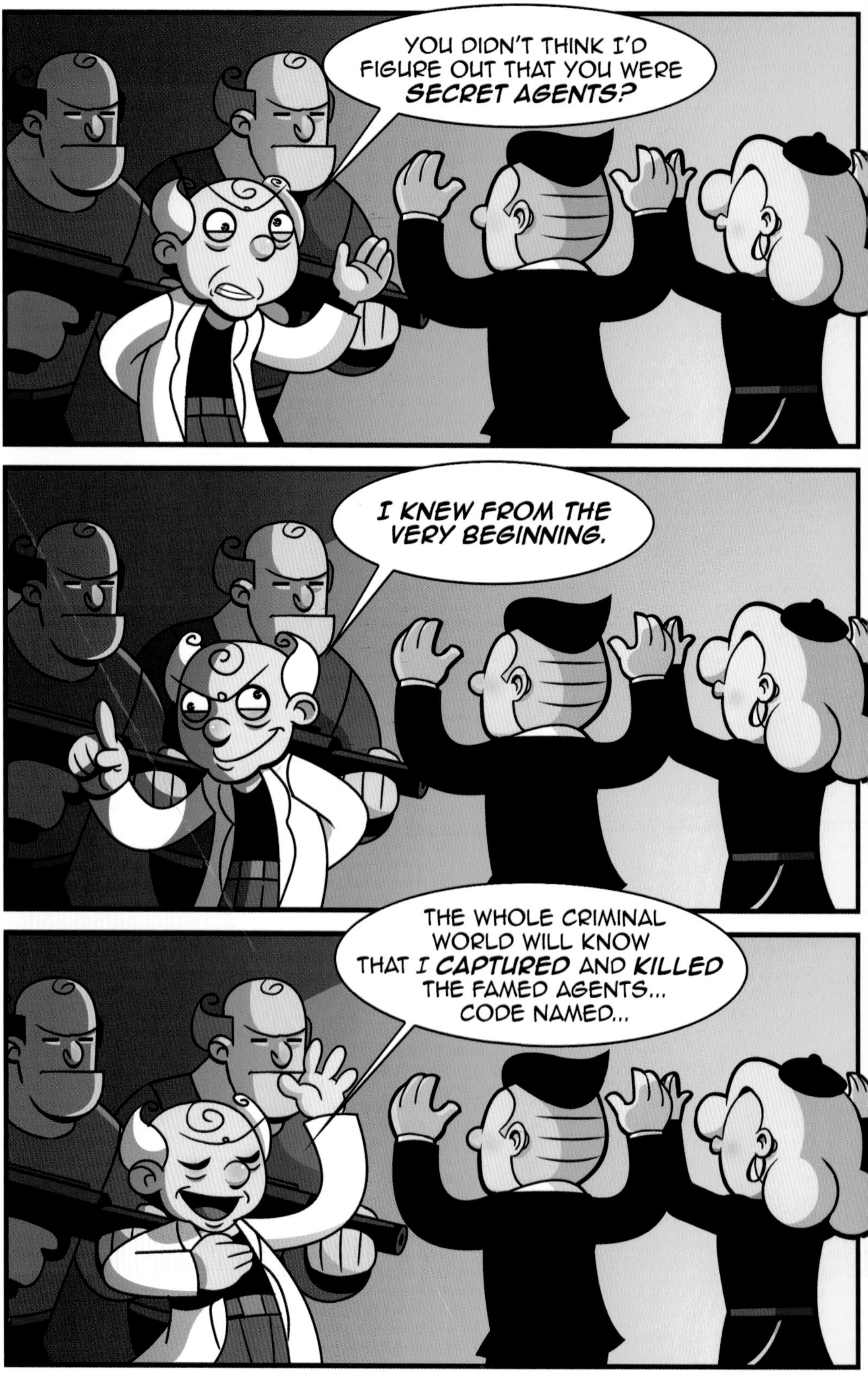
YOU DIDN'T THINK I'D FIGURE OUT THAT YOU WERE *SECRET AGENTS?*
I KNEW FROM THE VERY BEGINNING.
THE WHOLE CRIMINAL WORLD WILL KNOW THAT *I CAPTURED* AND *KILLED* THE FAMED AGENTS... CODE NAMED...

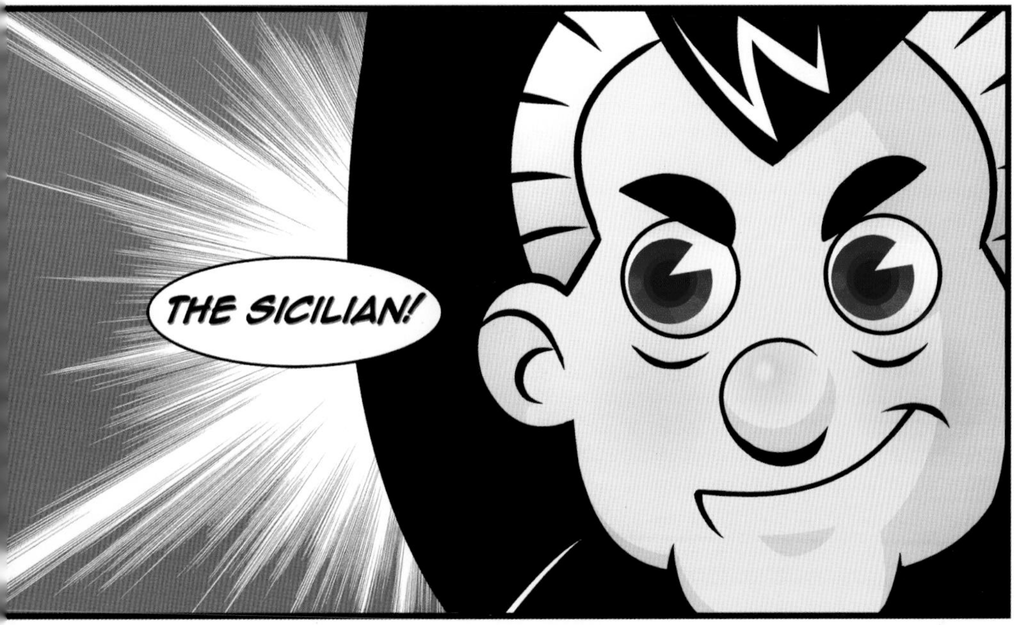
THE SICILIAN!

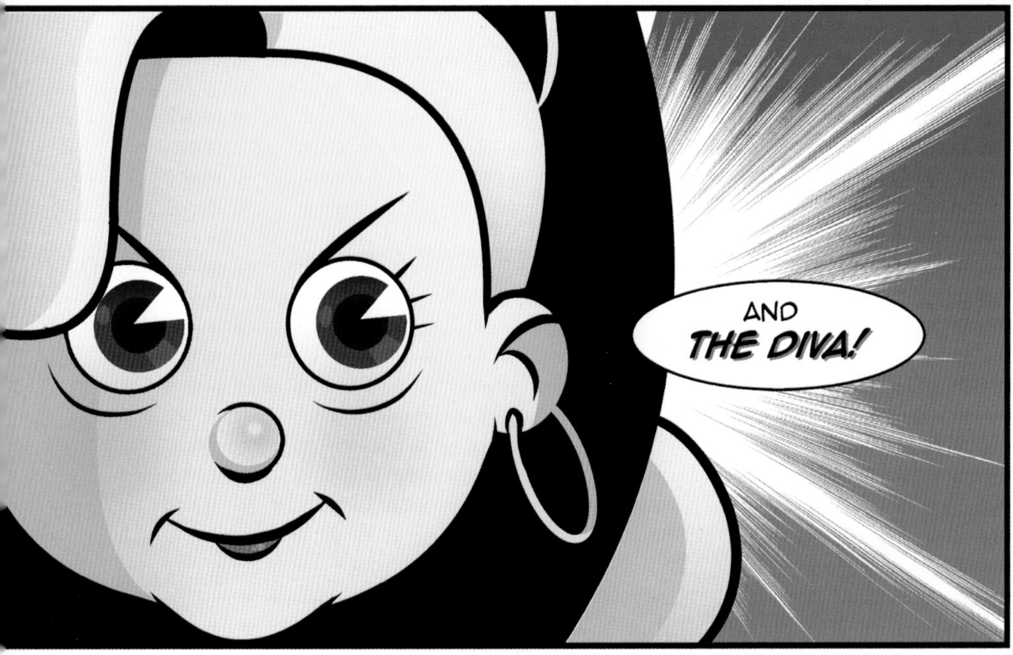
AND
THE DIVA!

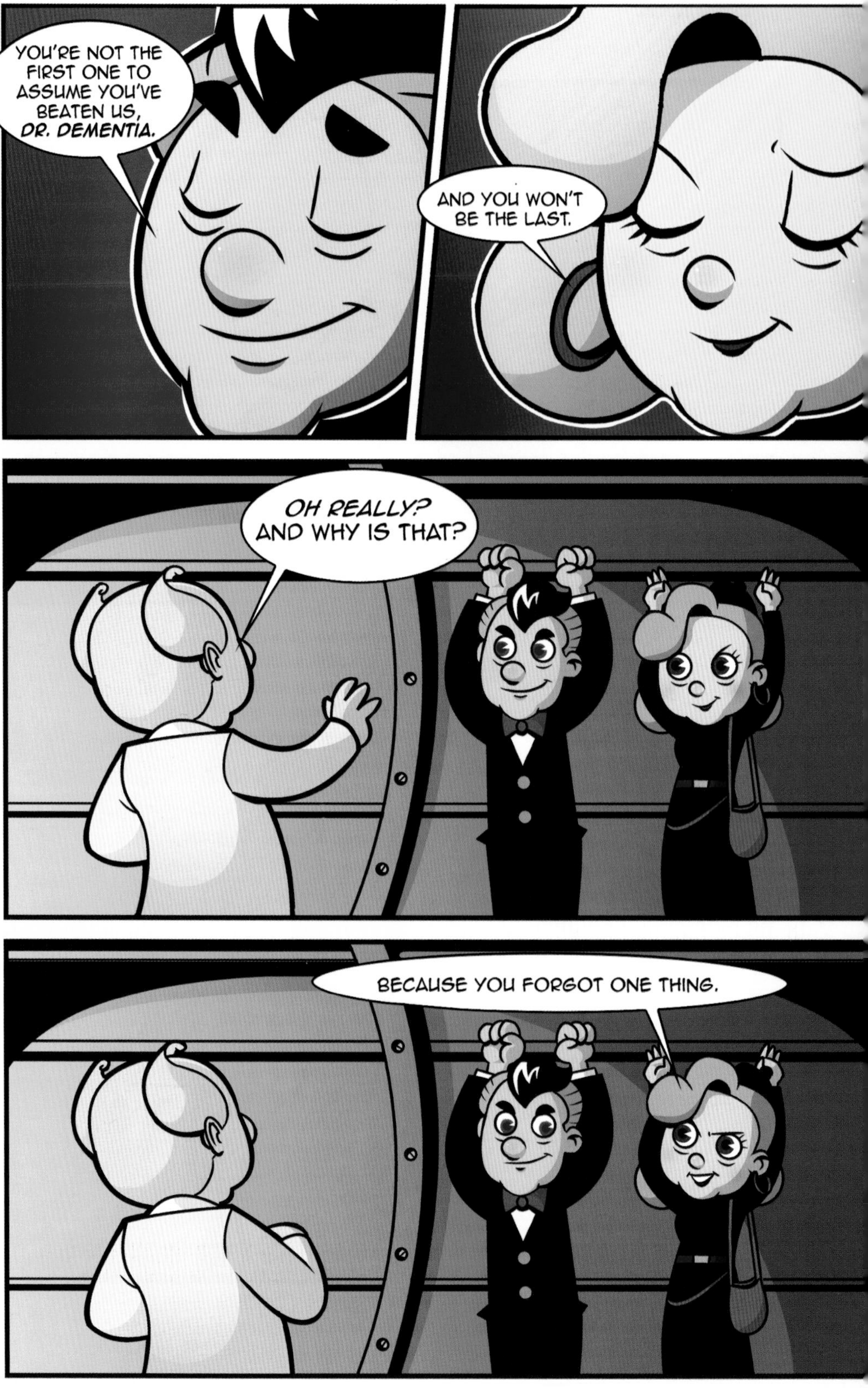
YOU'RE NOT THE FIRST ONE TO ASSUME YOU'VE BEATEN US, *DR. DEMENTIA.*
AND YOU WON'T BE THE LAST.
OH REALLY? AND WHY IS THAT?
BECAUSE YOU FORGOT ONE THING.

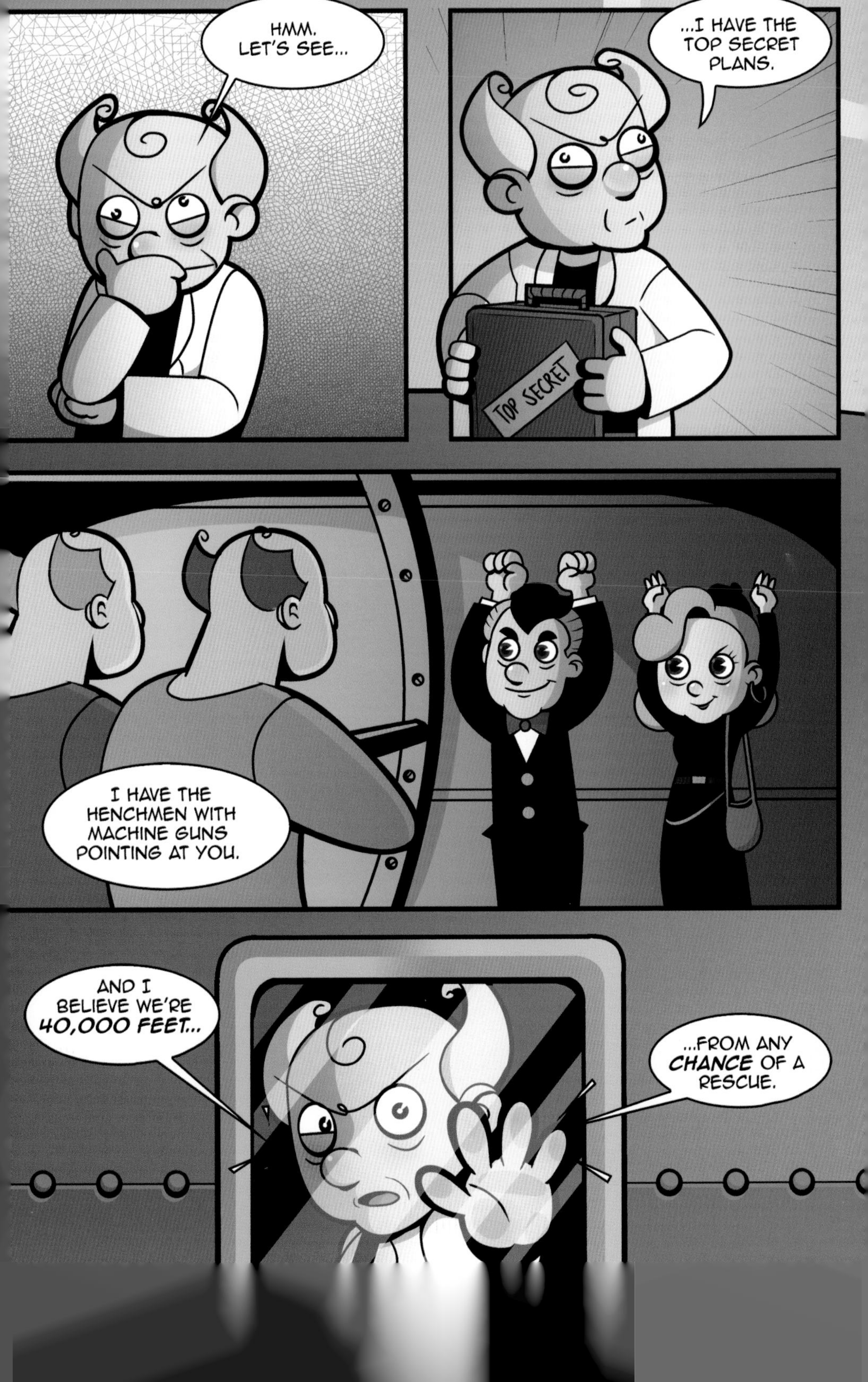
HMM. LET'S SEE...
...I HAVE THE TOP SECRET PLANS.
TOP SECRET
I HAVE THE HENCHMEN WITH MACHINE GUNS POINTING AT YOU.
AND I BELIEVE WE'RE 40,000 FEET...
...FROM ANY CHANCE OF A RESCUE.

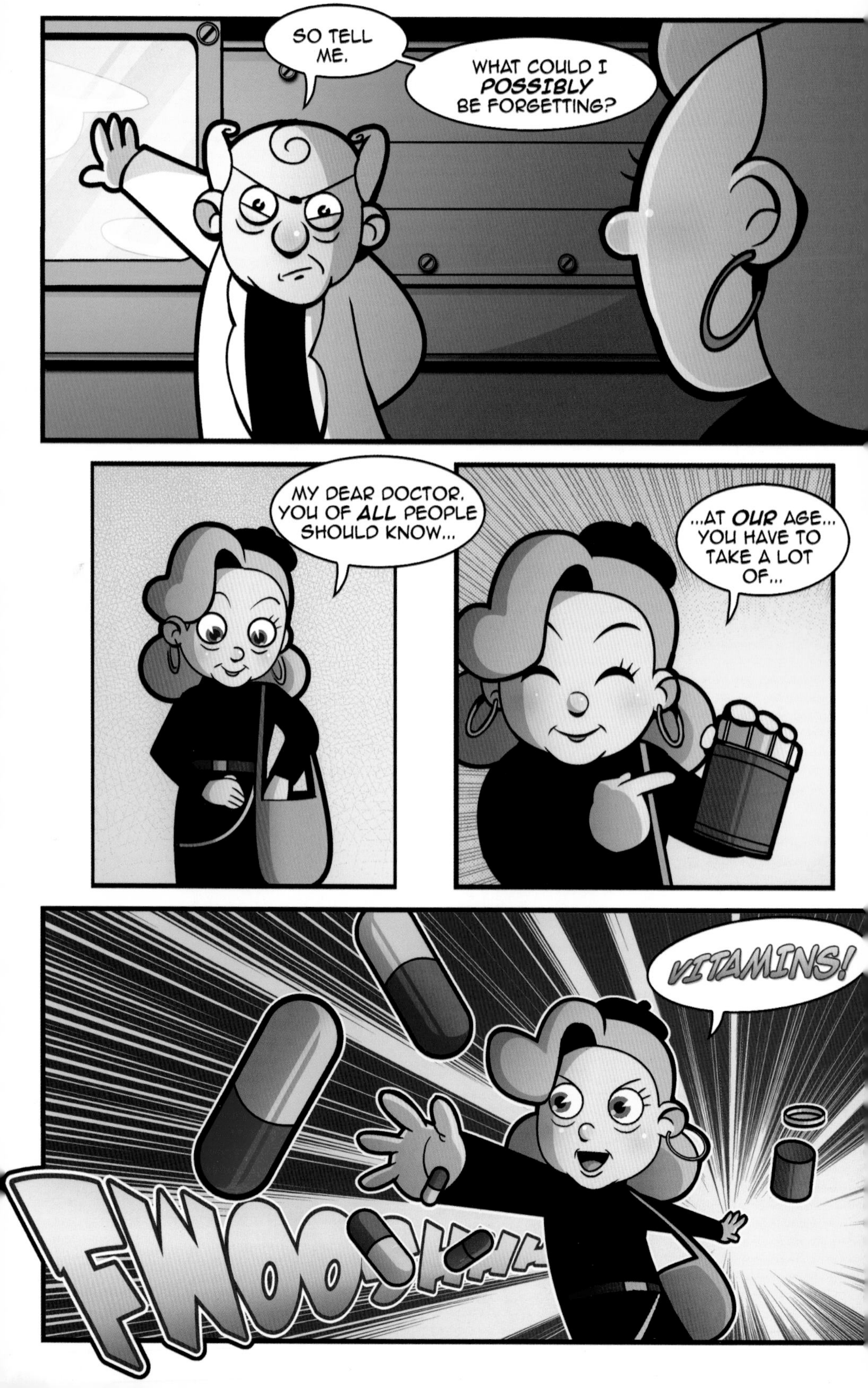
SO TELL ME.
WHAT COULD I POSSIBLY BE FORGETTING?
MY DEAR DOCTOR, YOU OF ALL PEOPLE SHOULD KNOW...
...AT OUR AGE... YOU HAVE TO TAKE A LOT OF...
VITAMINS!
FWOOSHHH

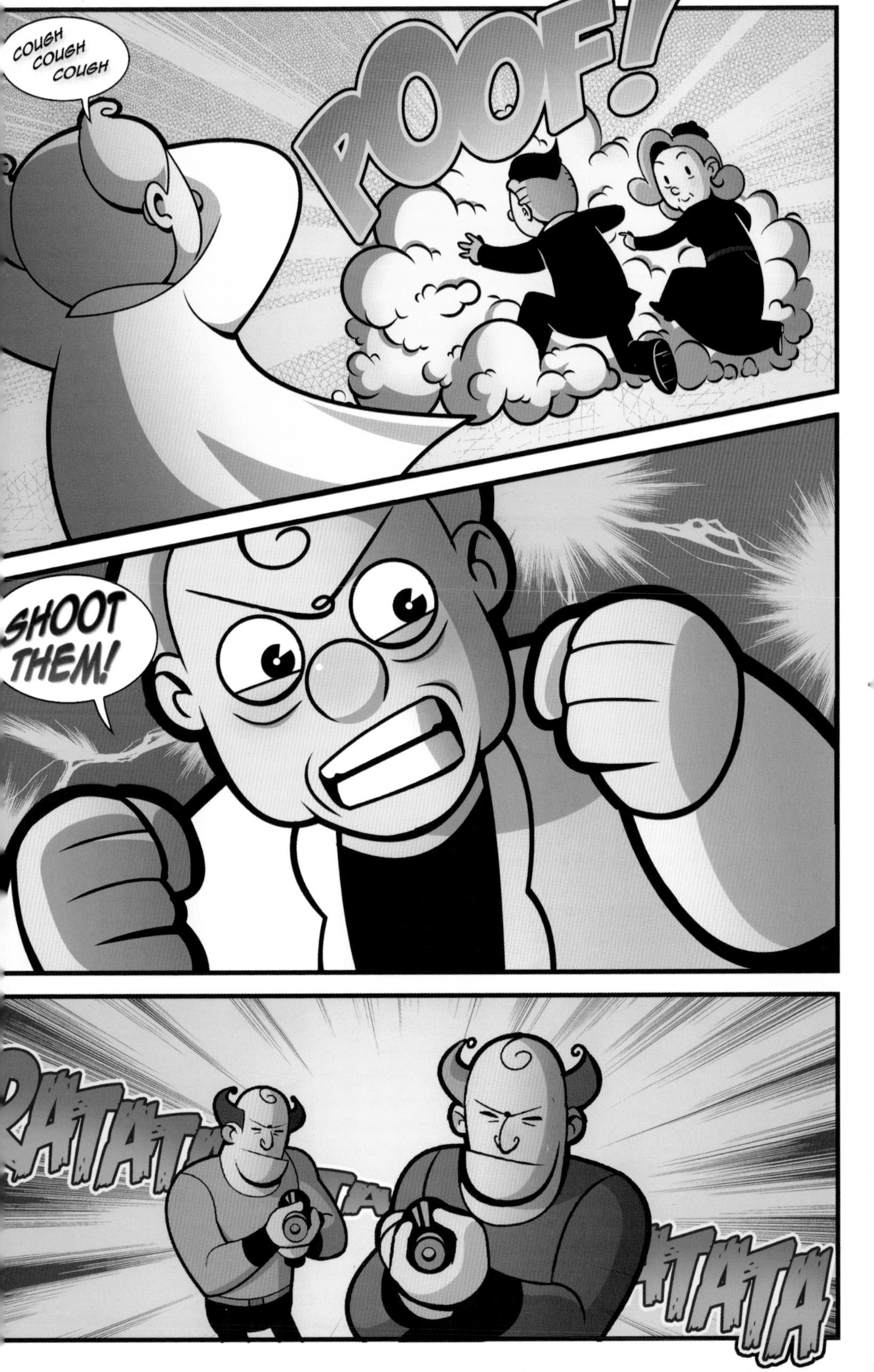
COUGH COUGH COUGH
POOF!
SHOOT THEM!
RATATATATATATA

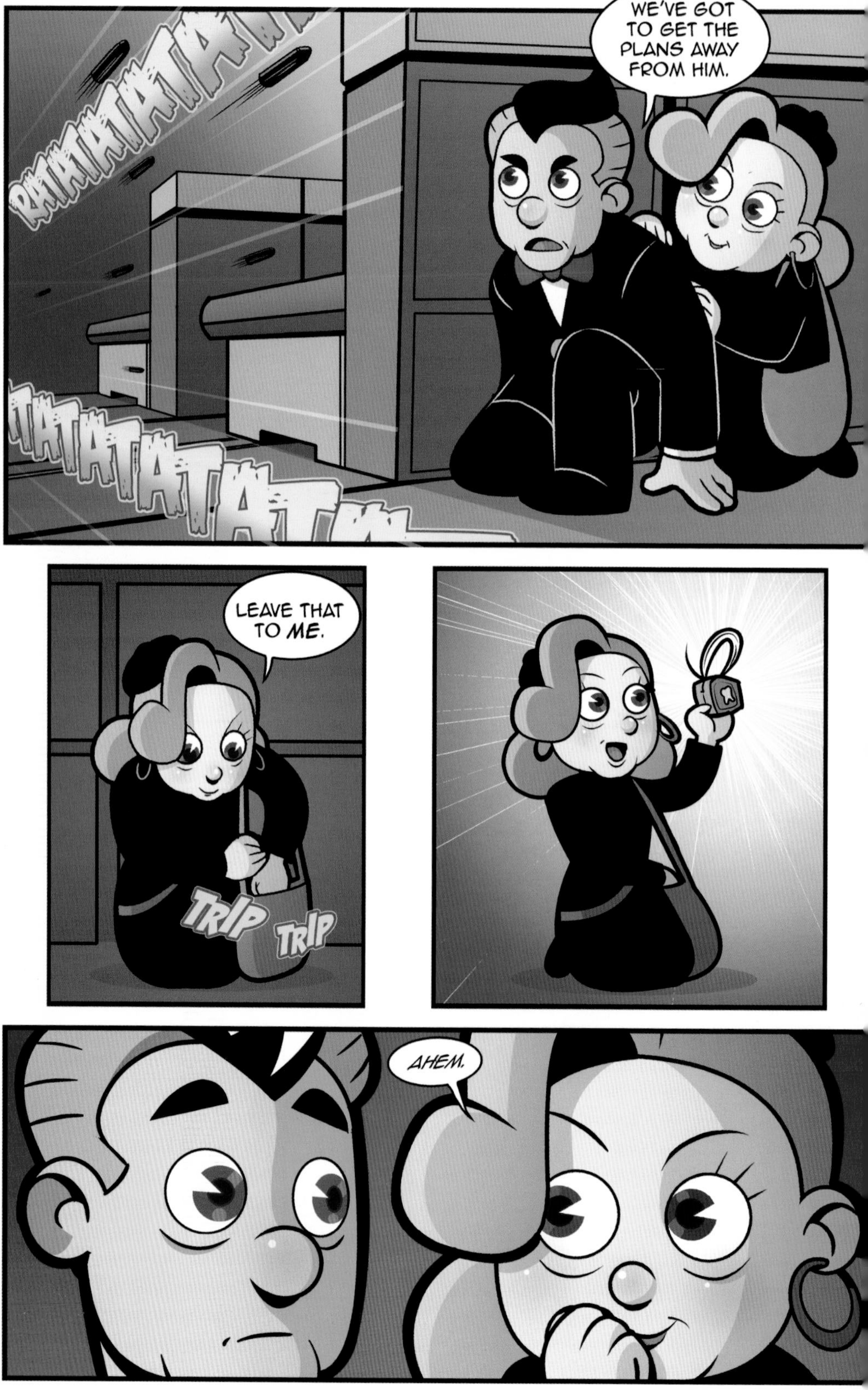
RATATATATATAT
WE'VE GOT TO GET THE PLANS AWAY FROM HIM.
TATATATATAT
LEAVE THAT TO *ME*.
TRIP
TRIP
AHEM.

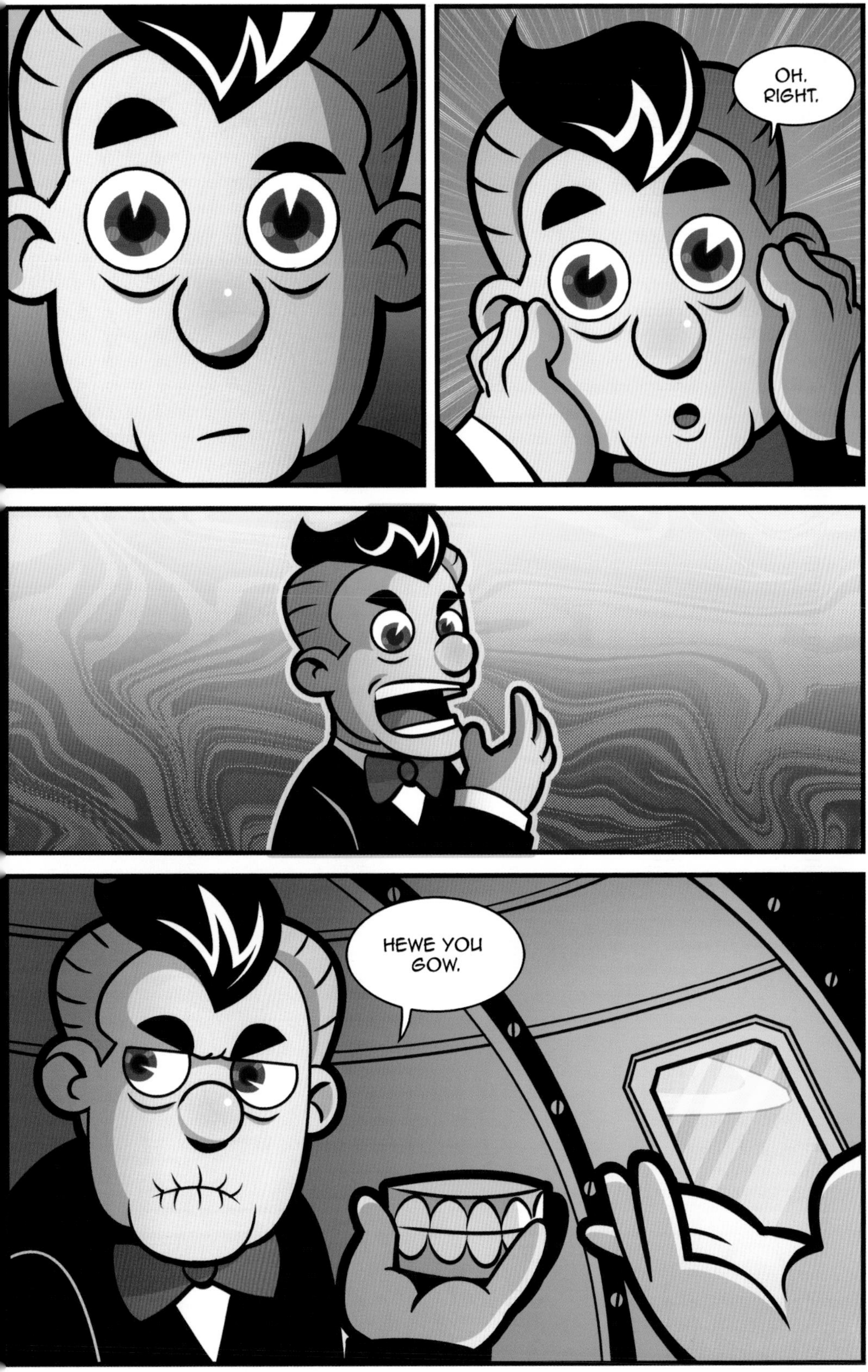
OH, RIGHT.
HEWE YOU GOW.

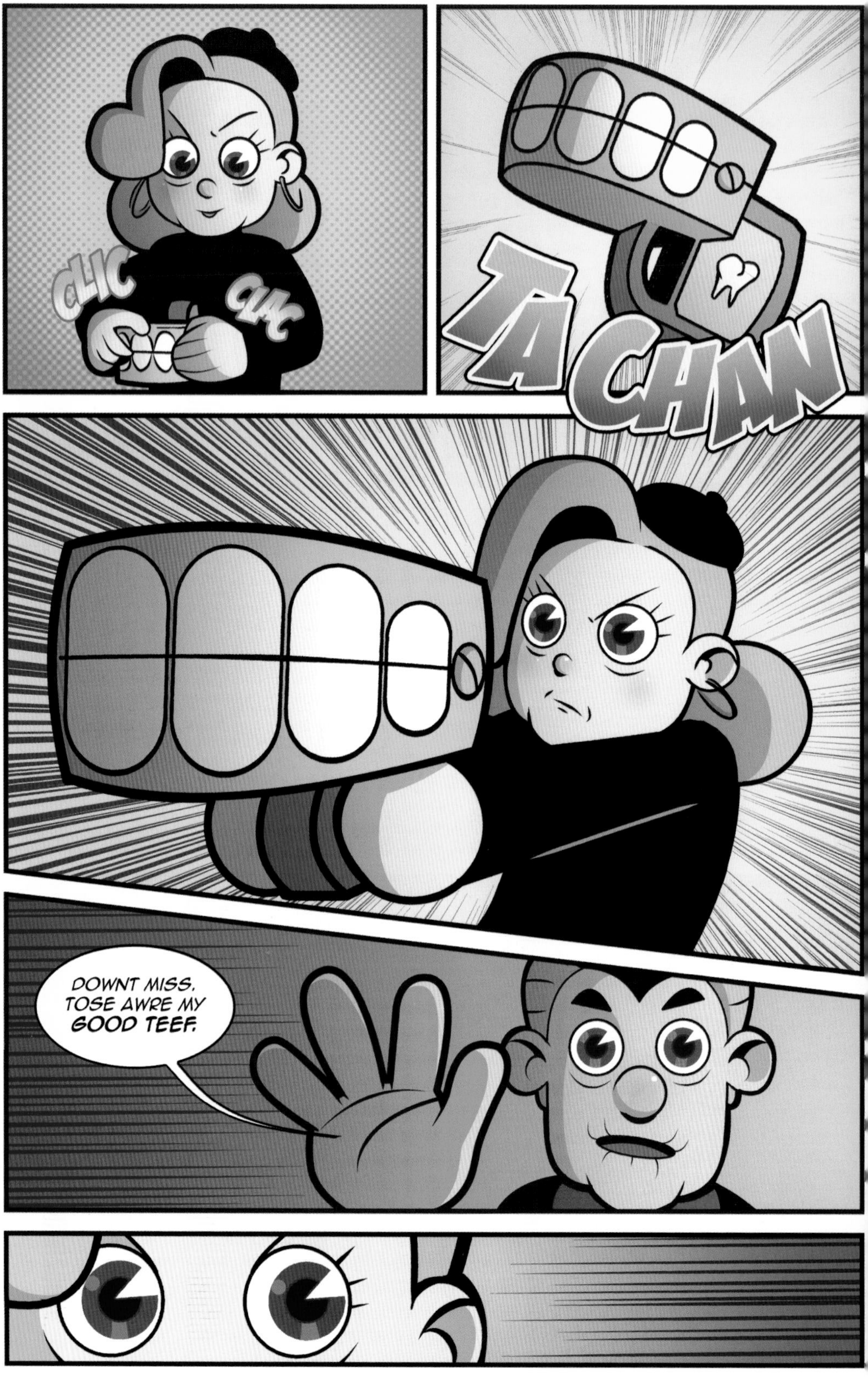
CLIC
CLIC
TA CHAN
DOWNT MISS. TOSE AWRE MY GOOD TEEF.

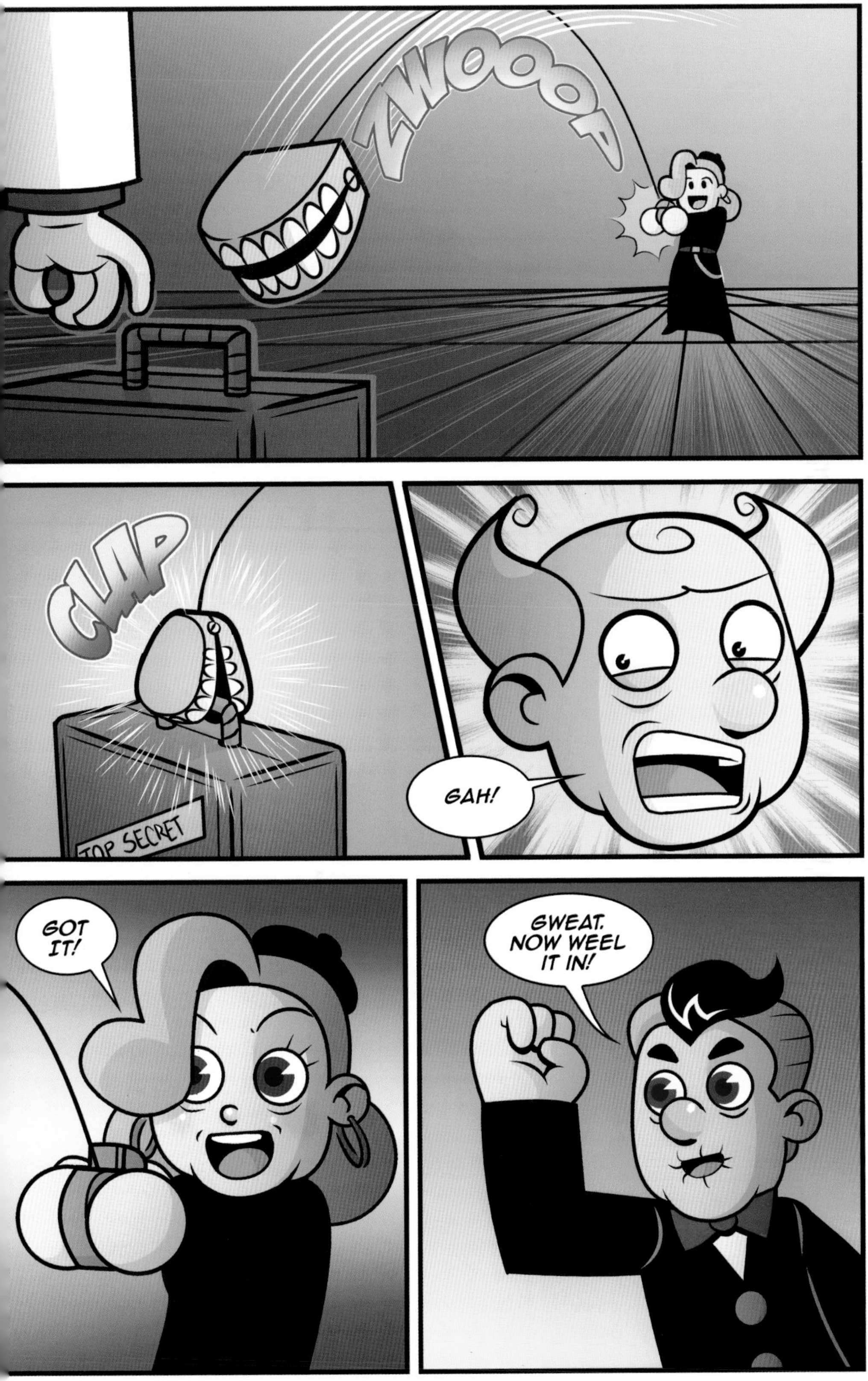
ZWOOOP
CLAP
TOP SECRET
GAH!
GOT IT!
GWEAT. NOW WEEL IT IN!

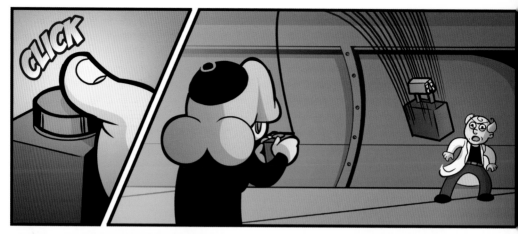

CLICK

NO! THE TOP SECRET PLANS!!

TOP SECRET

AH. MUCH BETTER.

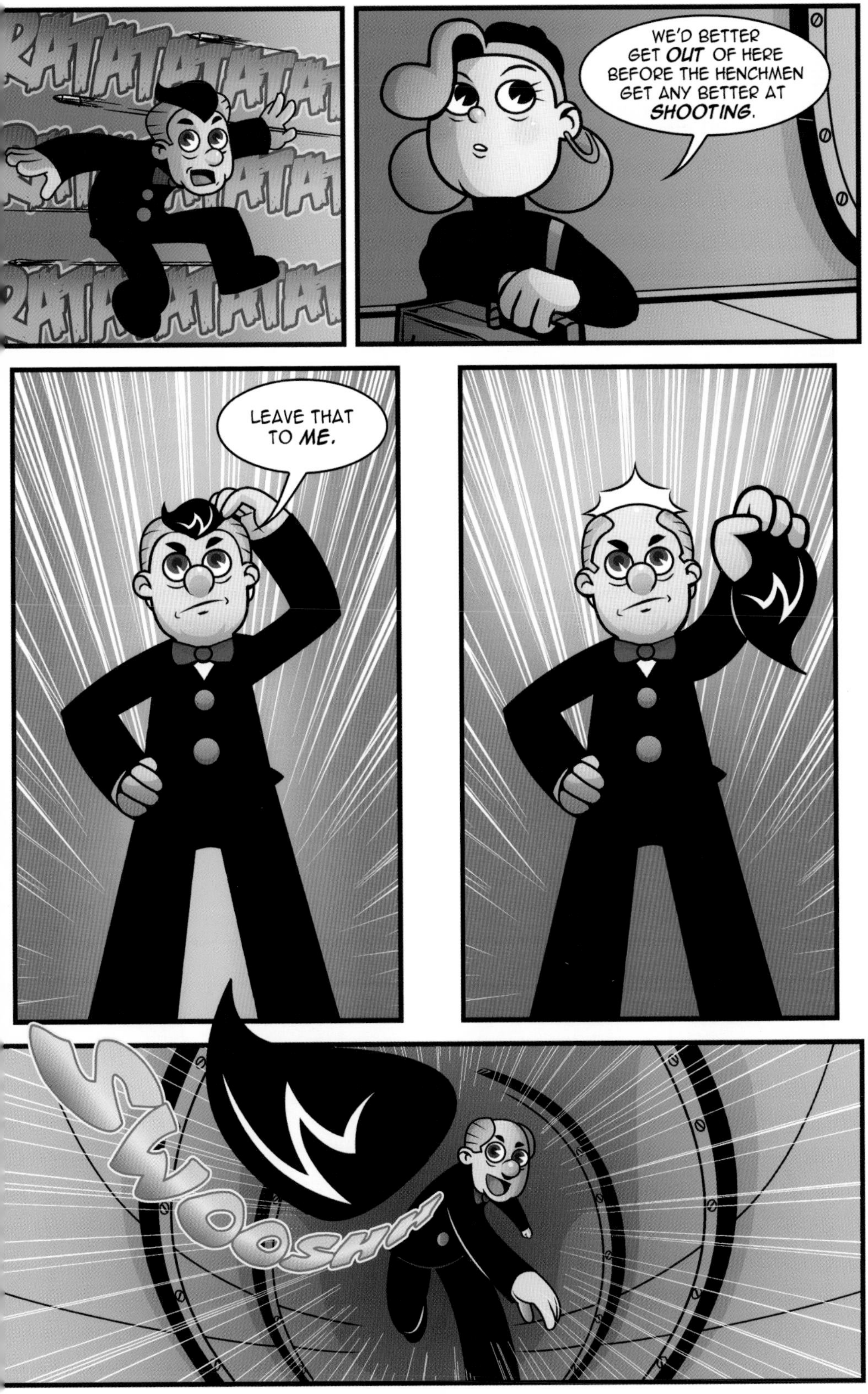
RATATATATATAT
WE'D BETTER GET OUT OF HERE BEFORE THE HENCHMEN GET ANY BETTER AT SHOOTING.
LEAVE THAT TO ME.
SWOOSHH

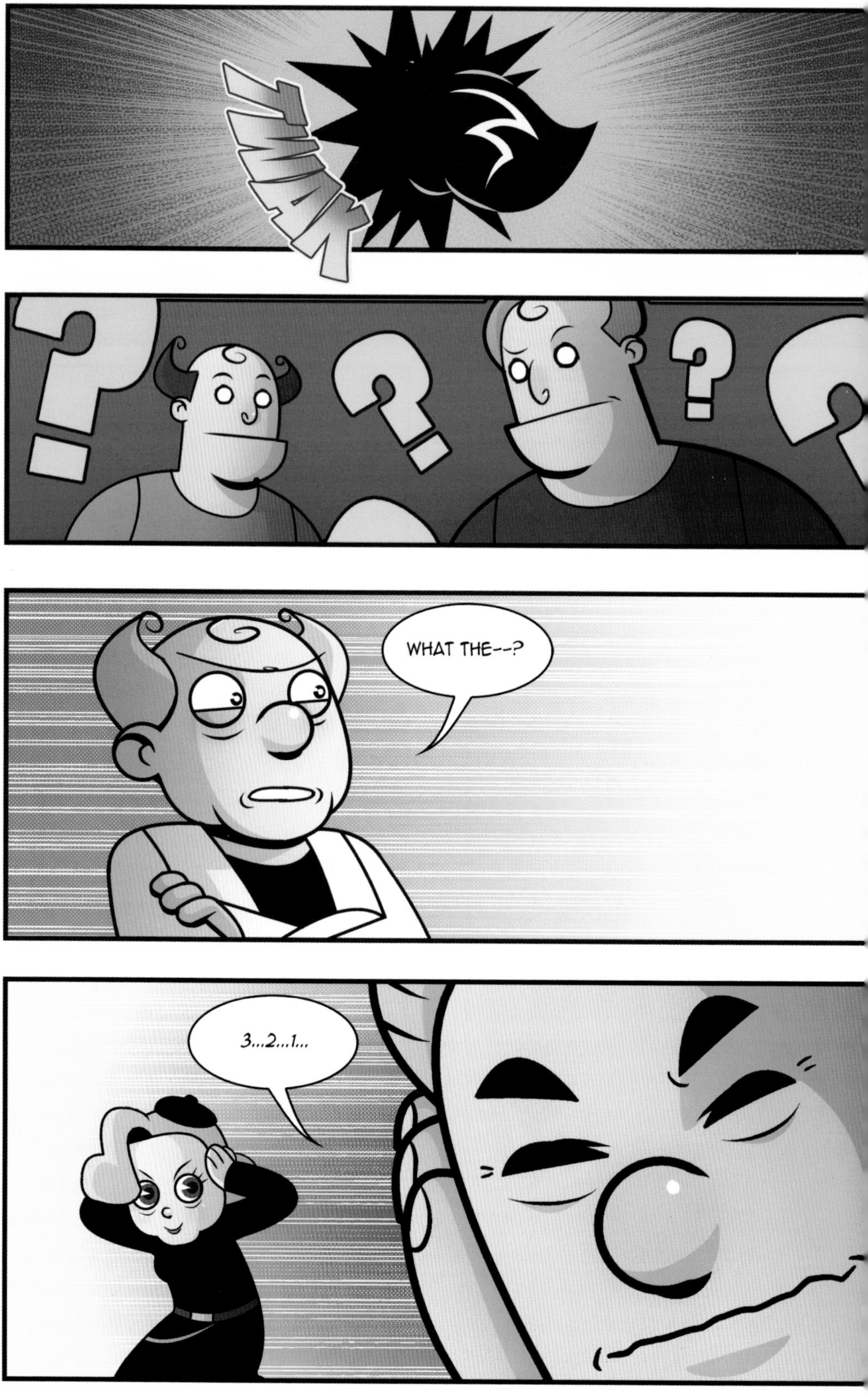
TWAK
WHAT THE--?
3...2...1...

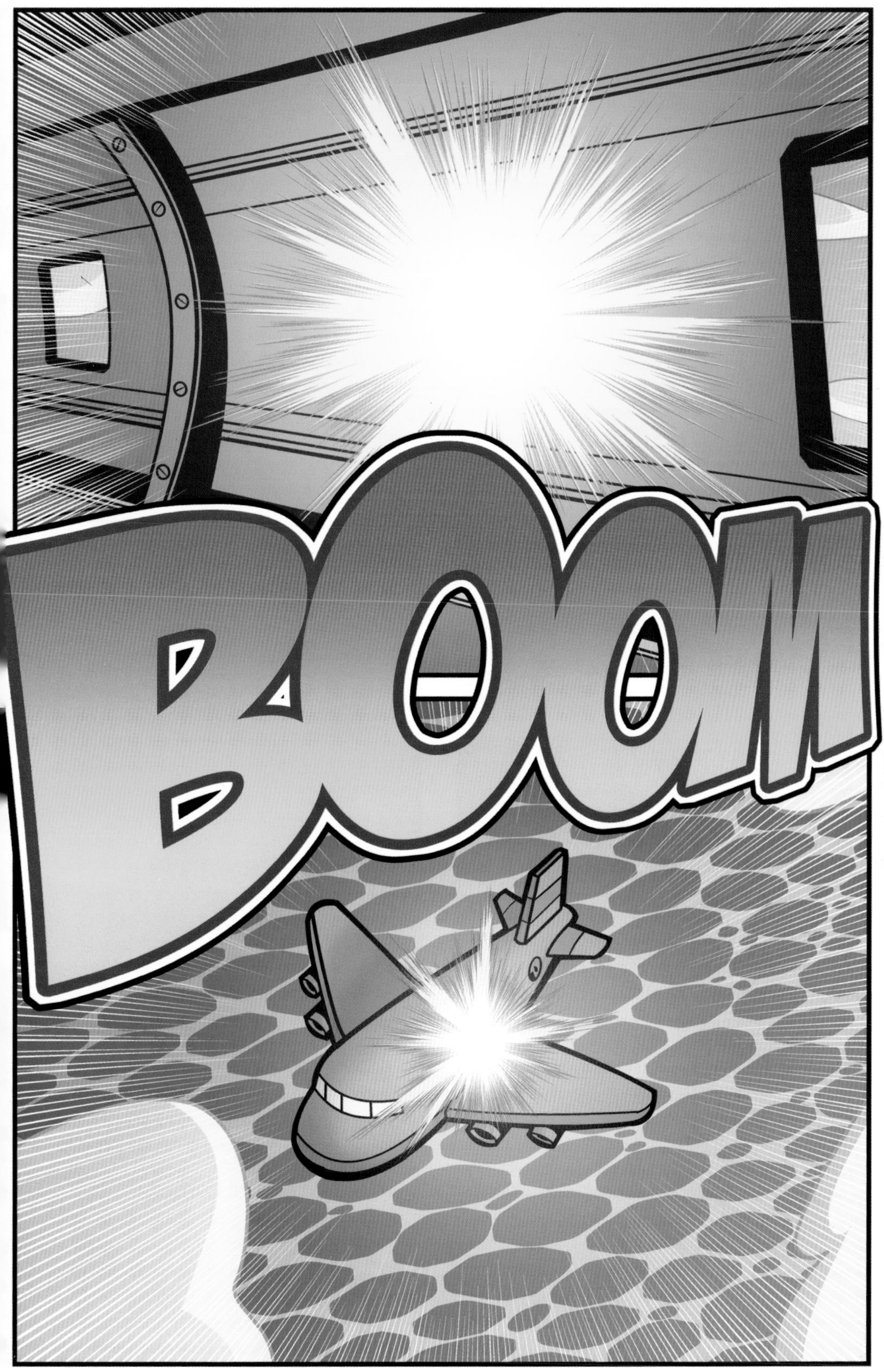
BOOM

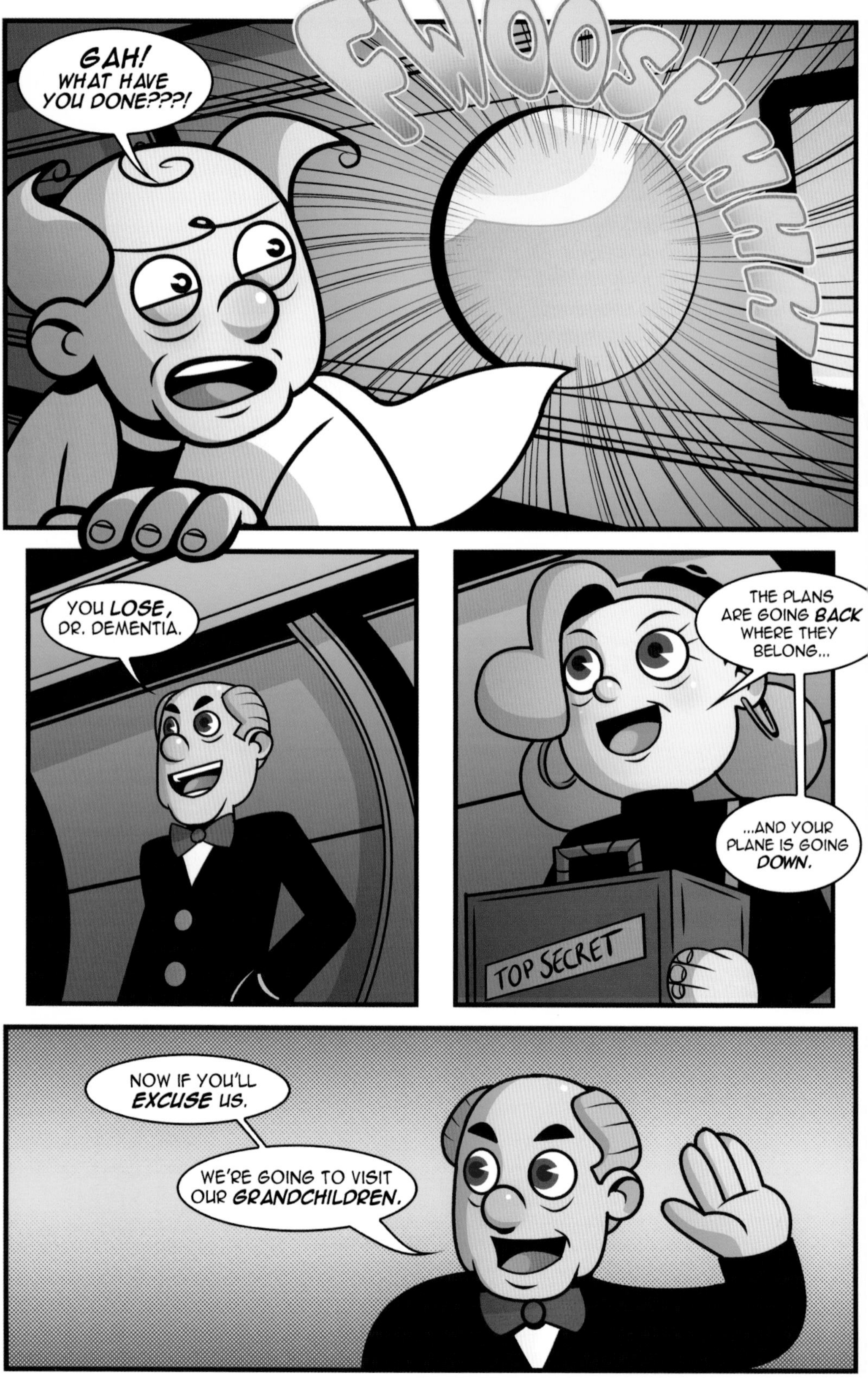
GAH! WHAT HAVE YOU DONE???!
FWOOSHHHH
YOU LOSE, DR. DEMENTIA.
THE PLANS ARE GOING BACK WHERE THEY BELONG...
...AND YOUR PLANE IS GOING DOWN.
TOP SECRET
NOW IF YOU'LL EXCUSE US.
WE'RE GOING TO VISIT OUR GRANDCHILDREN.

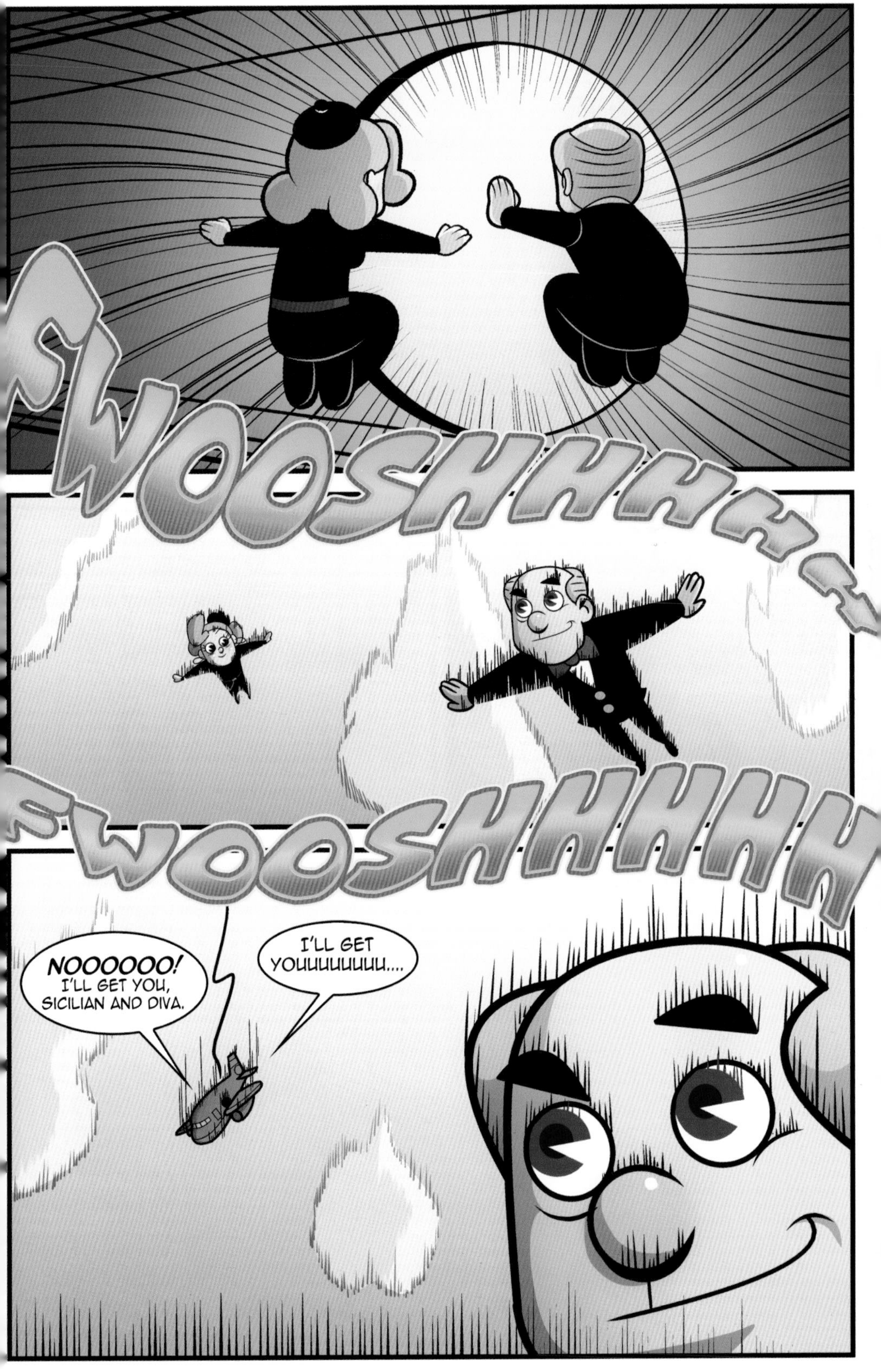
FWOOSHHHH~
FWOOSHHHHH
NOOOOOO! I'LL GET YOU, SICILIAN AND DIVA.
I'LL GET YOUUUUUUUU....

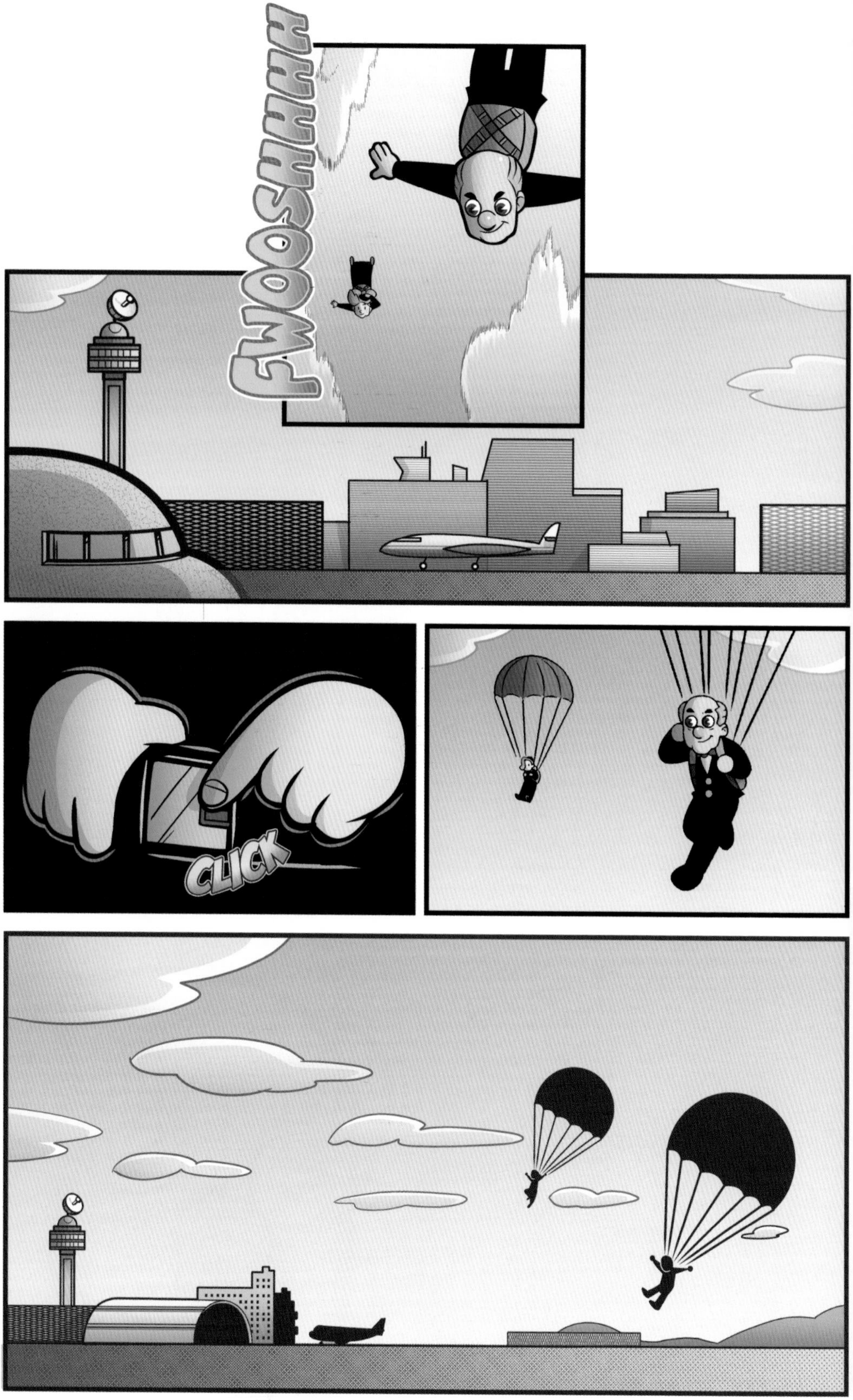
FWOOSHHHH
CLICK

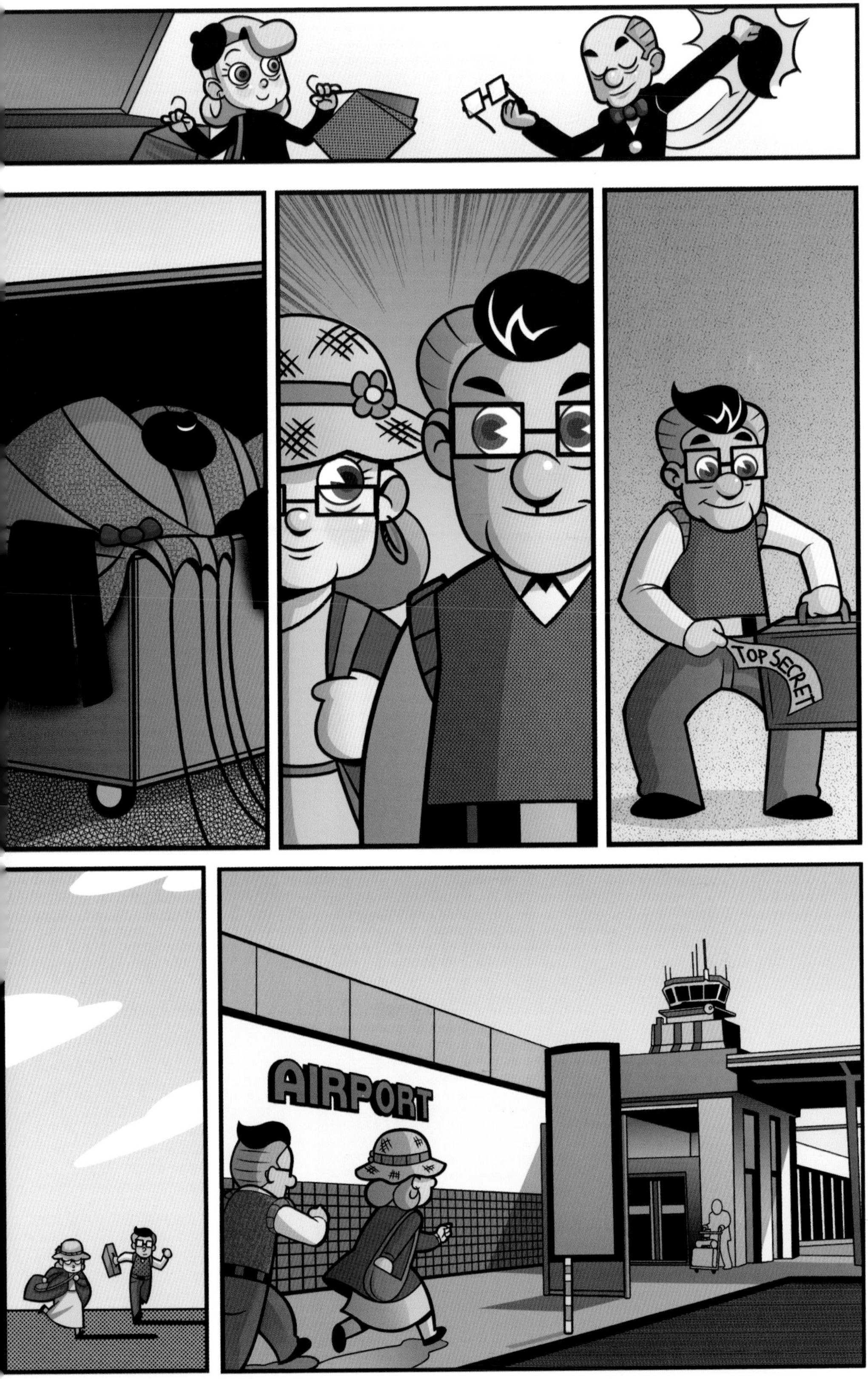
TOP SECRET
AIRPORT

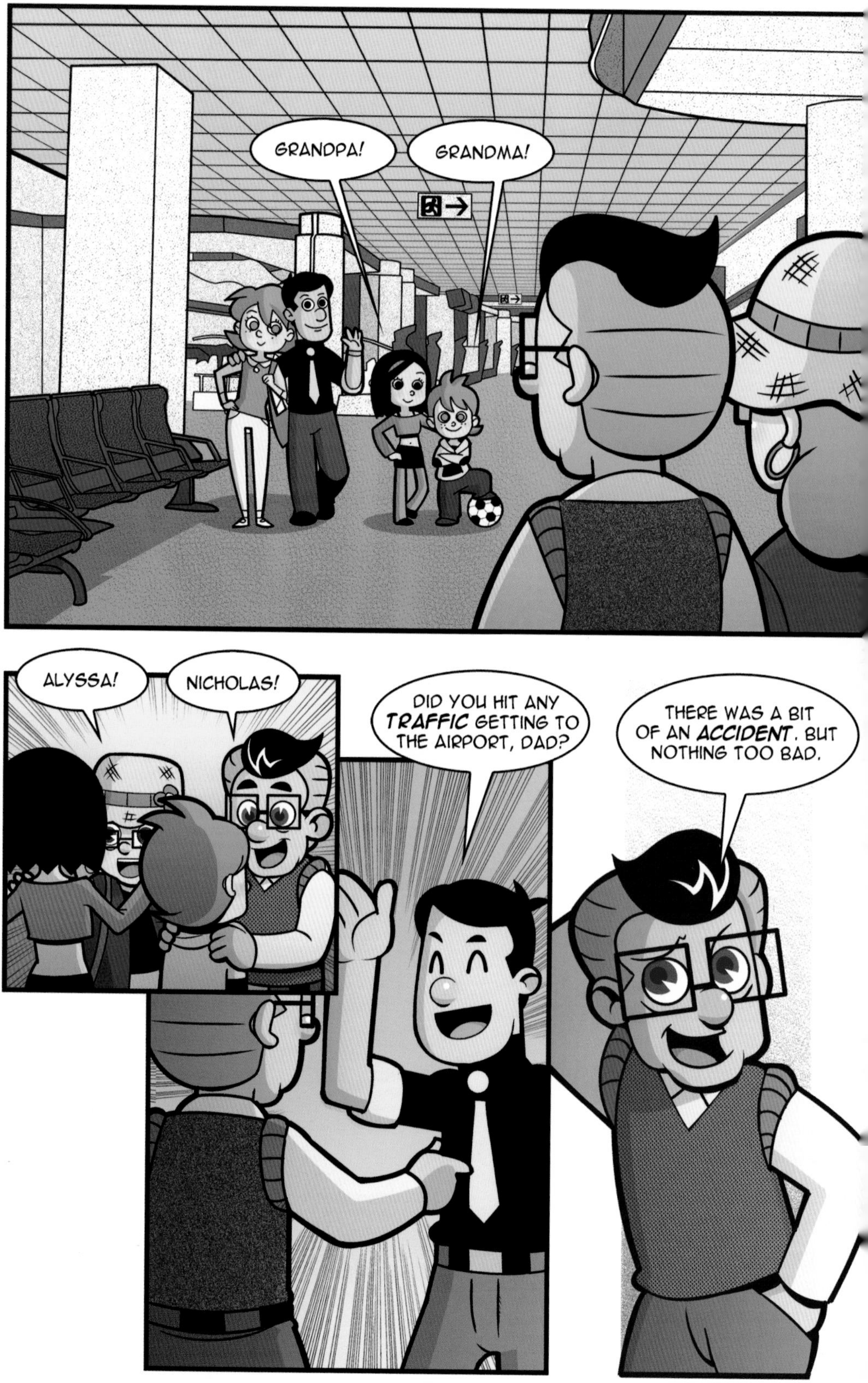
GRANDPA!
GRANDMA!
ALYSSA!
NICHOLAS!
DID YOU HIT ANY TRAFFIC GETTING TO THE AIRPORT, DAD?
THERE WAS A BIT OF AN ACCIDENT. BUT NOTHING TOO BAD.

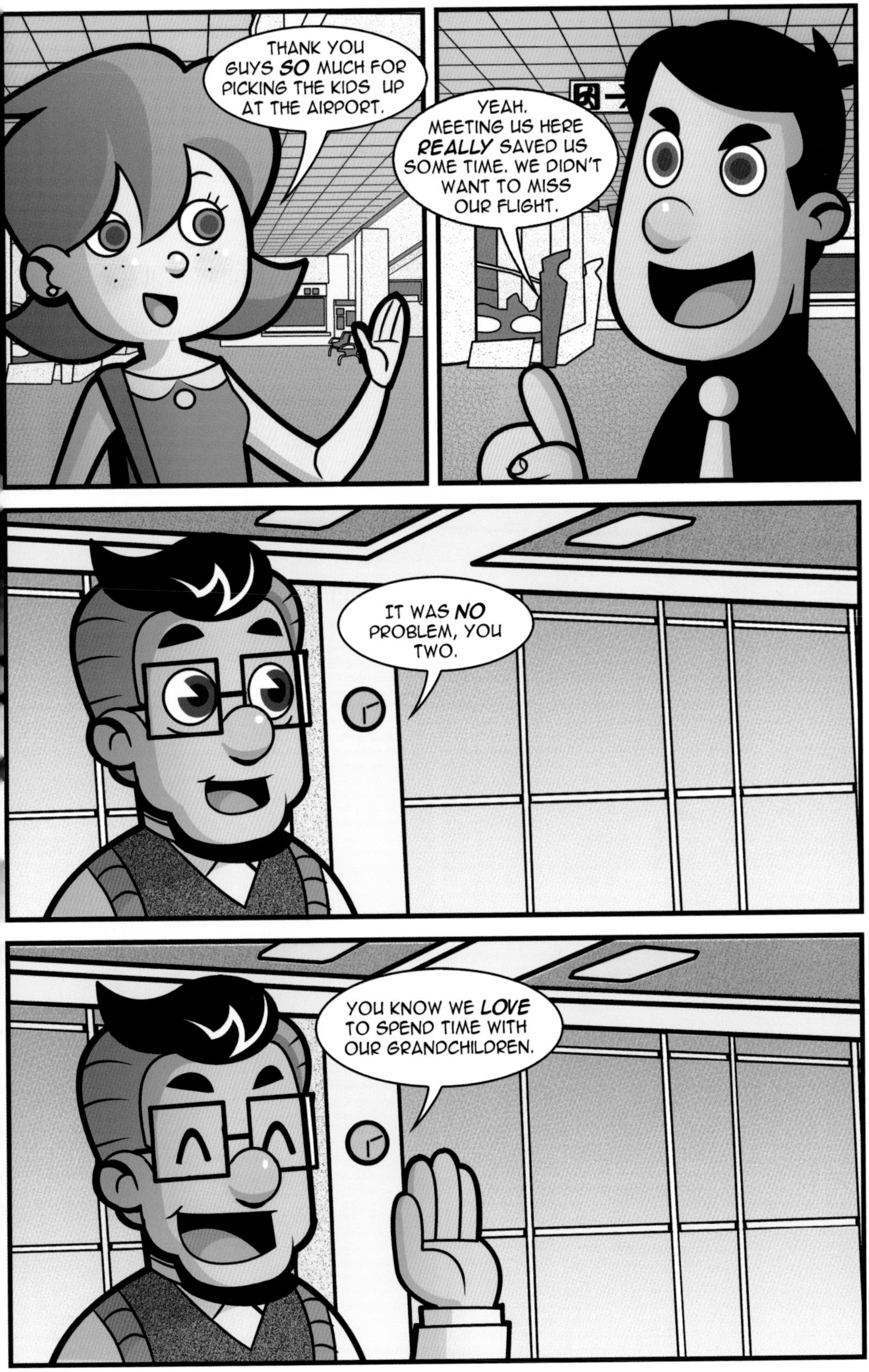
THANK YOU GUYS SO MUCH FOR PICKING THE KIDS UP AT THE AIRPORT.
YEAH. MEETING US HERE REALLY SAVED US SOME TIME. WE DIDN'T WANT TO MISS OUR FLIGHT.
IT WAS NO PROBLEM, YOU TWO.
YOU KNOW WE LOVE TO SPEND TIME WITH OUR GRANDCHILDREN.

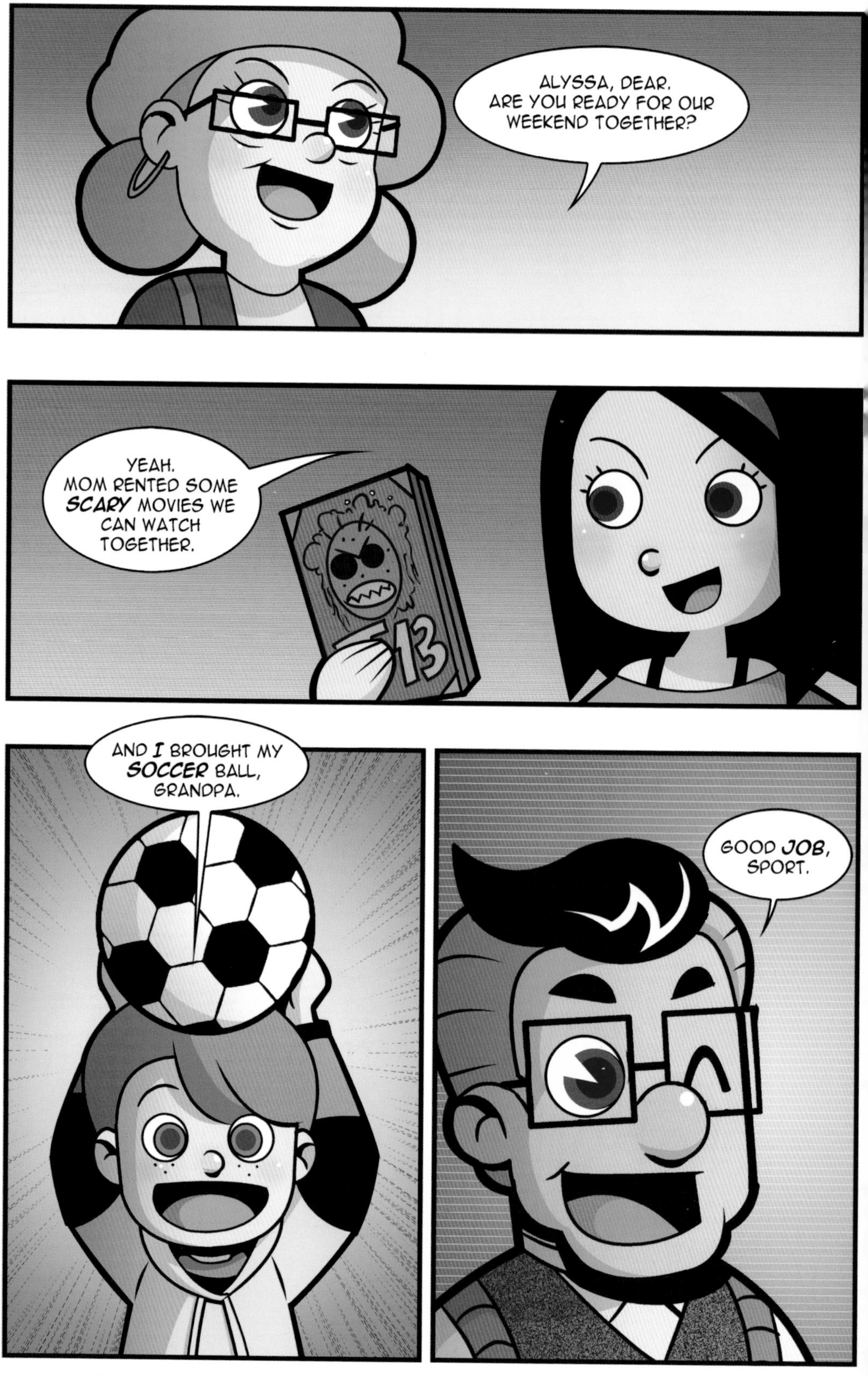

ALYSSA, DEAR. ARE YOU READY FOR OUR WEEKEND TOGETHER?
YEAH. MOM RENTED SOME **SCARY** MOVIES WE CAN WATCH TOGETHER.
13
AND **I** BROUGHT MY **SOCCER** BALL, GRANDPA.
GOOD **JOB**, SPORT.

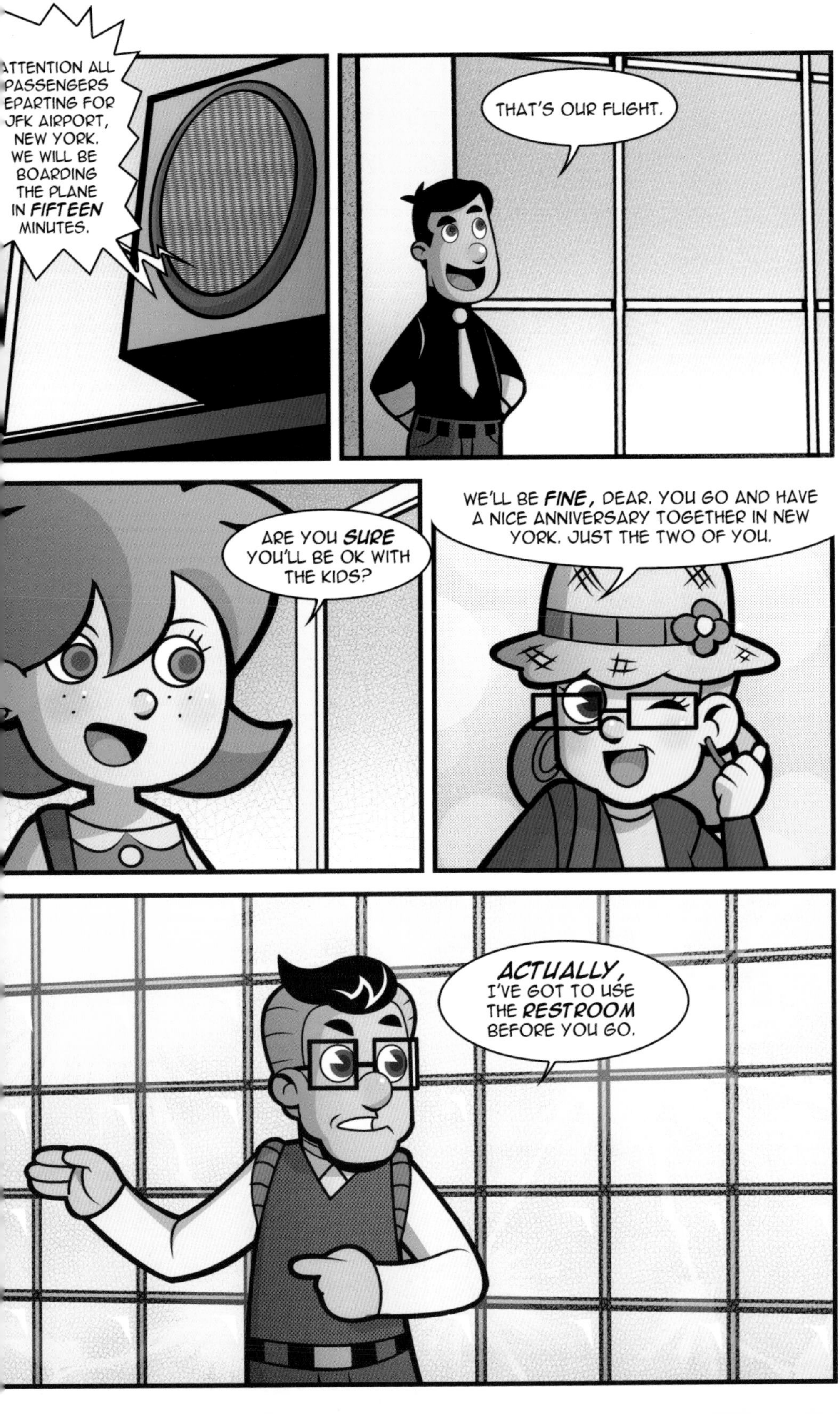
ATTENTION ALL PASSENGERS EPARTING FOR JFK AIRPORT, NEW YORK. WE WILL BE BOARDING THE PLANE IN FIFTEEN MINUTES.
THAT'S OUR FLIGHT.
ARE YOU SURE YOU'LL BE OK WITH THE KIDS?
WE'LL BE FINE, DEAR. YOU GO AND HAVE A NICE ANNIVERSARY TOGETHER IN NEW YORK. JUST THE TWO OF YOU.
ACTUALLY, I'VE GOT TO USE THE RESTROOM BEFORE YOU GO.

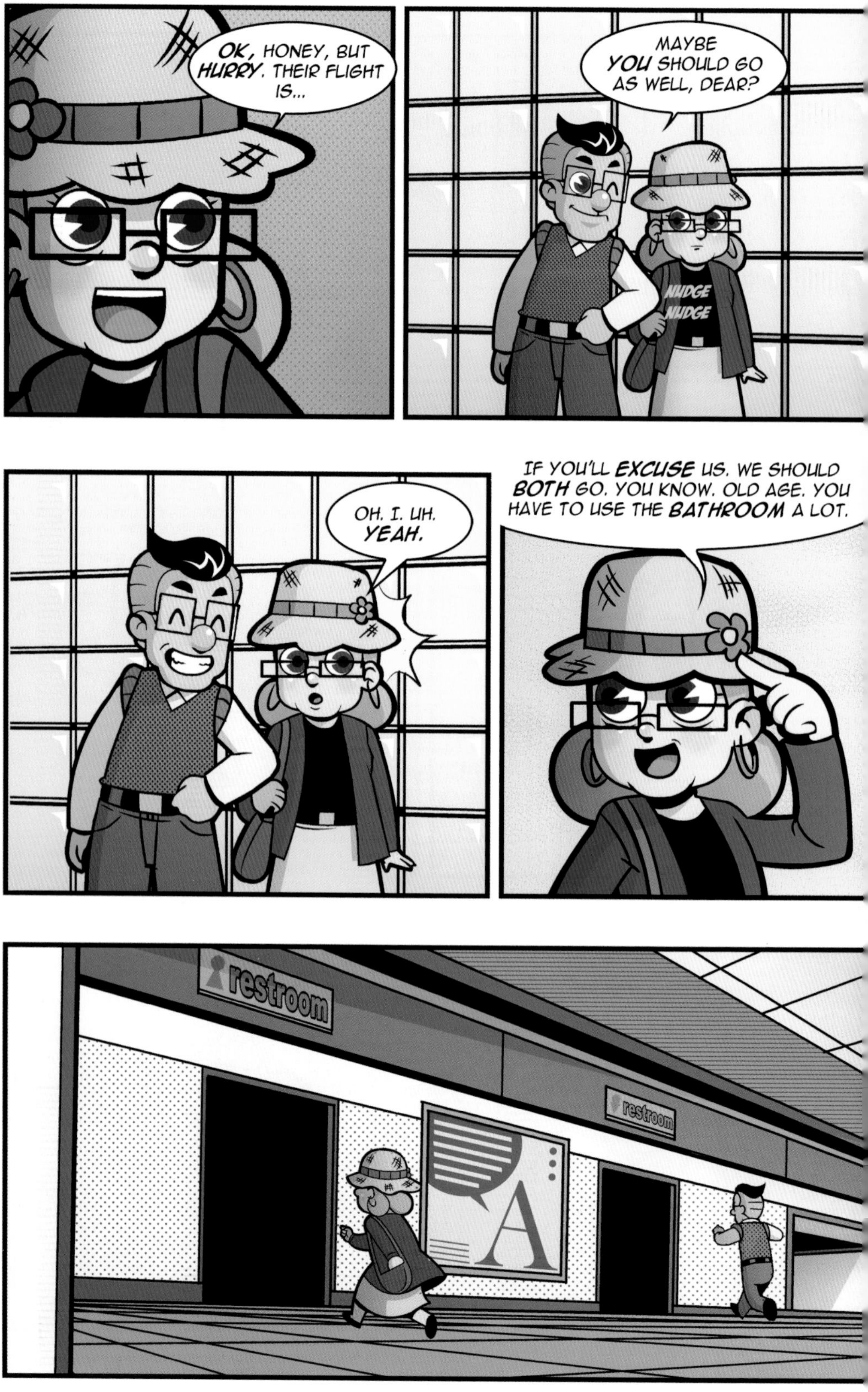
OK, HONEY, BUT HURRY. THEIR FLIGHT IS...
MAYBE YOU SHOULD GO AS WELL, DEAR?
NUDGE NUDGE
OH. I. UH. YEAH.
IF YOU'LL EXCUSE US. WE SHOULD BOTH GO. YOU KNOW. OLD AGE. YOU HAVE TO USE THE BATHROOM A LOT.
restroom
restroom
A

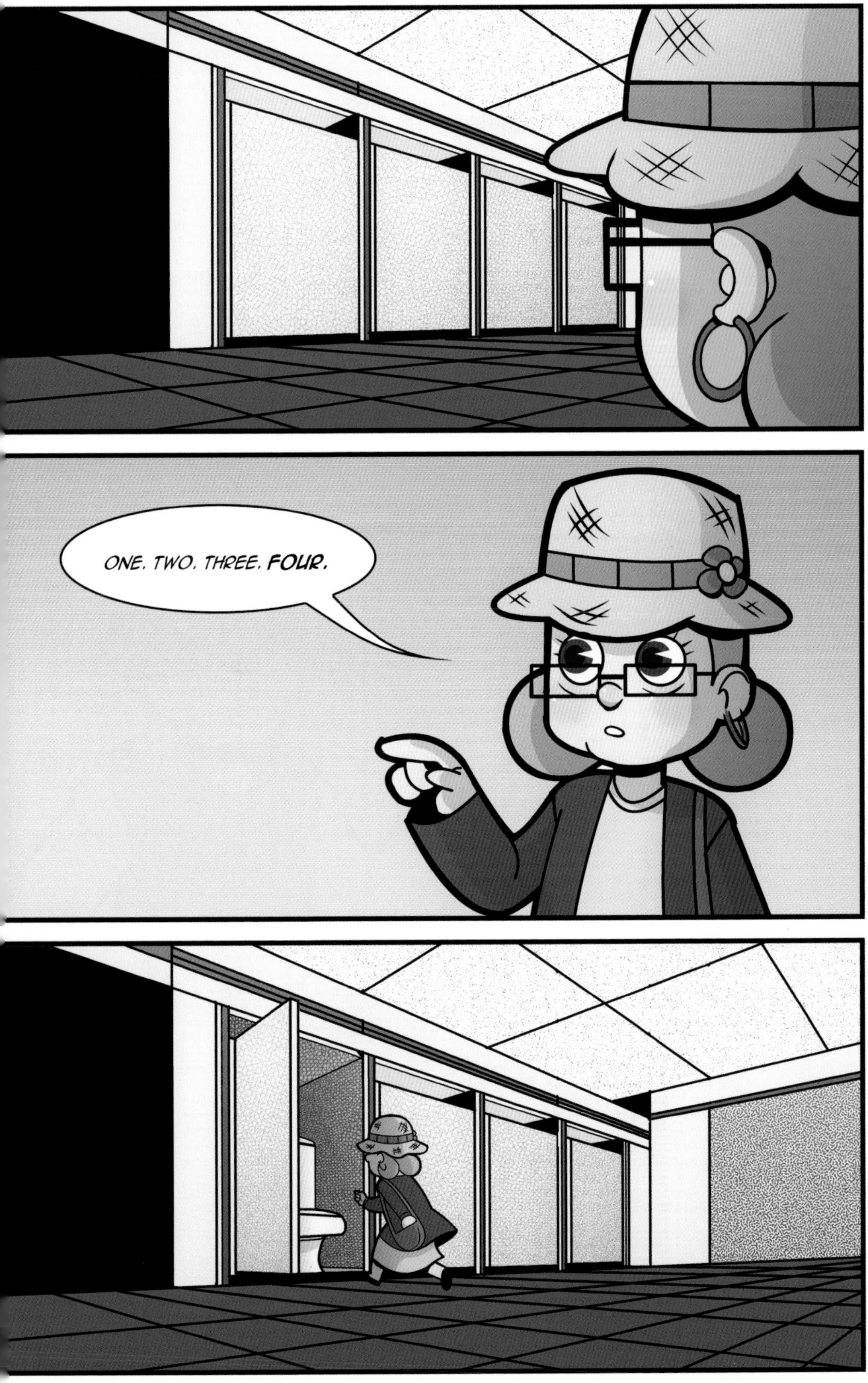
ONE. TWO. THREE. FOUR.

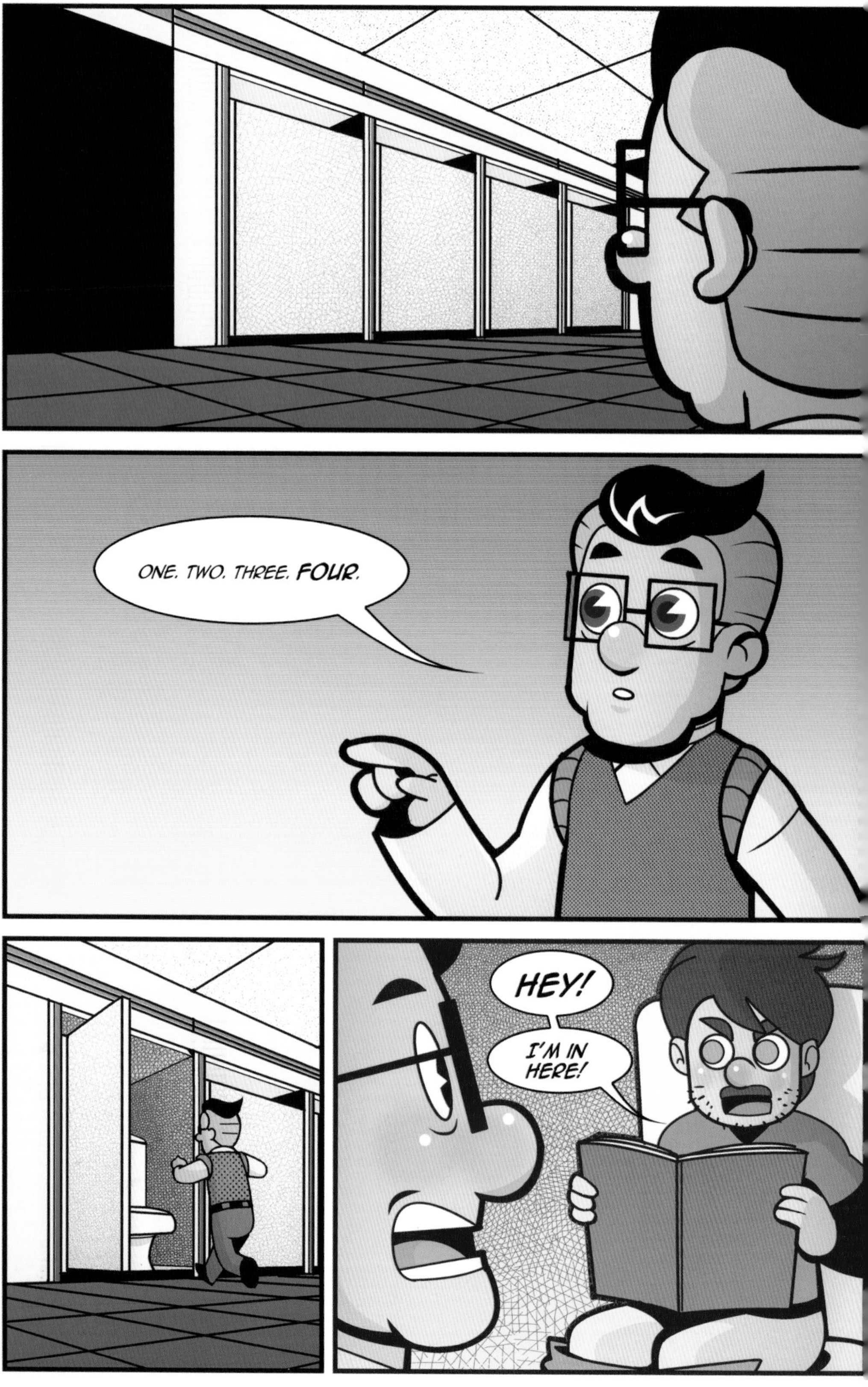
ONE. TWO. THREE. FOUR.
HEY!
I'M IN HERE!

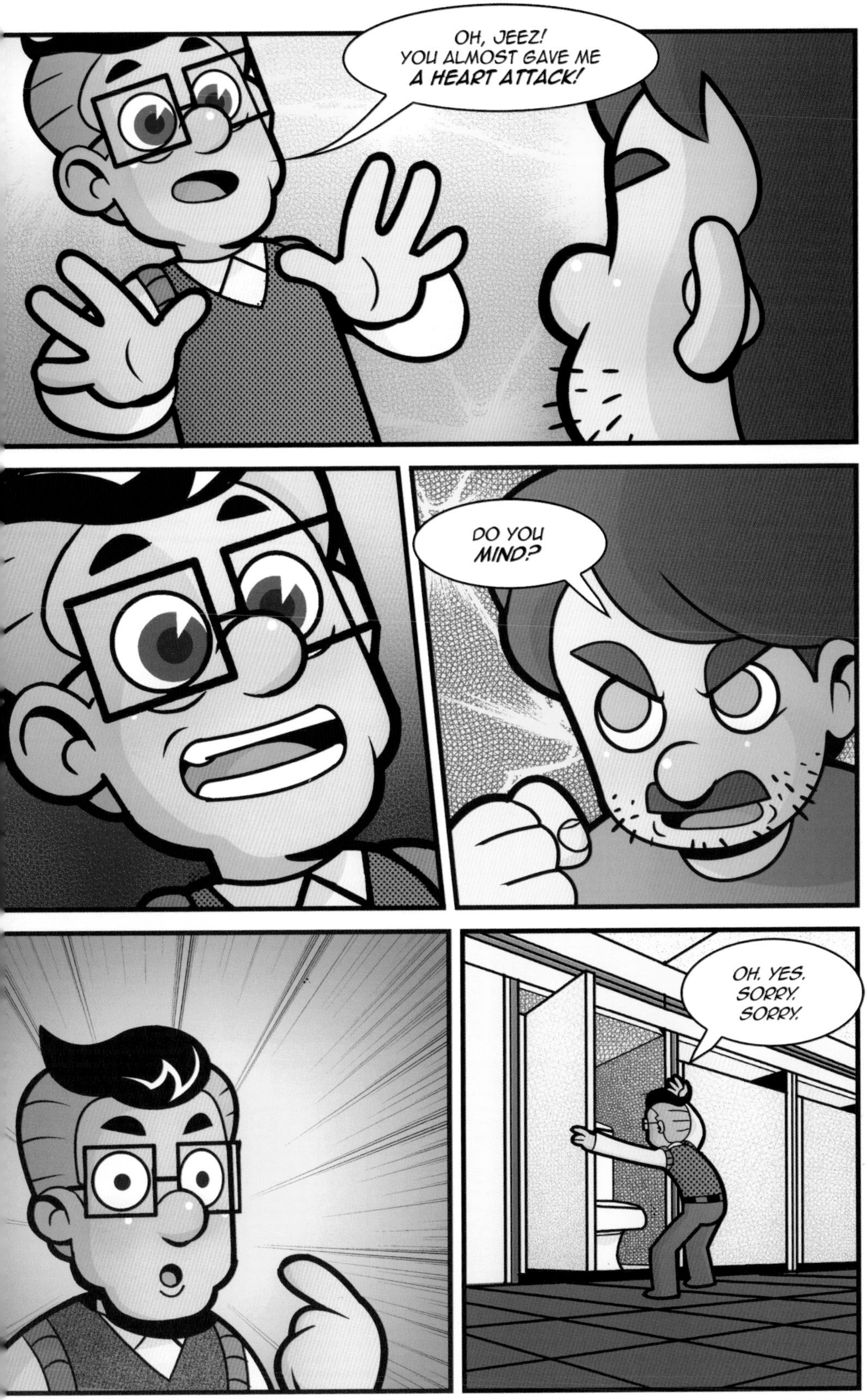
OH, JEEZ!
YOU ALMOST GAVE ME
A HEART ATTACK!
DO YOU
MIND?
OH. YES.
SORRY.
SORRY.

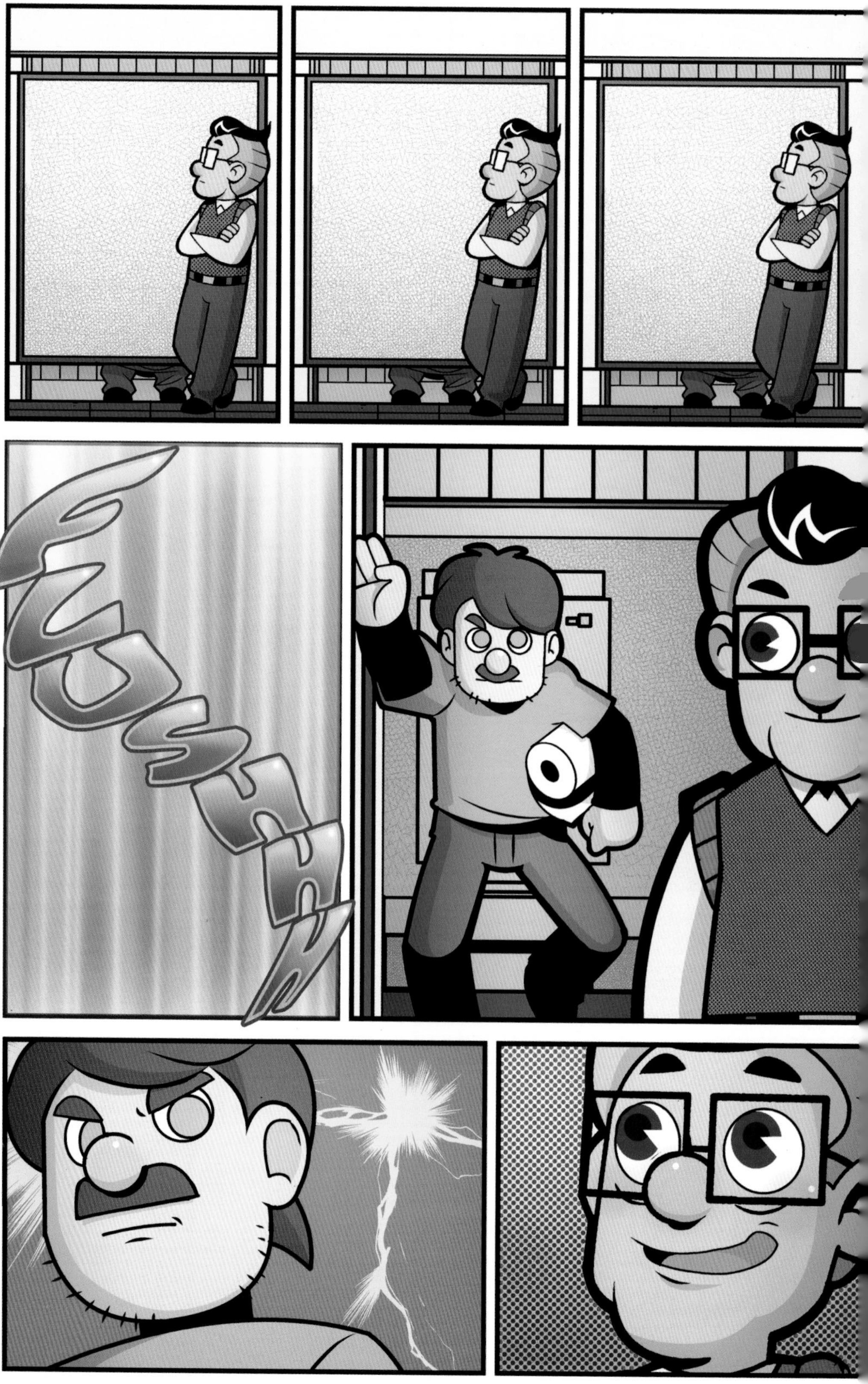
FLUSHHH

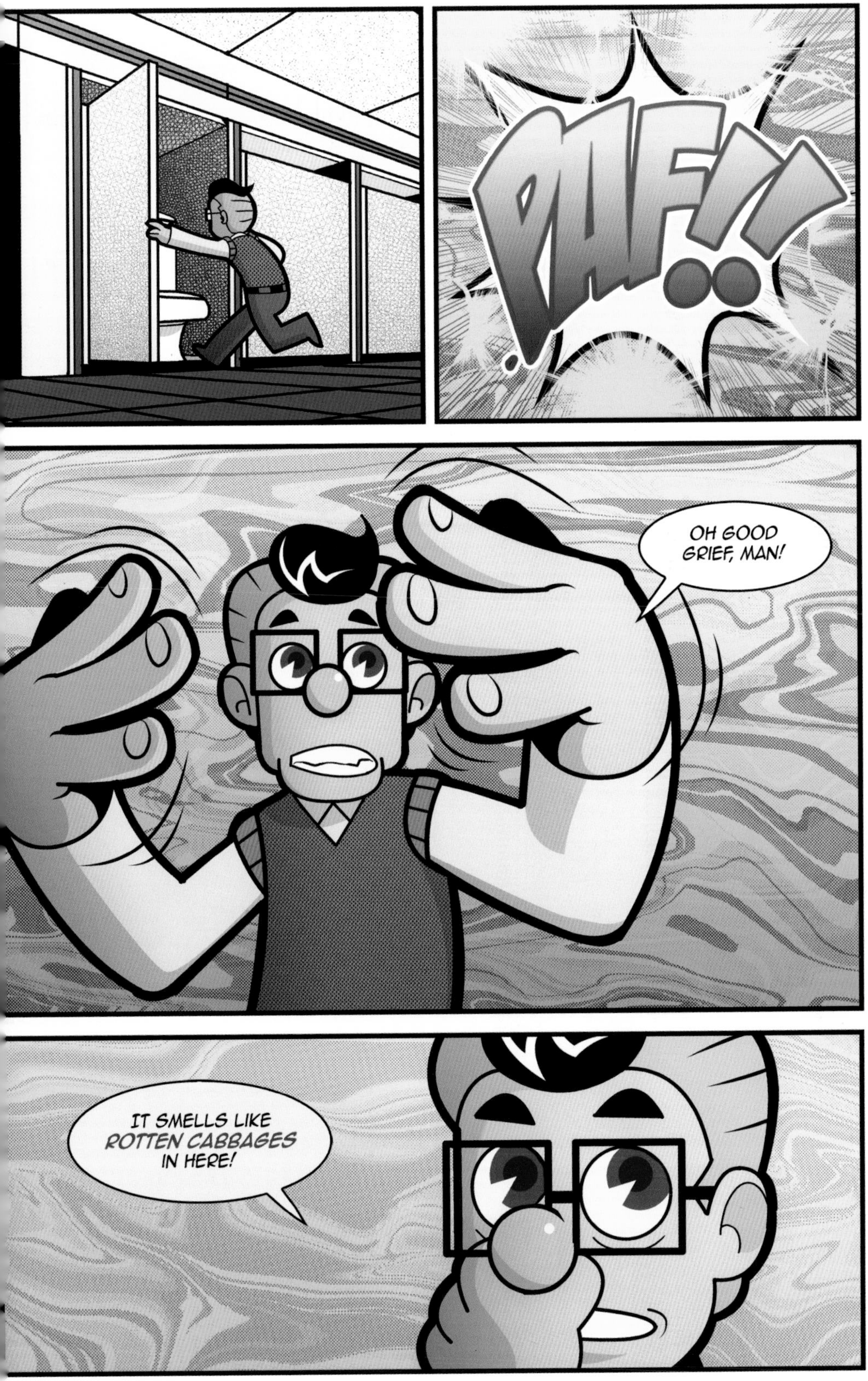
PAAF!!
OH GOOD GRIEF, MAN!
IT SMELLS LIKE ROTTEN CABBAGES IN HERE!

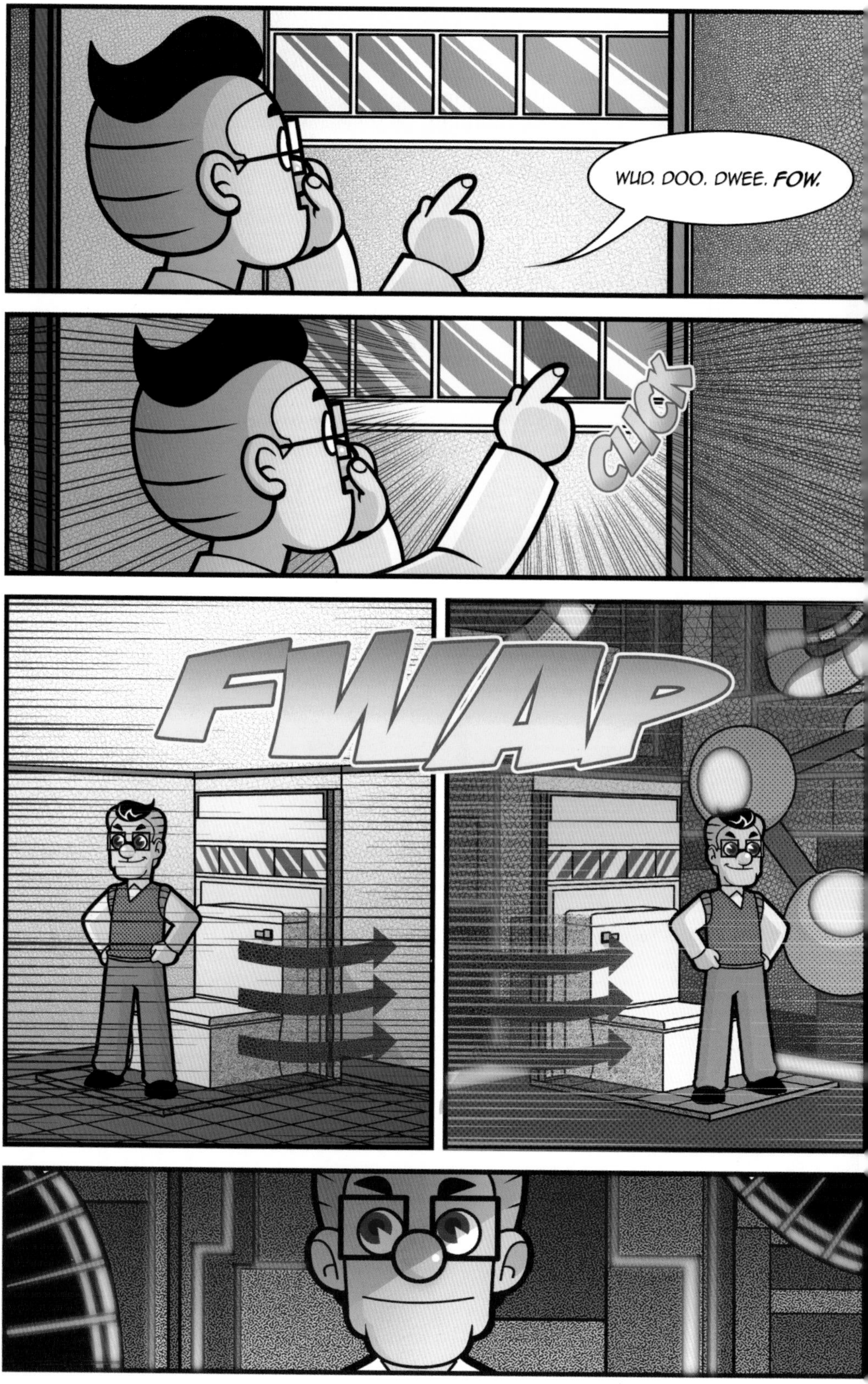
WUD. DOO. DWEE. FOW.
CLICK
FWAP

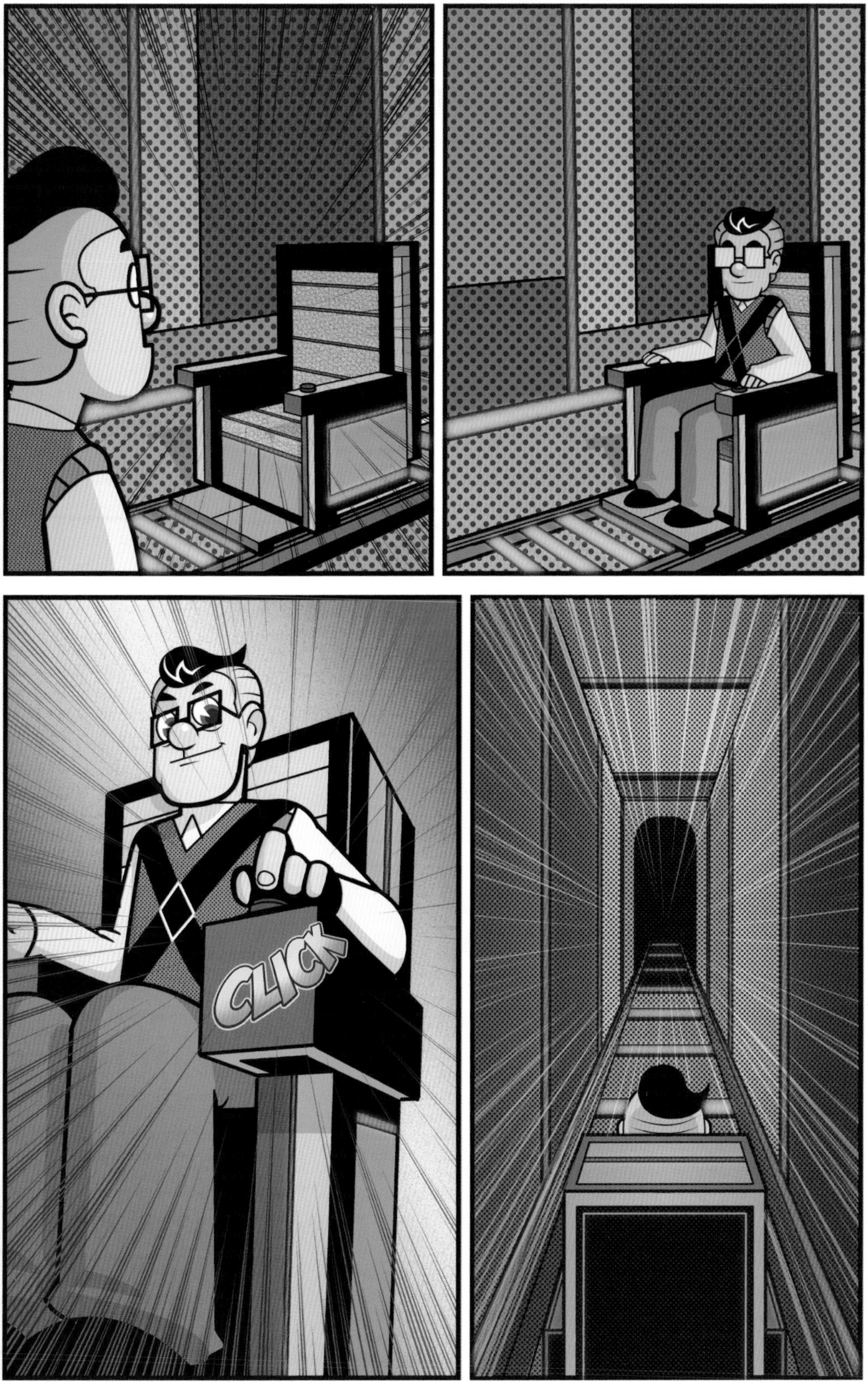
CLICK

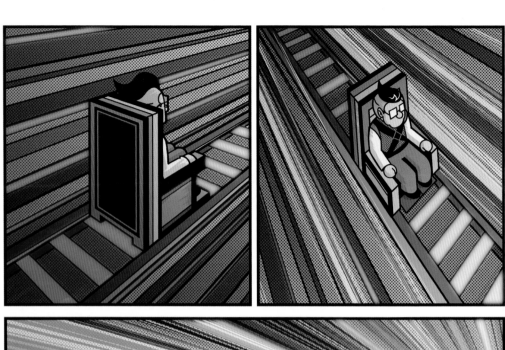

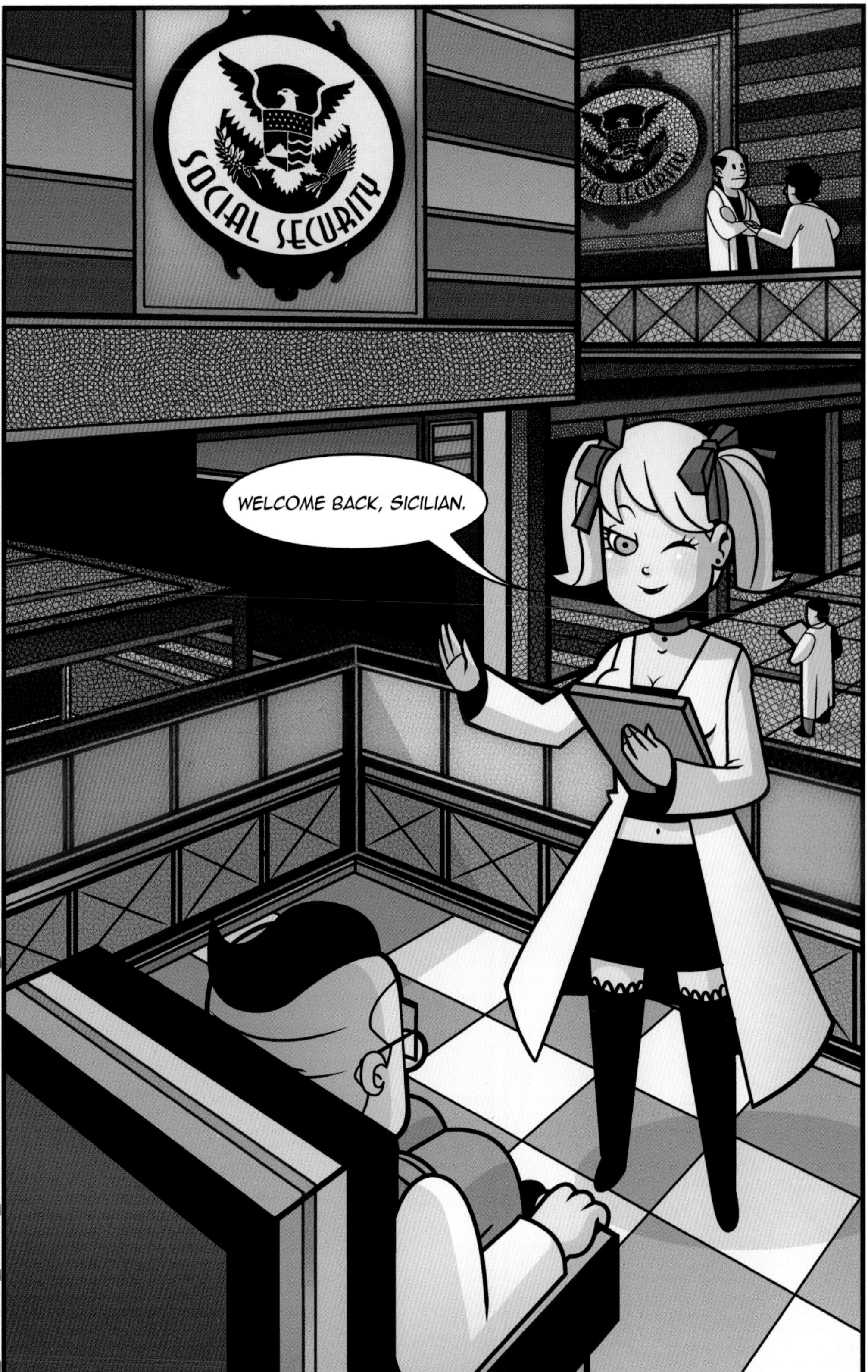
SOCIAL SECURITY
WELCOME BACK, SICILIAN.

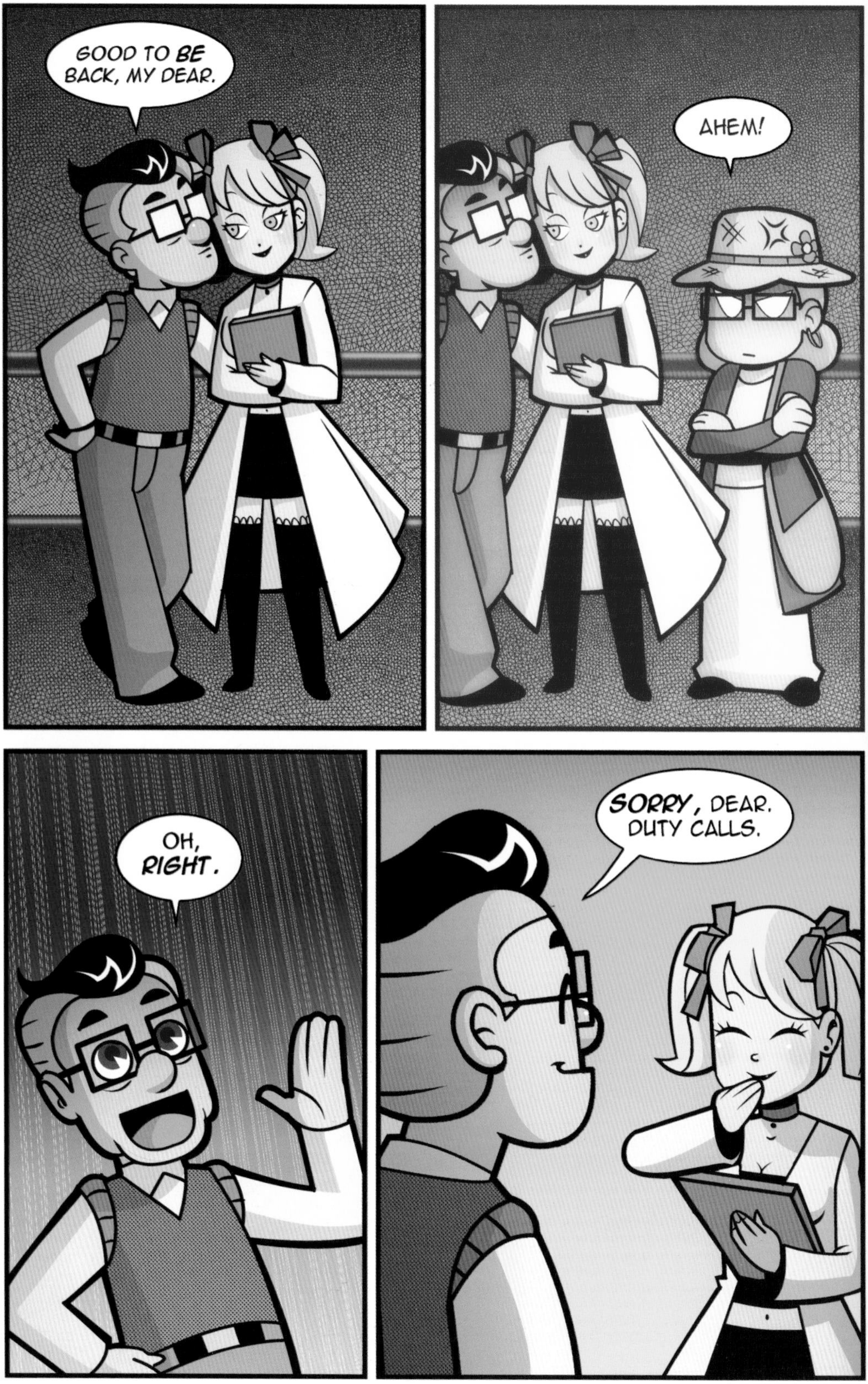
GOOD TO BE BACK, MY DEAR.
AHEM!
OH, RIGHT.
SORRY, DEAR. DUTY CALLS.

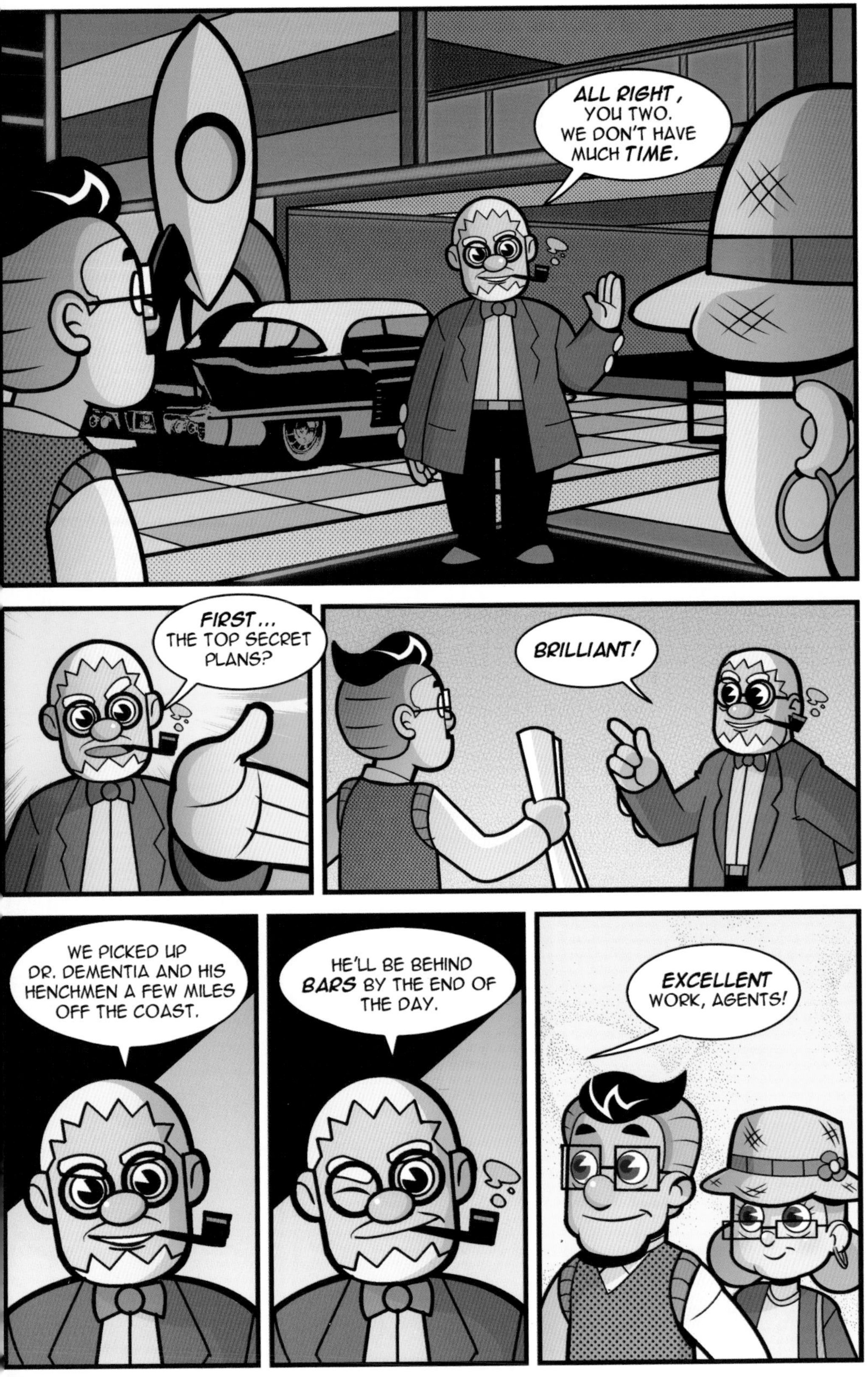
ALL RIGHT, YOU TWO. WE DON'T HAVE MUCH TIME.
FIRST... THE TOP SECRET PLANS?
BRILLIANT!
WE PICKED UP DR. DEMENTIA AND HIS HENCHMEN A FEW MILES OFF THE COAST.
HE'LL BE BEHIND BARS BY THE END OF THE DAY.
EXCELLENT WORK, AGENTS!

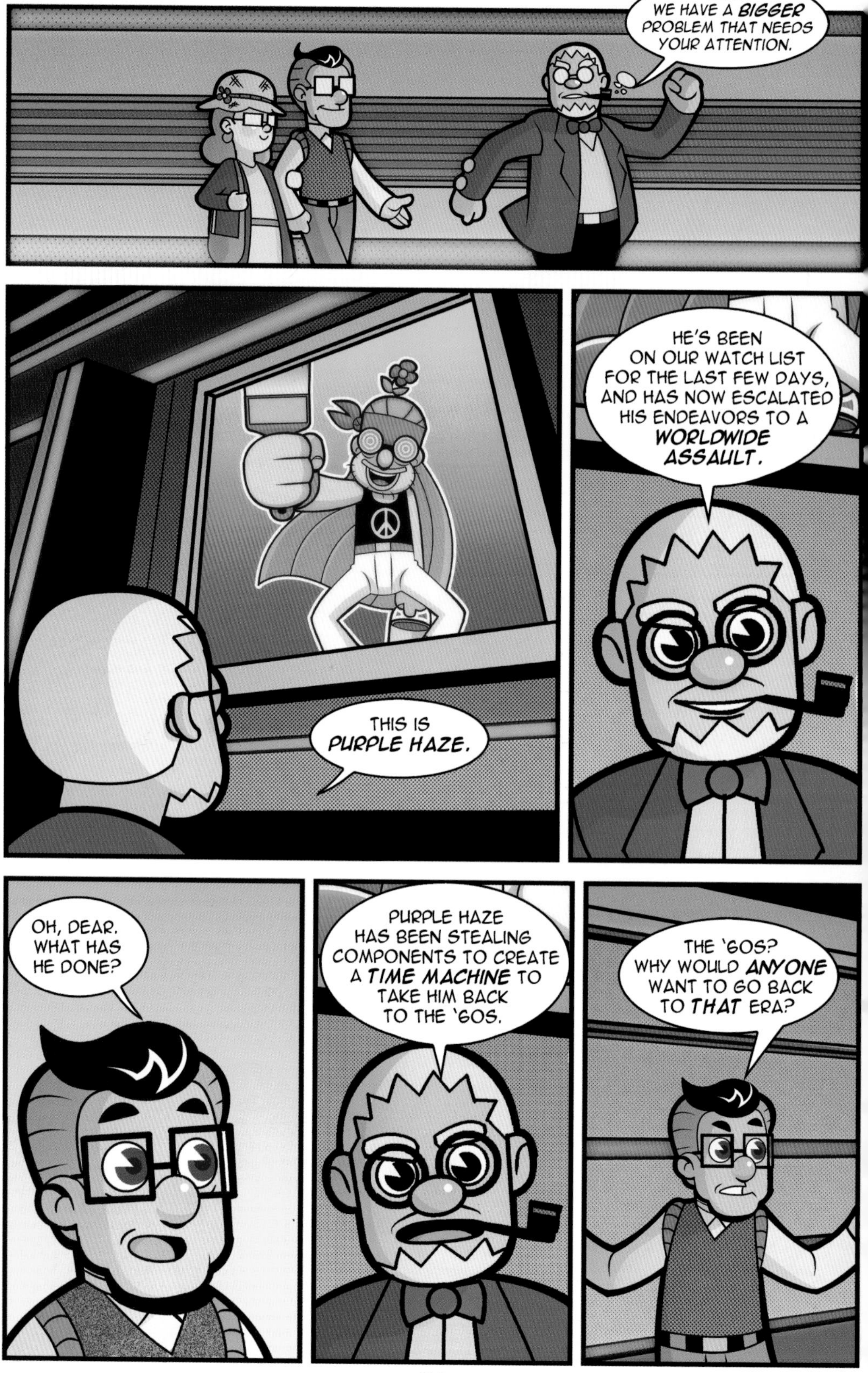
NOW. WE HAVE A BIGGER PROBLEM THAT NEEDS YOUR ATTENTION.
THIS IS PURPLE HAZE.
HE'S BEEN ON OUR WATCH LIST FOR THE LAST FEW DAYS, AND HAS NOW ESCALATED HIS ENDEAVORS TO A WORLDWIDE ASSAULT.
OH, DEAR. WHAT HAS HE DONE?
PURPLE HAZE HAS BEEN STEALING COMPONENTS TO CREATE A TIME MACHINE TO TAKE HIM BACK TO THE '60S.
THE '60S? WHY WOULD ANYONE WANT TO GO BACK TO THAT ERA?

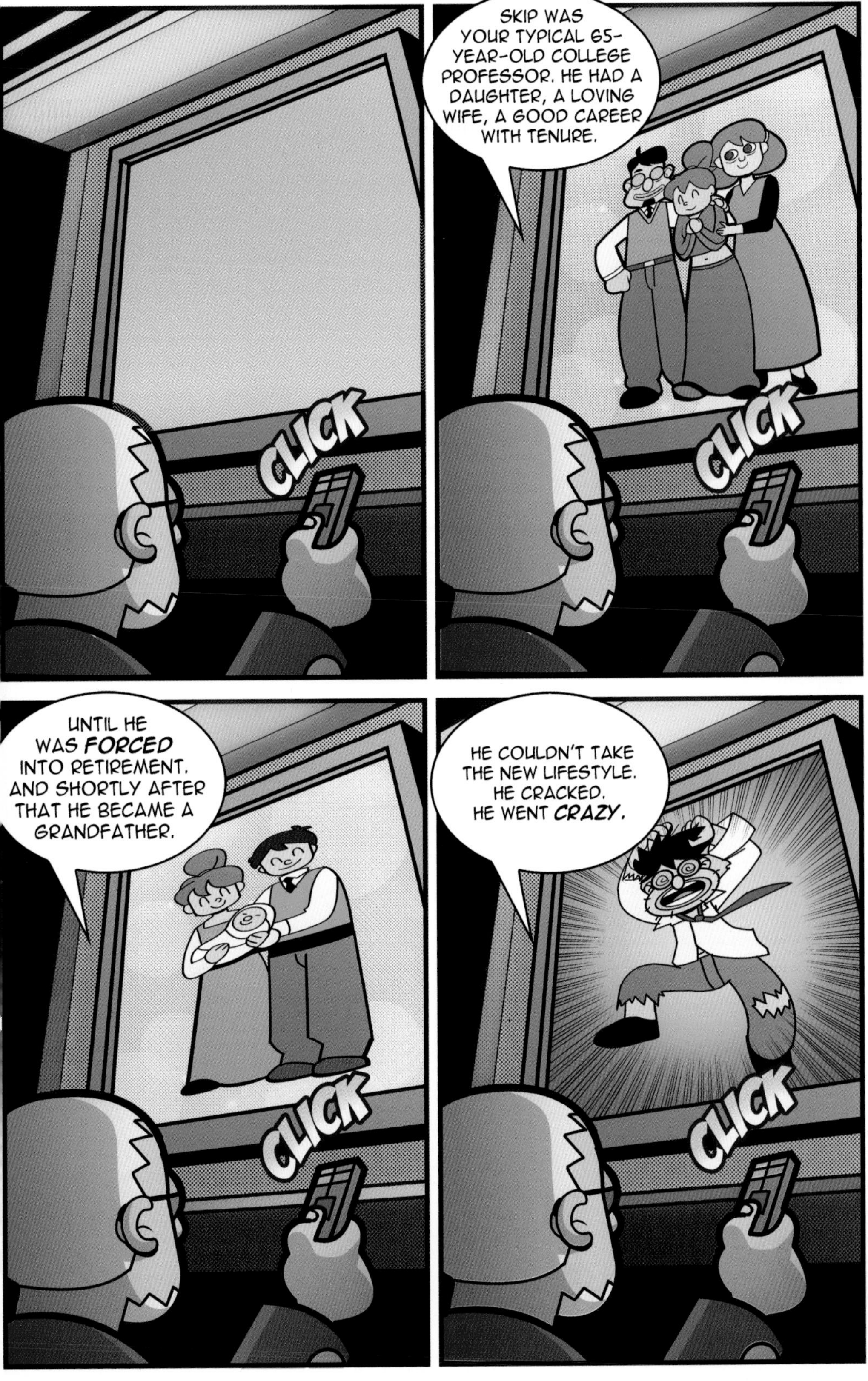
CLICK
SKIP WAS YOUR TYPICAL 65-YEAR-OLD COLLEGE PROFESSOR. HE HAD A DAUGHTER, A LOVING WIFE, A GOOD CAREER WITH TENURE.
CLICK
UNTIL HE WAS FORCED INTO RETIREMENT. AND SHORTLY AFTER THAT HE BECAME A GRANDFATHER.
CLICK
HE COULDN'T TAKE THE NEW LIFESTYLE. HE CRACKED. HE WENT CRAZY.
CLICK

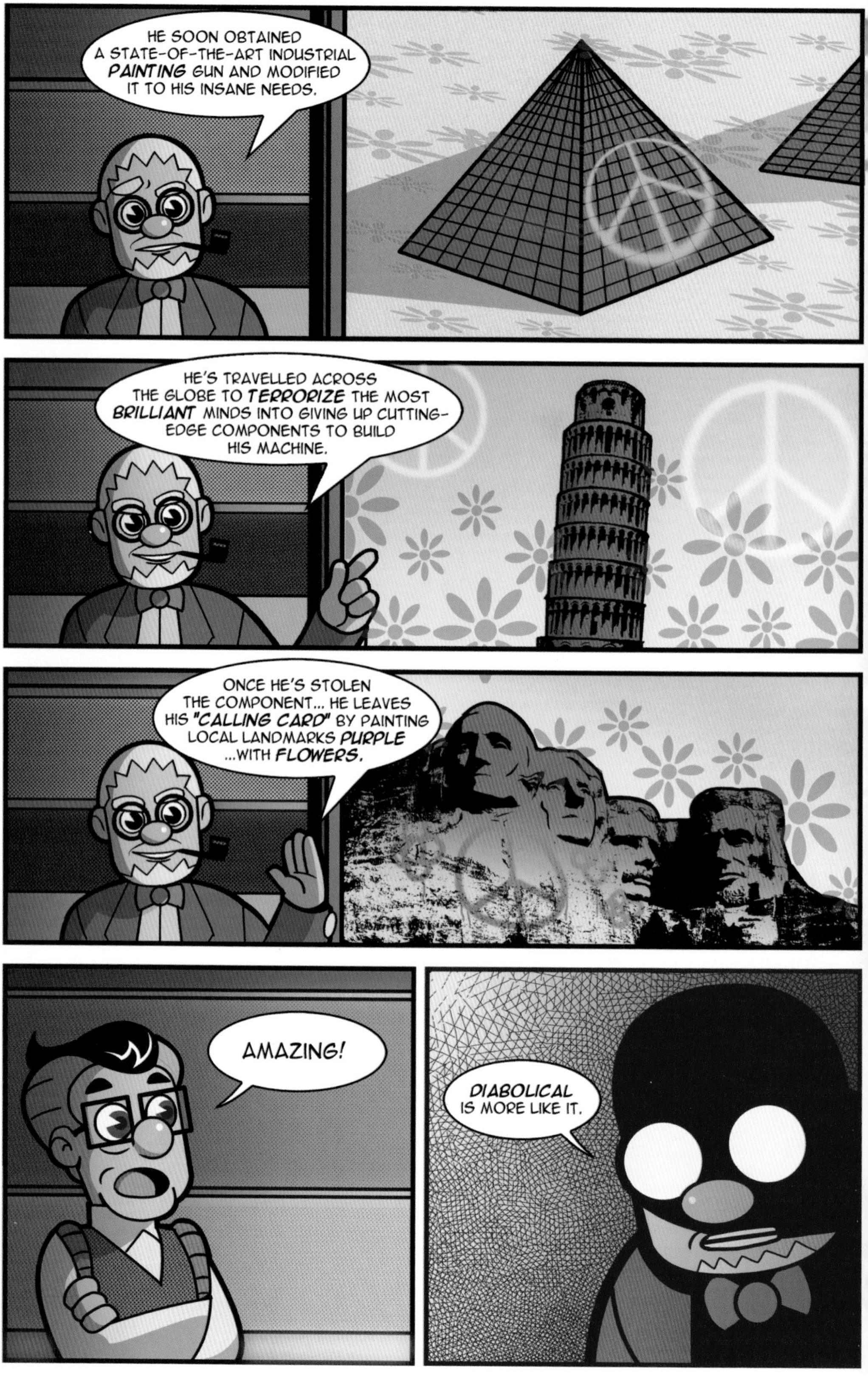
HE SOON OBTAINED A STATE-OF-THE-ART INDUSTRIAL PAINTING GUN AND MODIFIED IT TO HIS INSANE NEEDS.
HE'S TRAVELLED ACROSS THE GLOBE TO TERRORIZE THE MOST BRILLIANT MINDS INTO GIVING UP CUTTING-EDGE COMPONENTS TO BUILD HIS MACHINE.
ONCE HE'S STOLEN THE COMPONENT... HE LEAVES HIS "CALLING CARD" BY PAINTING LOCAL LANDMARKS PURPLE ...WITH FLOWERS.
AMAZING!
DIABOLICAL IS MORE LIKE IT.

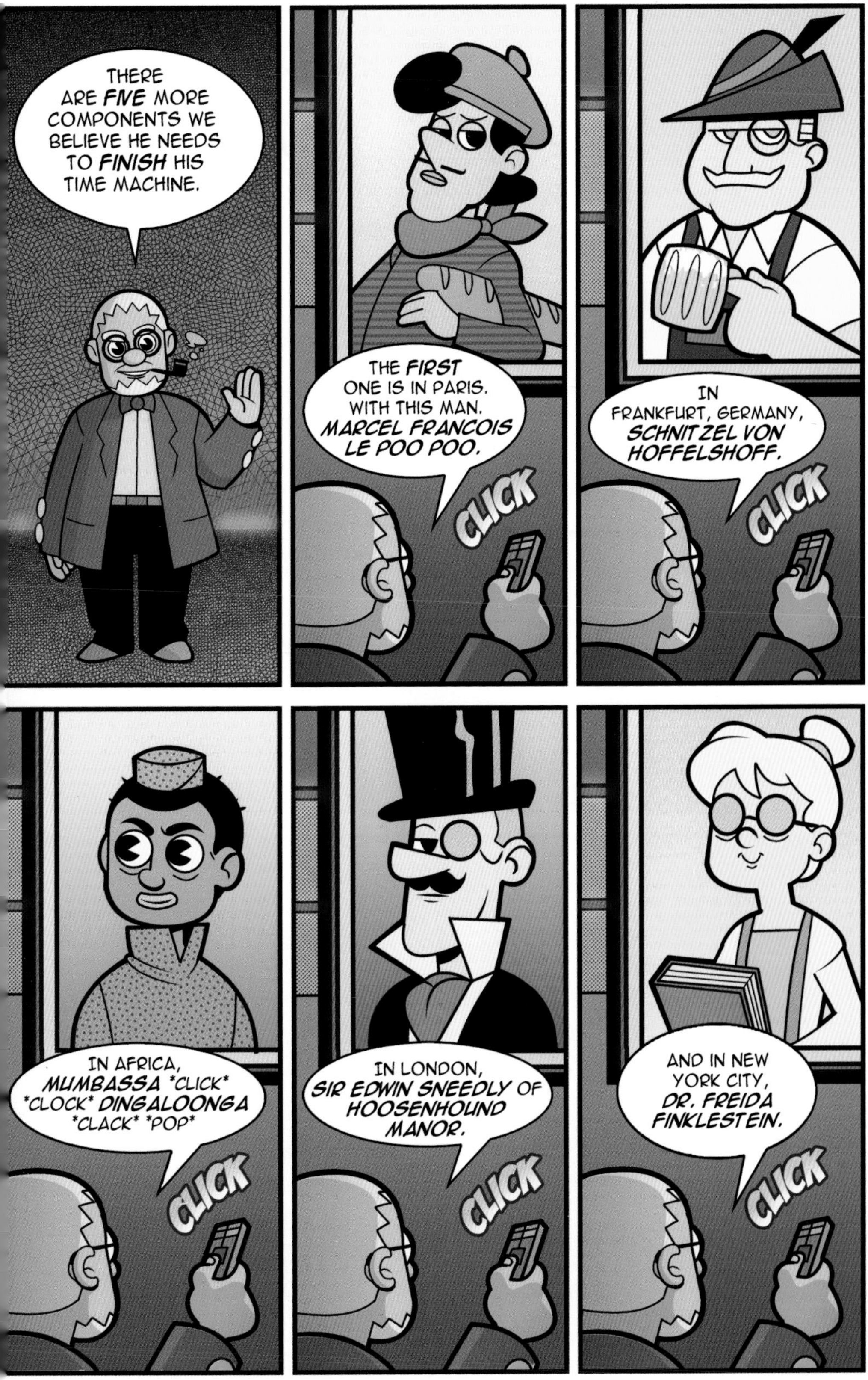
THERE ARE FIVE MORE COMPONENTS WE BELIEVE HE NEEDS TO FINISH HIS TIME MACHINE.
THE FIRST ONE IS IN PARIS. WITH THIS MAN. MARCEL FRANCOIS LE POO POO.
CLICK
IN FRANKFURT, GERMANY, SCHNITZEL VON HOFFELSHOFF.
CLICK
IN AFRICA, MUMBASSA *CLICK* *CLOCK* DINGALOONGA *CLACK* *POP*
CLICK
IN LONDON, SIR EDWIN SNEEDLY OF HOOSENHOUND MANOR.
CLICK
AND IN NEW YORK CITY, DR. FREIDA FINKLESTEIN.
CLICK

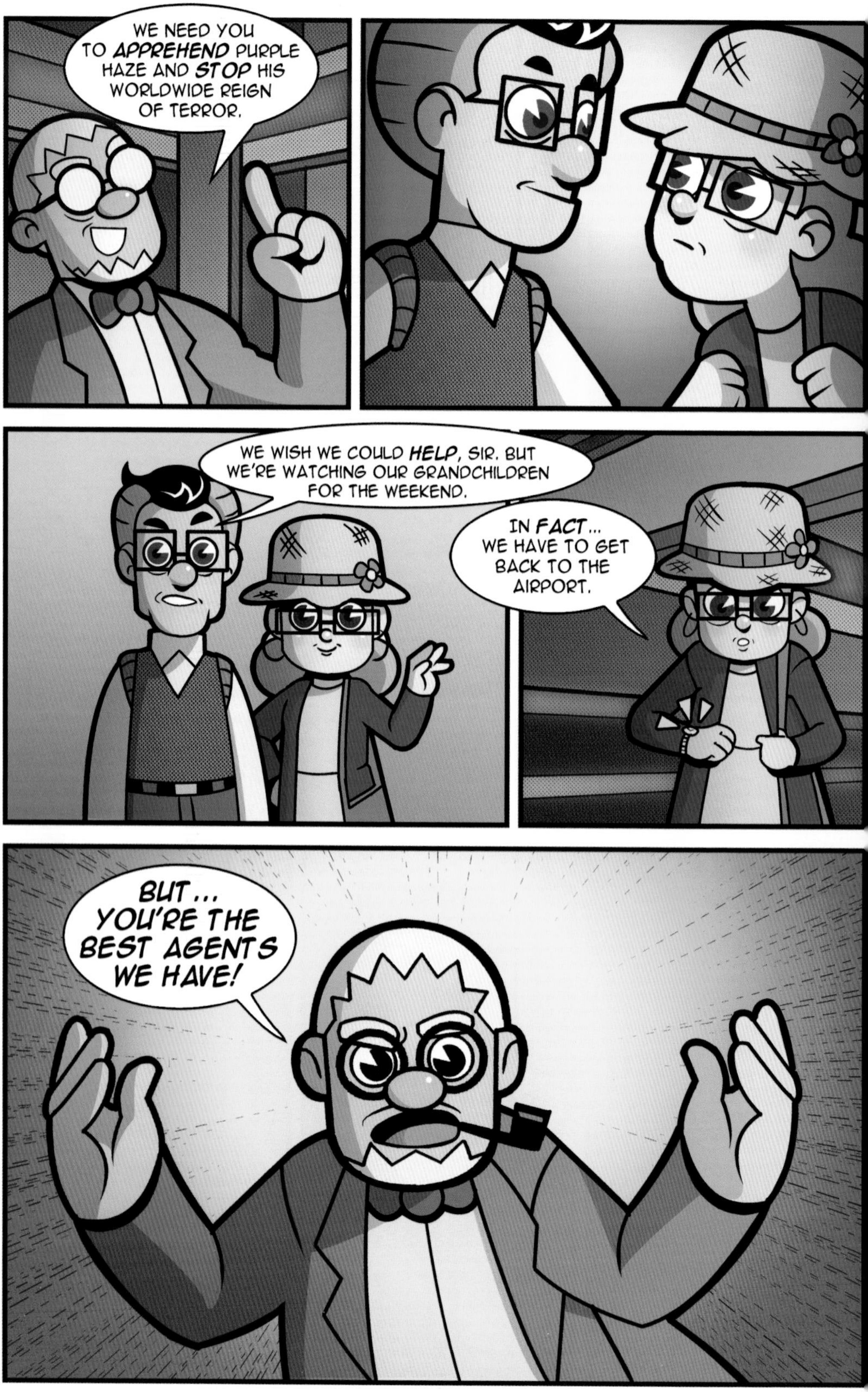
WE NEED YOU TO APPREHEND PURPLE HAZE AND STOP HIS WORLDWIDE REIGN OF TERROR.
WE WISH WE COULD HELP, SIR. BUT WE'RE WATCHING OUR GRANDCHILDREN FOR THE WEEKEND.
IN FACT... WE HAVE TO GET BACK TO THE AIRPORT.
BUT... YOU'RE THE BEST AGENTS WE HAVE!

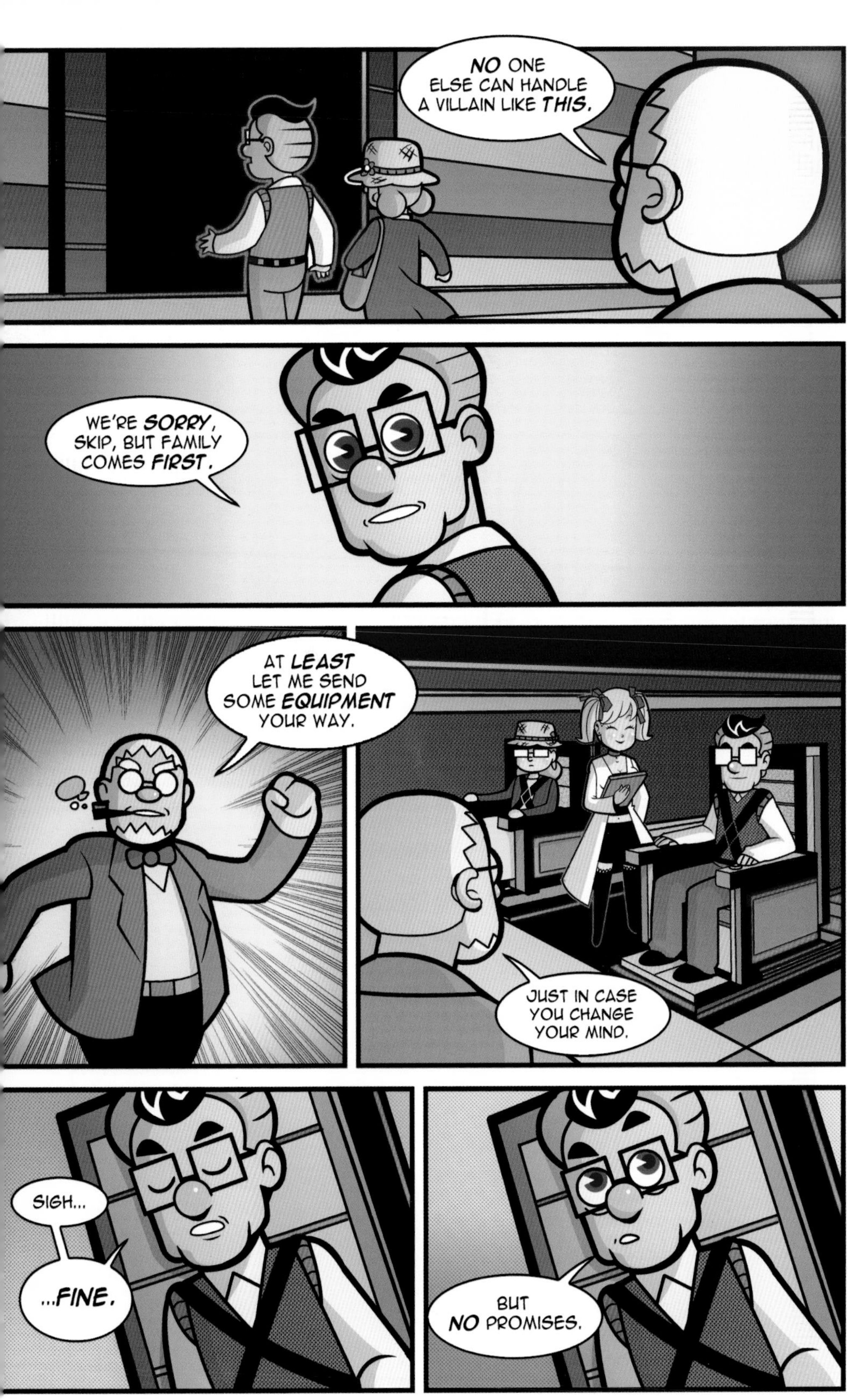
NO ONE ELSE CAN HANDLE A VILLAIN LIKE THIS.
WE'RE SORRY, SKIP, BUT FAMILY COMES FIRST.
AT LEAST LET ME SEND SOME EQUIPMENT YOUR WAY.
JUST IN CASE YOU CHANGE YOUR MIND.
SIGH...
...FINE.
BUT NO PROMISES.

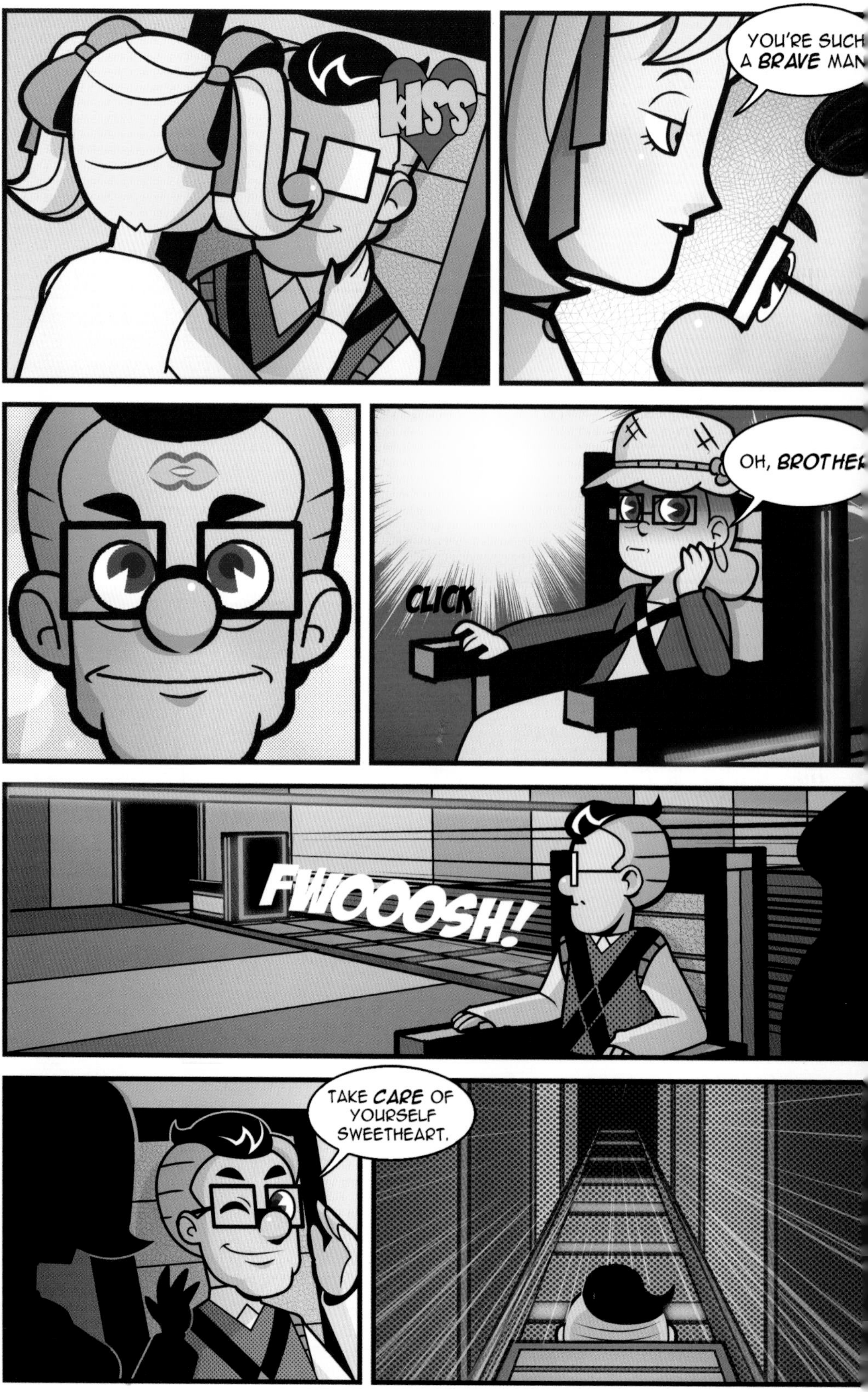
KISS
YOU'RE SUCH A BRAVE MAN
OH, BROTHER
CLICK
FWOOOSH!
TAKE CARE OF YOURSELF SWEETHEART.

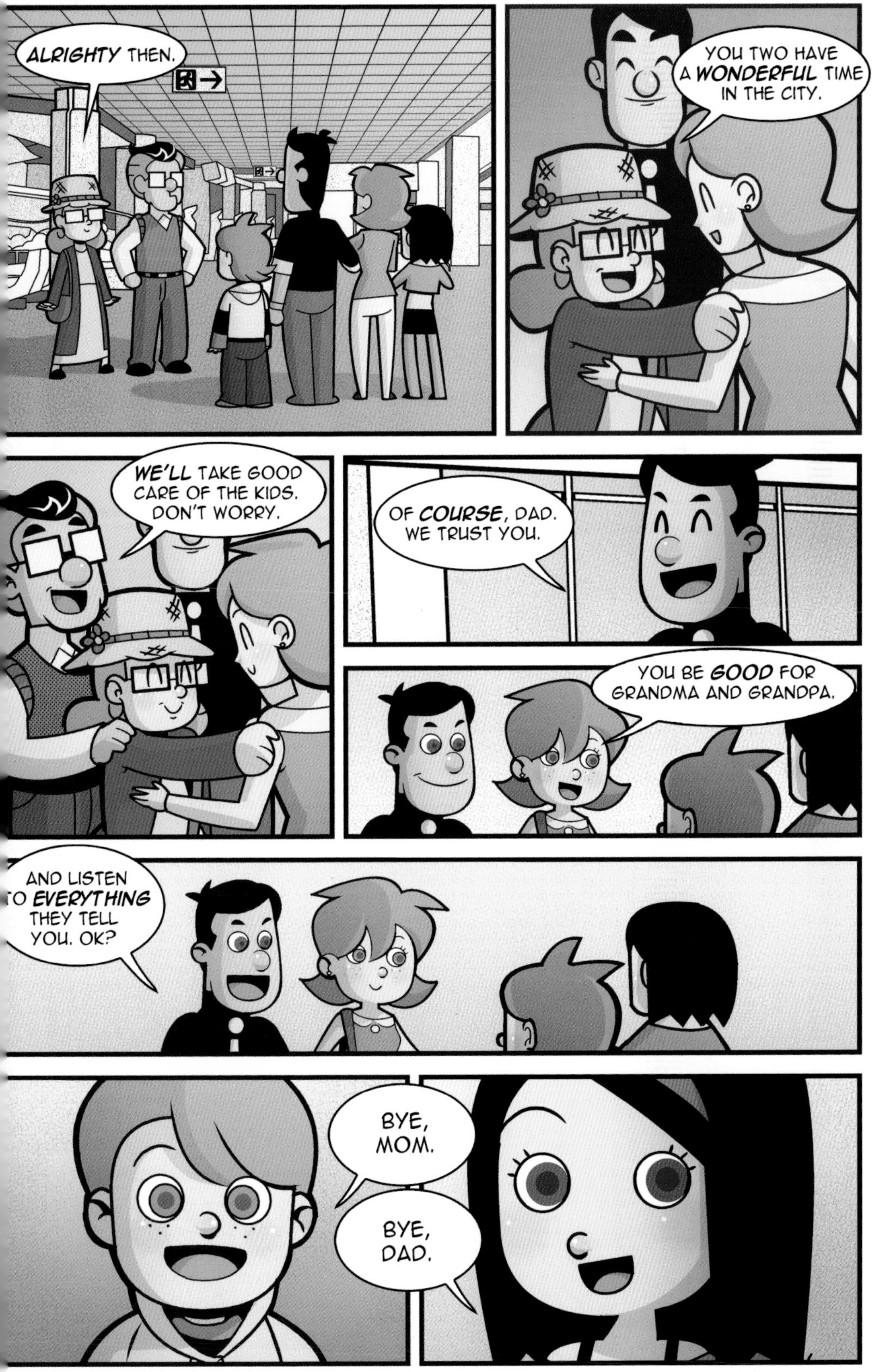
ALRIGHTY THEN.
YOU TWO HAVE A WONDERFUL TIME IN THE CITY.
WE'LL TAKE GOOD CARE OF THE KIDS. DON'T WORRY.
OF COURSE, DAD. WE TRUST YOU.
YOU BE GOOD FOR GRANDMA AND GRANDPA.
AND LISTEN TO EVERYTHING THEY TELL YOU. OK?
BYE, MOM.
BYE, DAD.

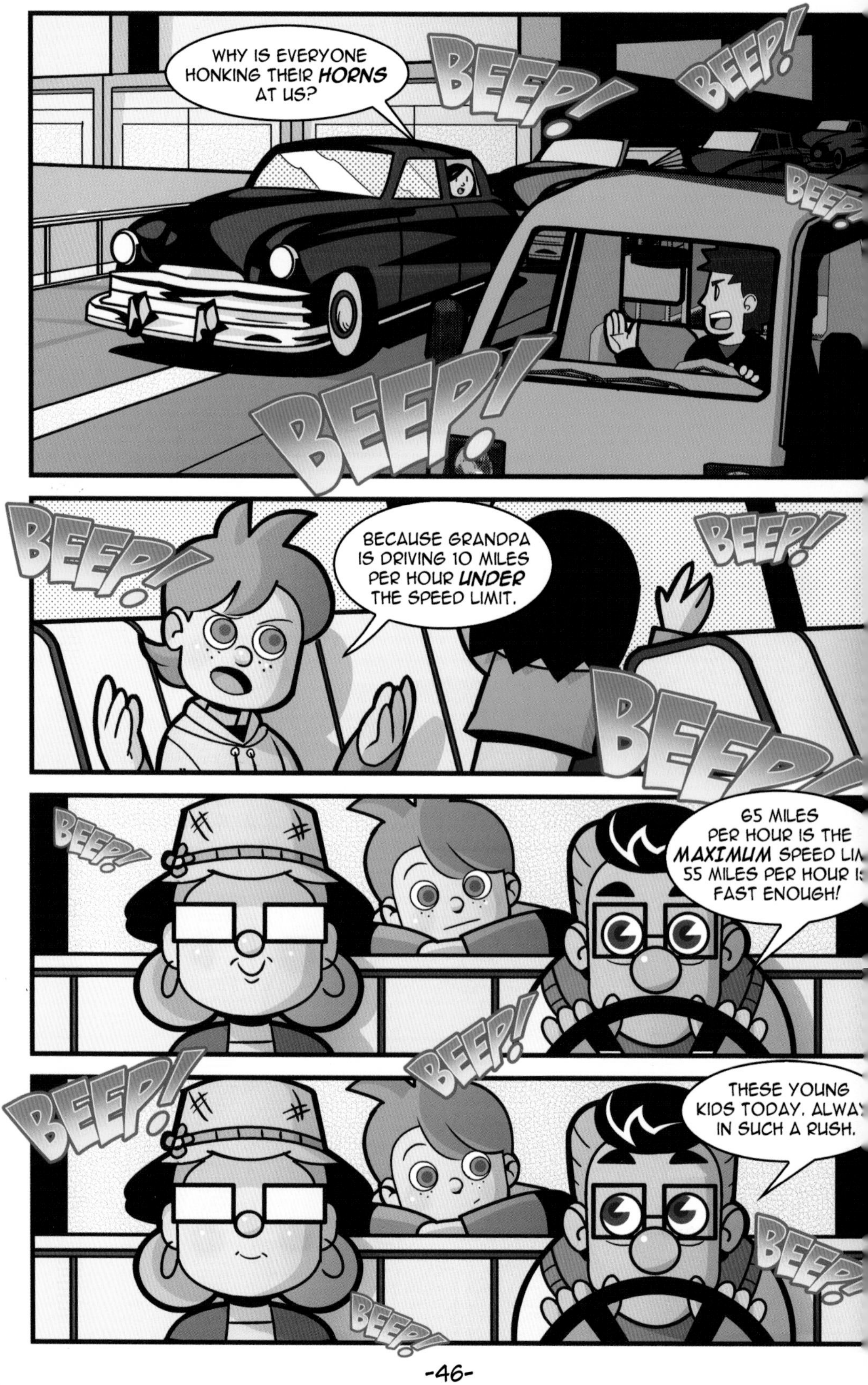
WHY IS EVERYONE HONKING THEIR HORNS AT US?
BEEP!
BEEP!
BEEP!
BEEP!
BEEP!
BECAUSE GRANDPA IS DRIVING 10 MILES PER HOUR UNDER THE SPEED LIMIT.
BEEP!
BEEP!
65 MILES PER HOUR IS THE MAXIMUM SPEED LIM
55 MILES PER HOUR I
FAST ENOUGH!
BEEP!
BEEP!
BEEP!
THESE YOUNG KIDS TODAY. ALWA
IN SUCH A RUSH.
BEEP!

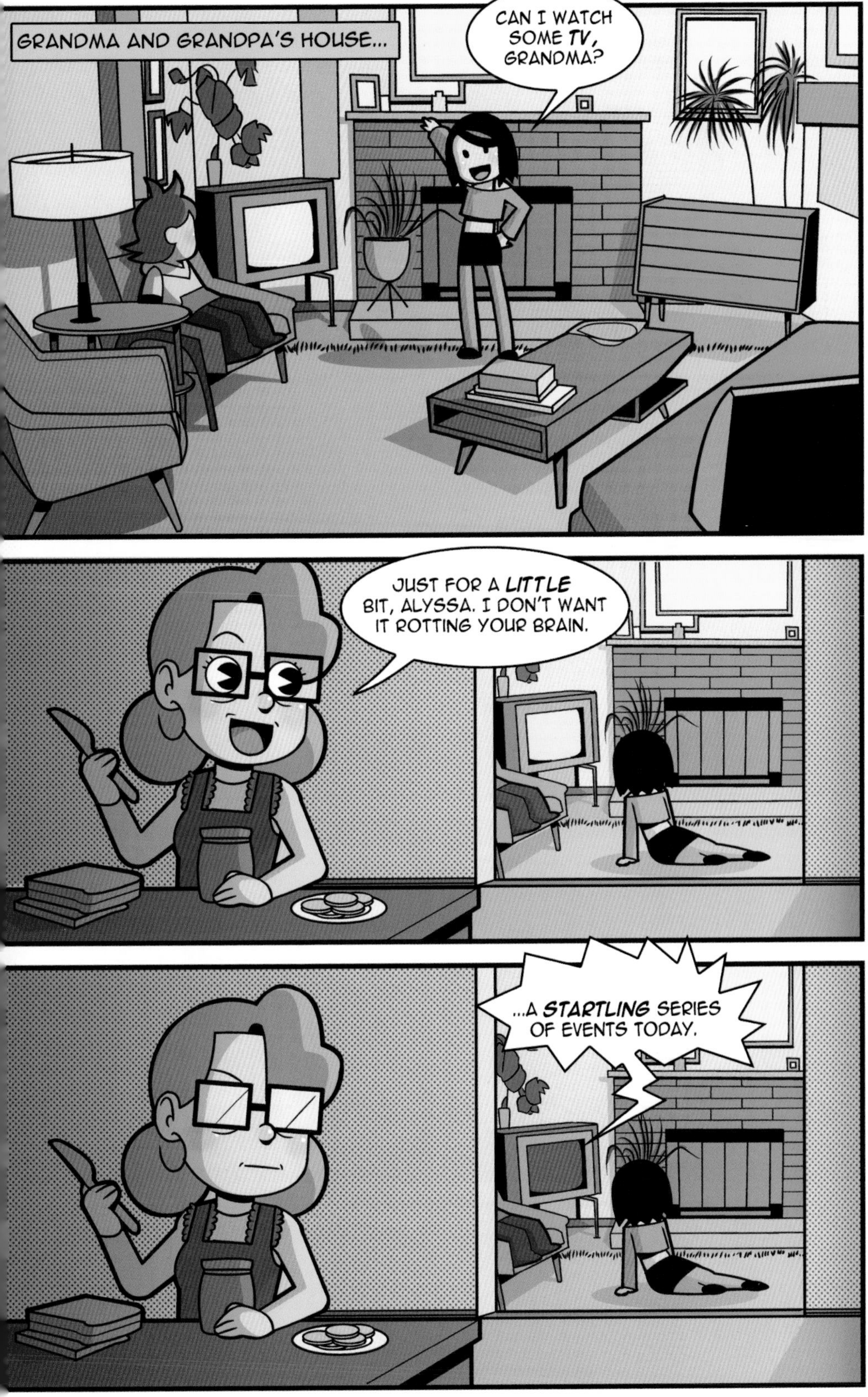
GRANDMA AND GRANDPA'S HOUSE...
CAN I WATCH SOME TV, GRANDMA?
JUST FOR A LITTLE BIT, ALYSSA. I DON'T WANT IT ROTTING YOUR BRAIN.
...A STARTLING SERIES OF EVENTS TODAY.

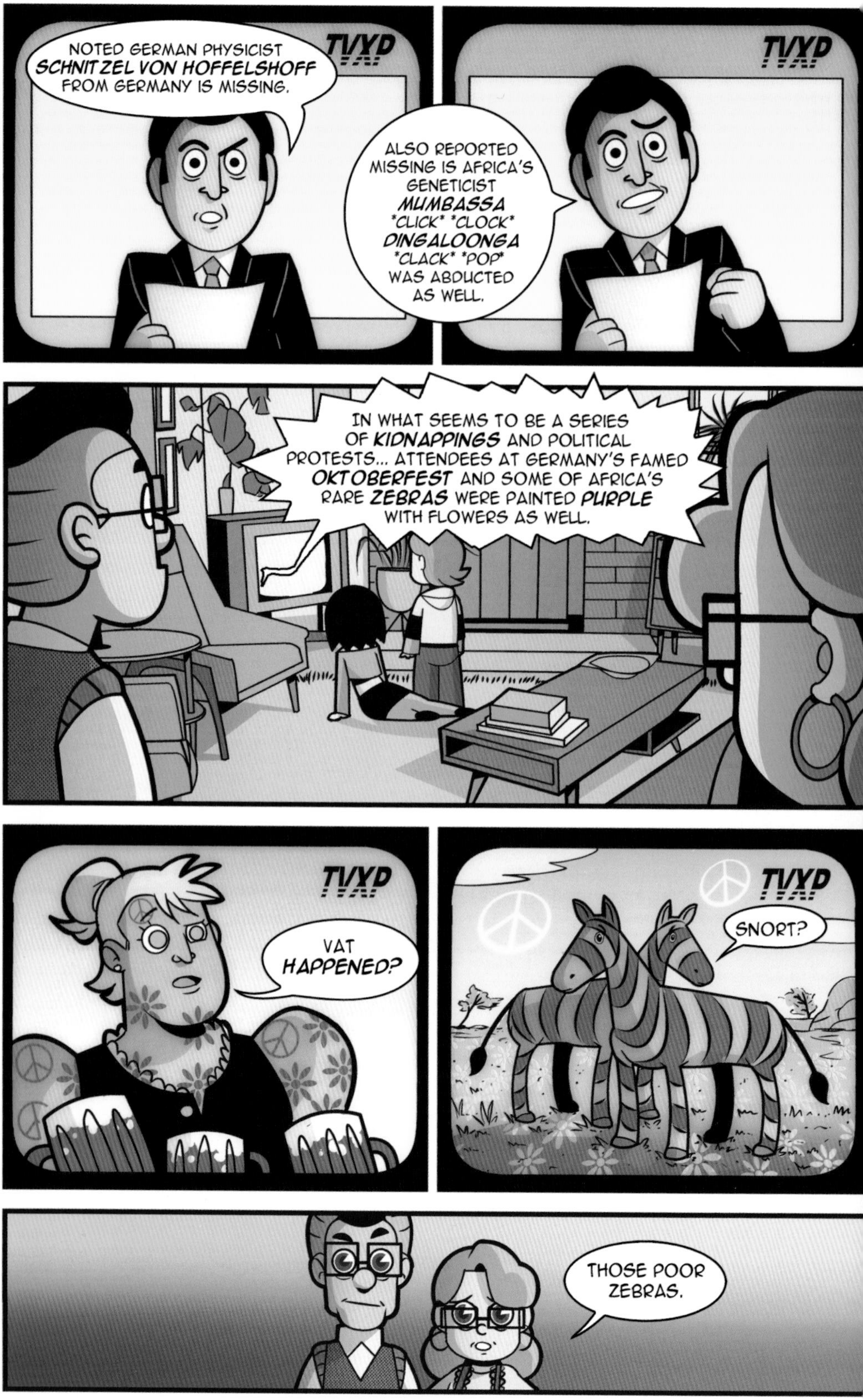
TVXD
NOTED GERMAN PHYSICIST SCHNITZEL VON HOFFELSHOFF FROM GERMANY IS MISSING.
TVXD
ALSO REPORTED MISSING IS AFRICA'S GENETICIST MUMBASSA *CLICK* *CLOCK* DINGALOONGA *CLACK* *POP* WAS ABDUCTED AS WELL.
IN WHAT SEEMS TO BE A SERIES OF KIDNAPPINGS AND POLITICAL PROTESTS... ATTENDEES AT GERMANY'S FAMED OKTOBERFEST AND SOME OF AFRICA'S RARE ZEBRAS WERE PAINTED PURPLE WITH FLOWERS AS WELL.
TVXD
VAT HAPPENED?
TVXD
SNORT?
THOSE POOR ZEBRAS.

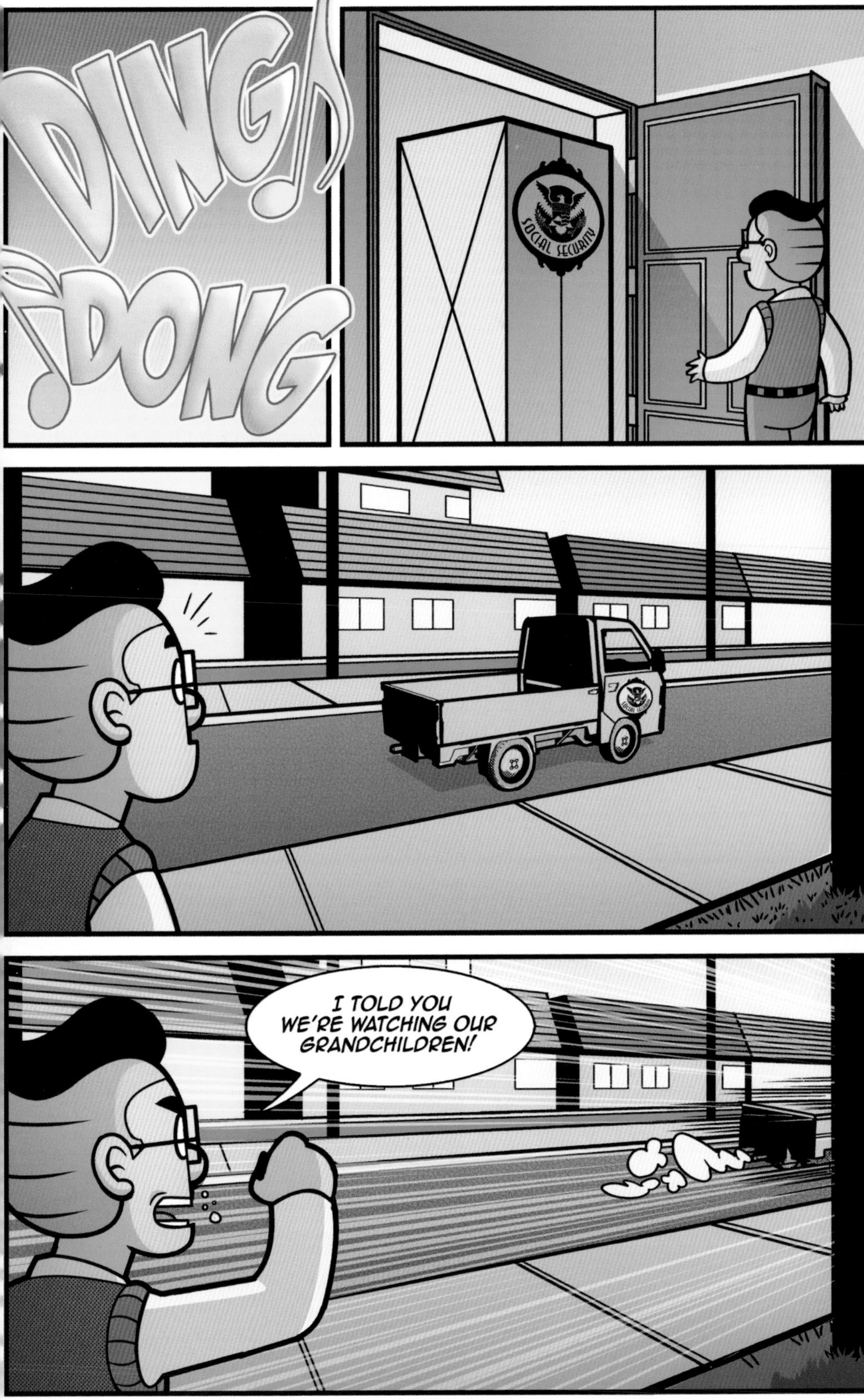
DING
DONG
SOCIAL SECURITY
I TOLD YOU WE'RE WATCHING OUR GRANDCHILDREN!

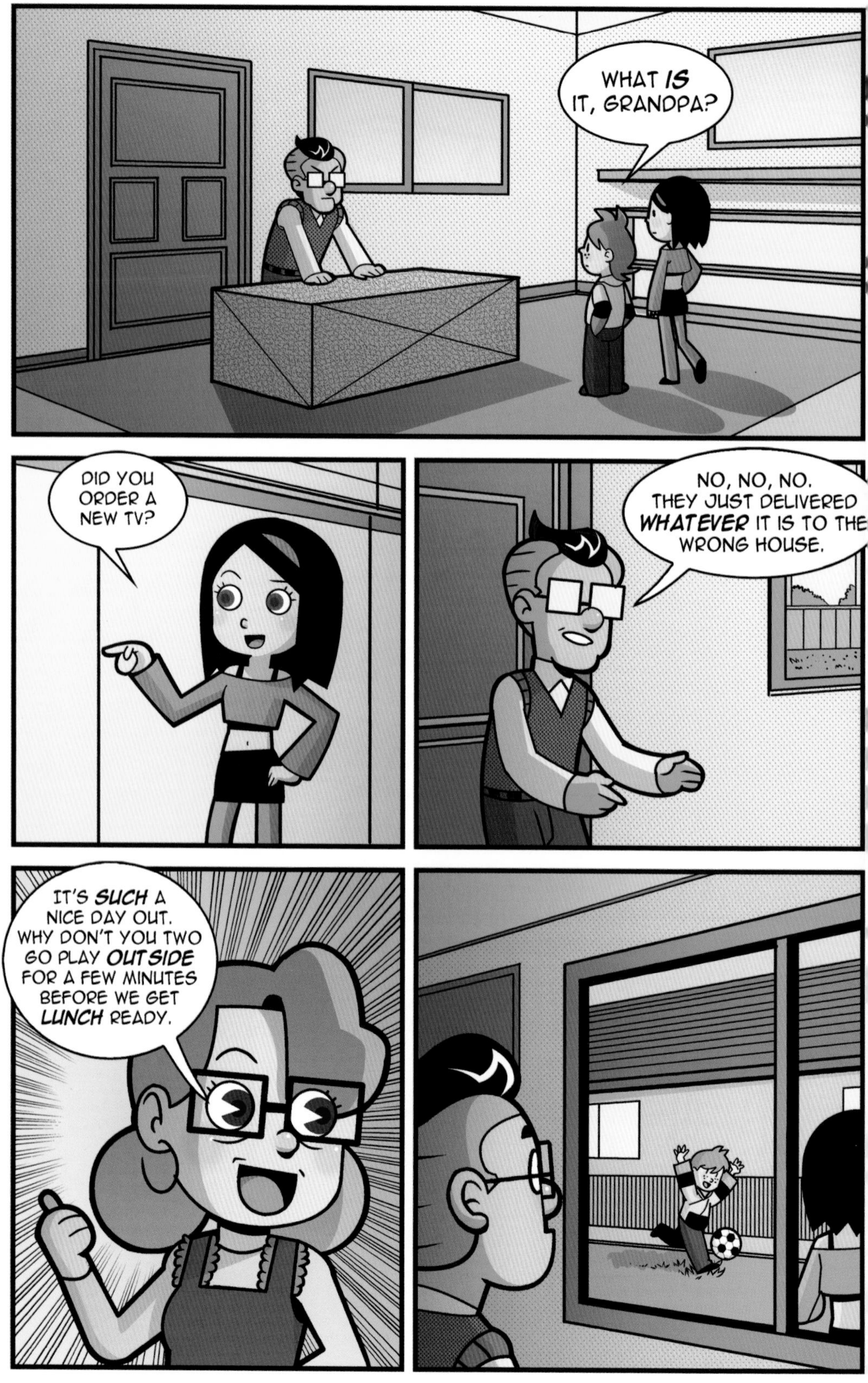
WHAT IS IT, GRANDPA?
DID YOU ORDER A NEW TV?
NO, NO, NO. THEY JUST DELIVERED WHATEVER IT IS TO THE WRONG HOUSE.
IT'S SUCH A NICE DAY OUT. WHY DON'T YOU TWO GO PLAY OUTSIDE FOR A FEW MINUTES BEFORE WE GET LUNCH READY.

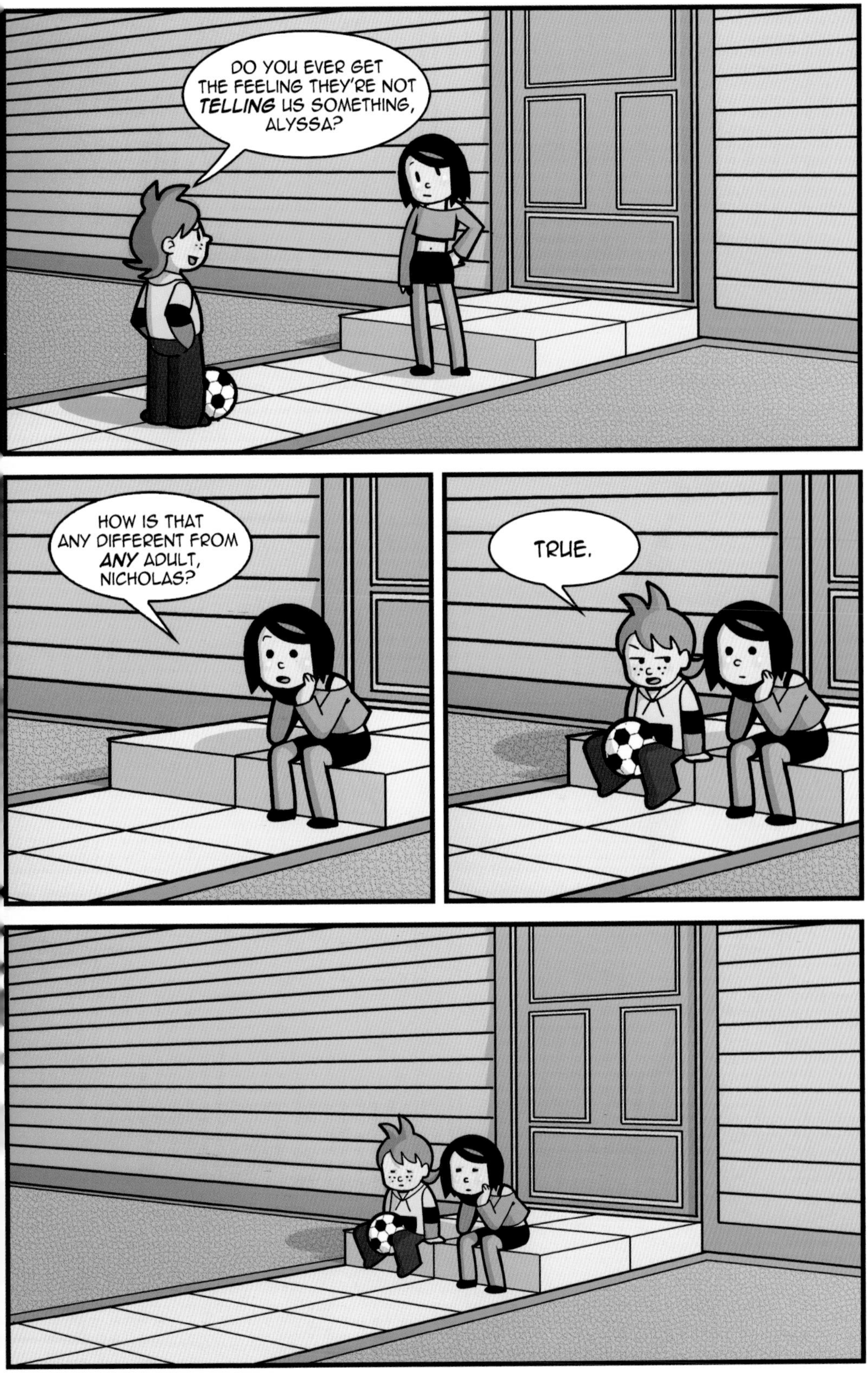
DO YOU EVER GET THE FEELING THEY'RE NOT *TELLING* US SOMETHING, ALYSSA?
HOW IS THAT ANY DIFFERENT FROM *ANY* ADULT, NICHOLAS?
TRUE.

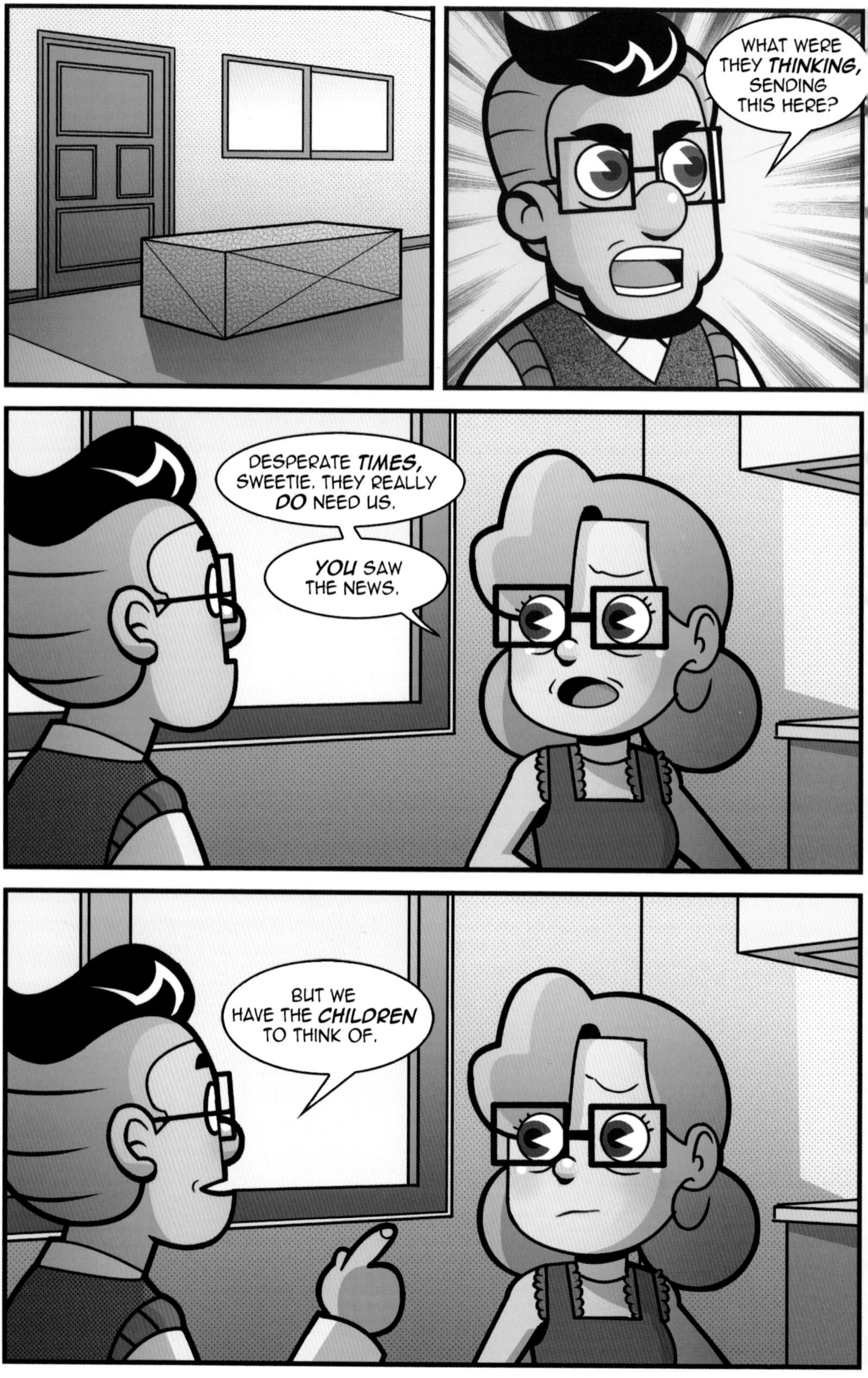
WHAT WERE THEY THINKING, SENDING THIS HERE?
DESPERATE TIMES, SWEETIE. THEY REALLY DO NEED US.
YOU SAW THE NEWS.
BUT WE HAVE THE CHILDREN TO THINK OF.

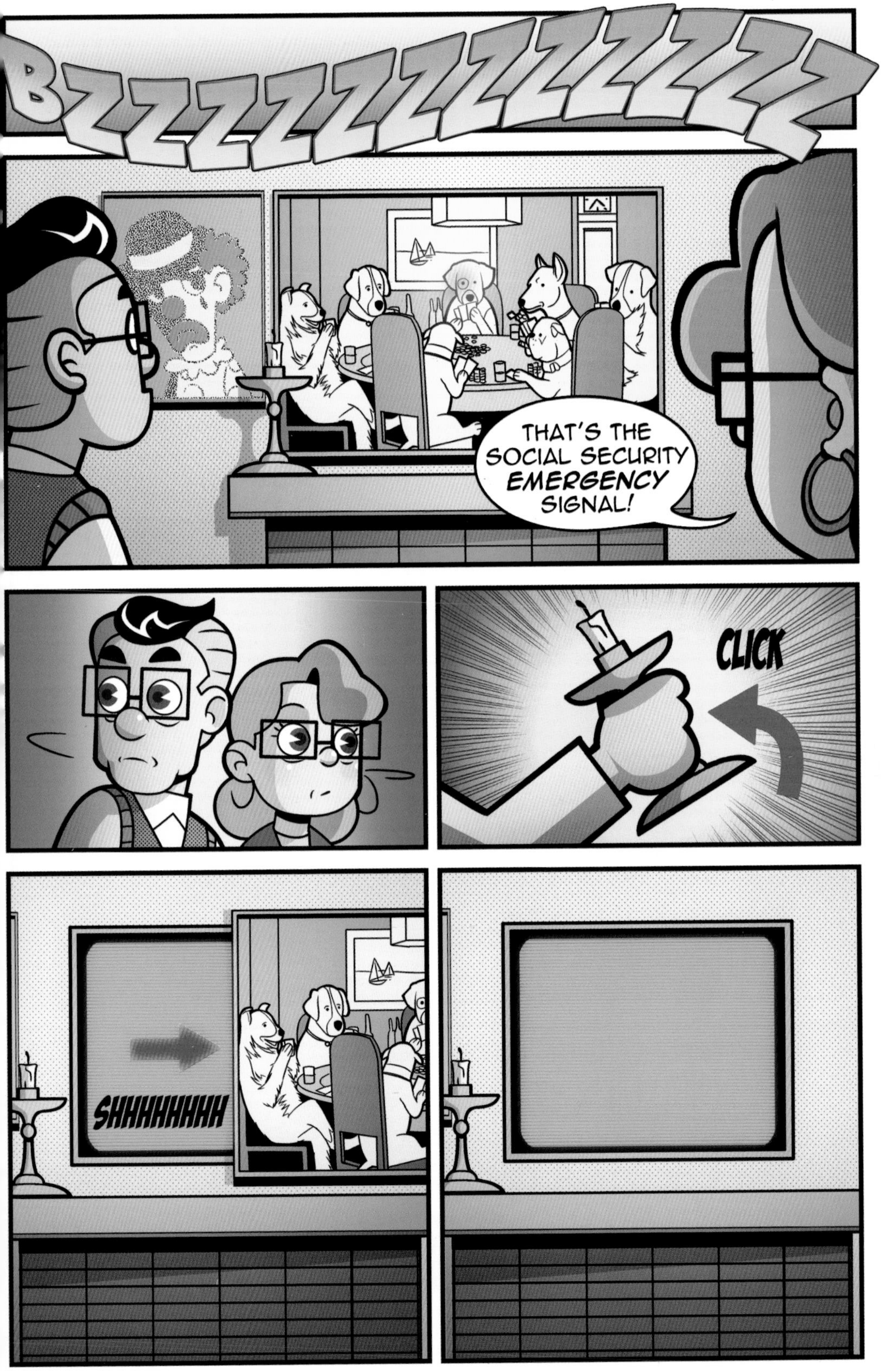
BZZZZZZZZZZZZZZ
THAT'S THE SOCIAL SECURITY EMERGENCY SIGNAL!
CLICK
SHHHHHHHH

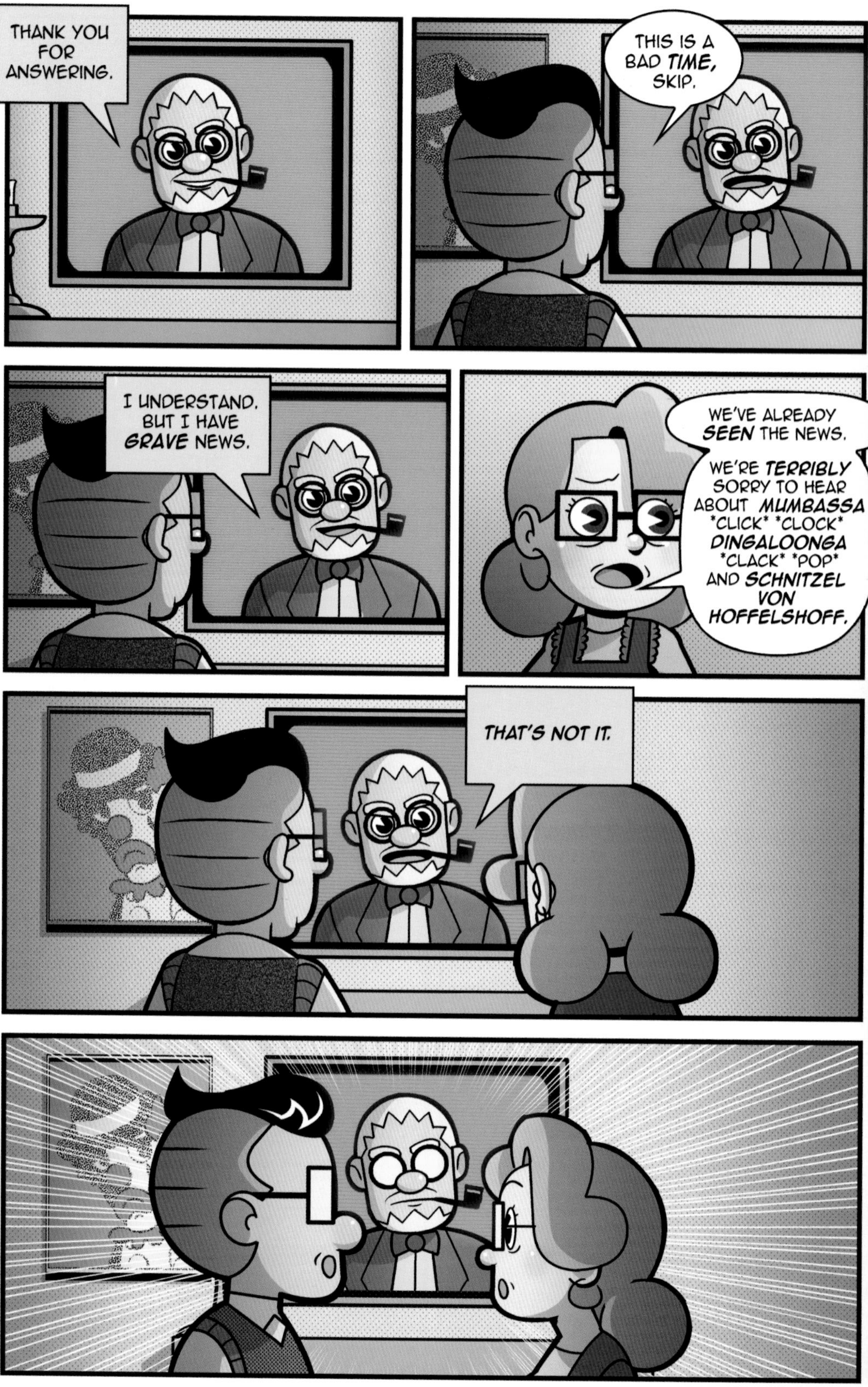
THANK YOU FOR ANSWERING.
THIS IS A BAD TIME, SKIP.
I UNDERSTAND. BUT I HAVE GRAVE NEWS.
WE'VE ALREADY SEEN THE NEWS.
WE'RE TERRIBLY SORRY TO HEAR ABOUT MUMBASSA *CLICK* *CLOCK* DINGALOONGA *CLACK* *POP* AND SCHNITZEL VON HOFFELSHOFF.
THAT'S NOT IT.

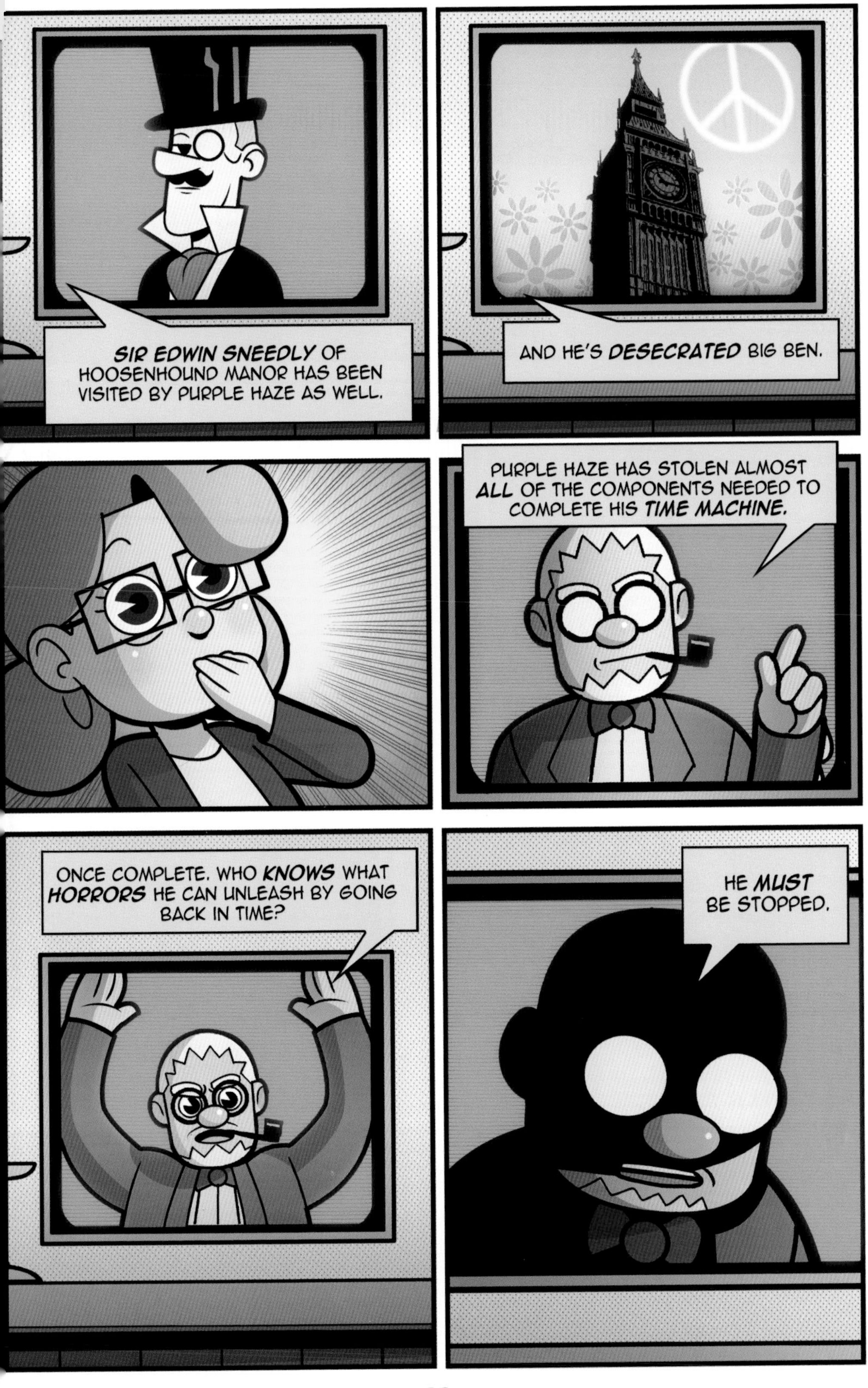
SIR EDWIN SNEEDLY OF HOOSENHOUND MANOR HAS BEEN VISITED BY PURPLE HAZE AS WELL.
AND HE'S DESECRATED BIG BEN.
PURPLE HAZE HAS STOLEN ALMOST ALL OF THE COMPONENTS NEEDED TO COMPLETE HIS TIME MACHINE.
ONCE COMPLETE. WHO KNOWS WHAT HORRORS HE CAN UNLEASH BY GOING BACK IN TIME?
HE MUST BE STOPPED.

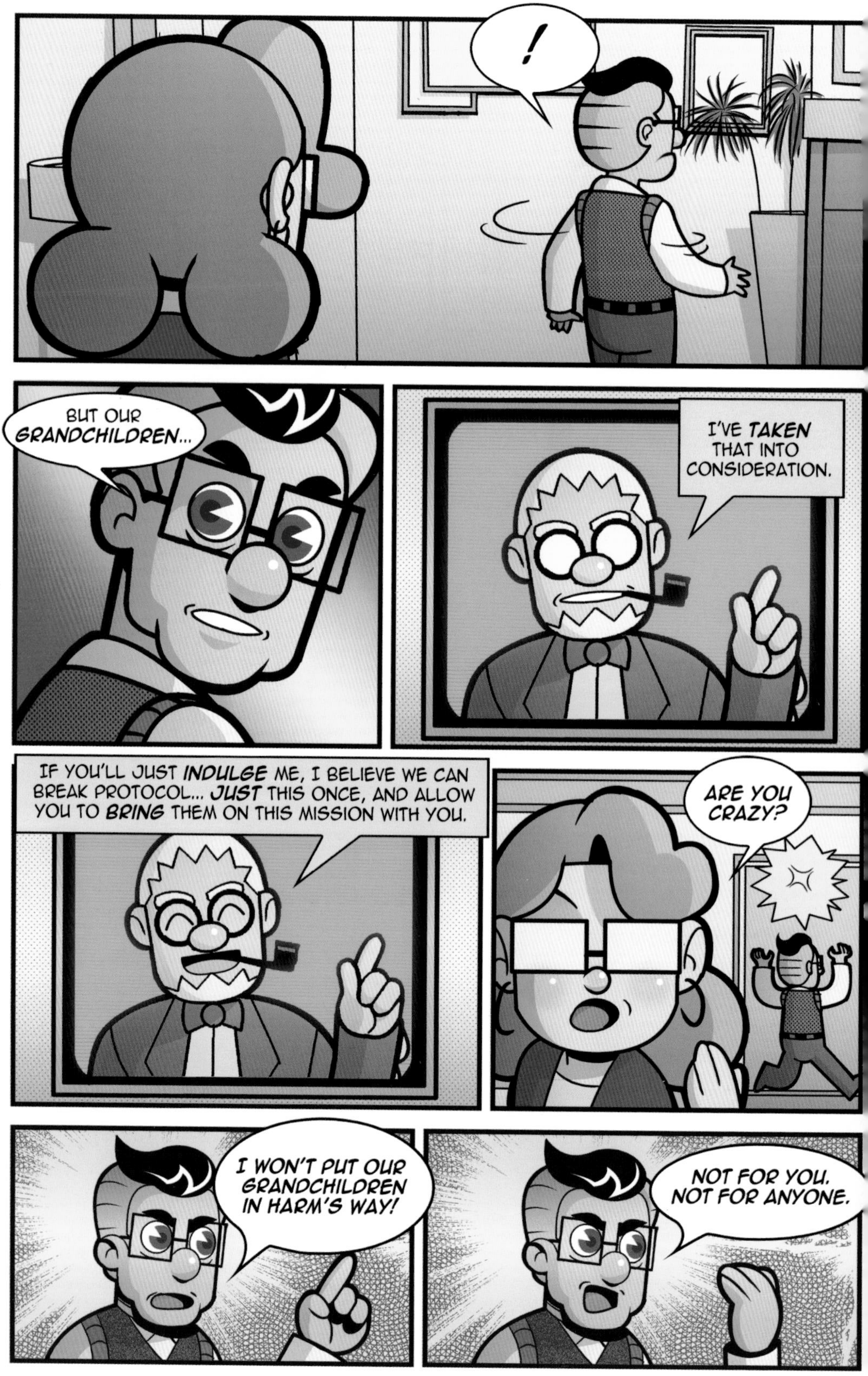
!
BUT OUR GRANDCHILDREN...
I'VE TAKEN THAT INTO CONSIDERATION.
IF YOU'LL JUST INDULGE ME, I BELIEVE WE CAN BREAK PROTOCOL... JUST THIS ONCE, AND ALLOW YOU TO BRING THEM ON THIS MISSION WITH YOU.
ARE YOU CRAZY?
I WON'T PUT OUR GRANDCHILDREN IN HARM'S WAY!
NOT FOR YOU. NOT FOR ANYONE.

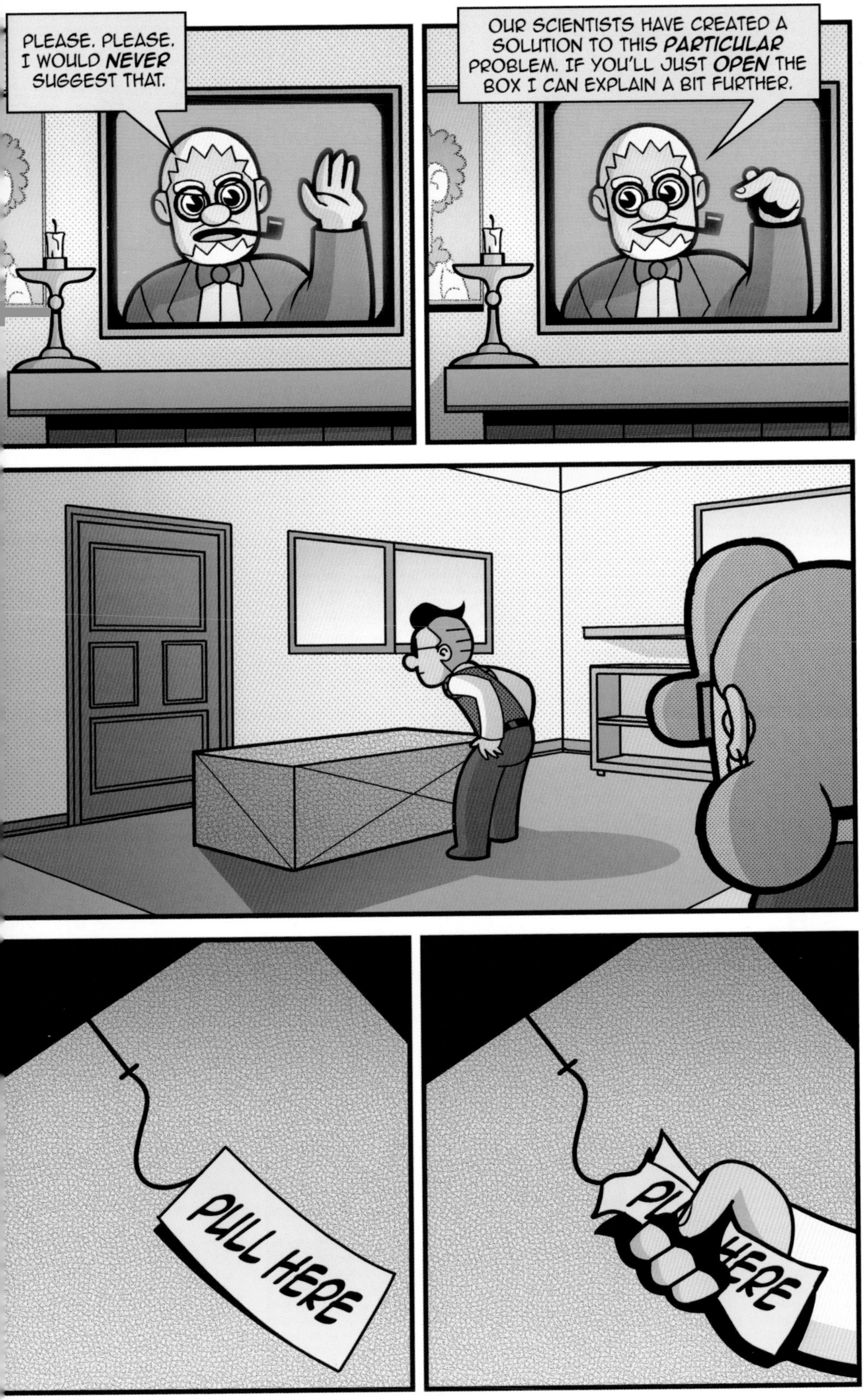
PLEASE. PLEASE. I WOULD NEVER SUGGEST THAT.
OUR SCIENTISTS HAVE CREATED A SOLUTION TO THIS PARTICULAR PROBLEM. IF YOU'LL JUST OPEN THE BOX I CAN EXPLAIN A BIT FURTHER.
PULL HERE

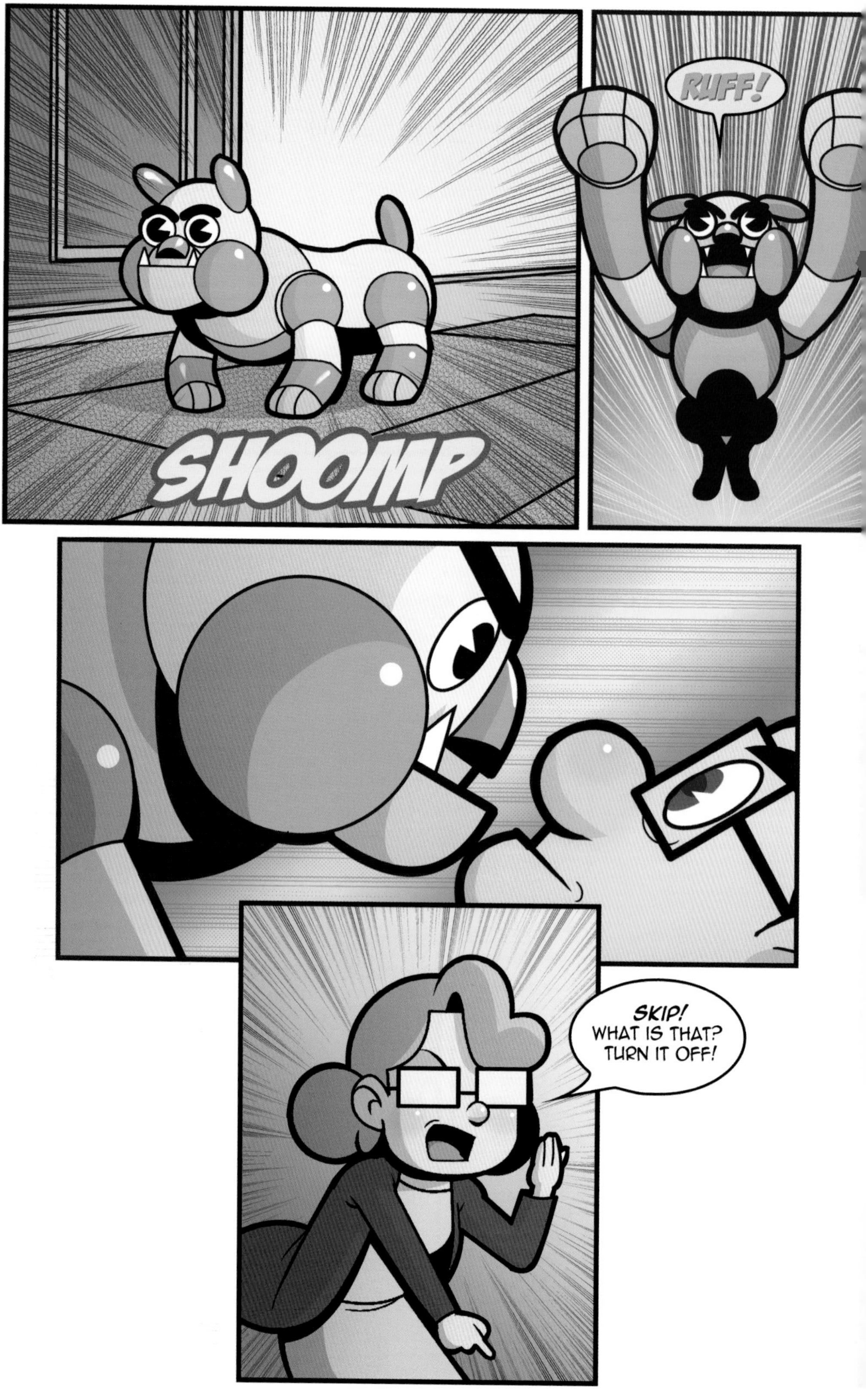
SHOOMP
RUFF!
SKIP! WHAT IS THAT? TURN IT OFF!

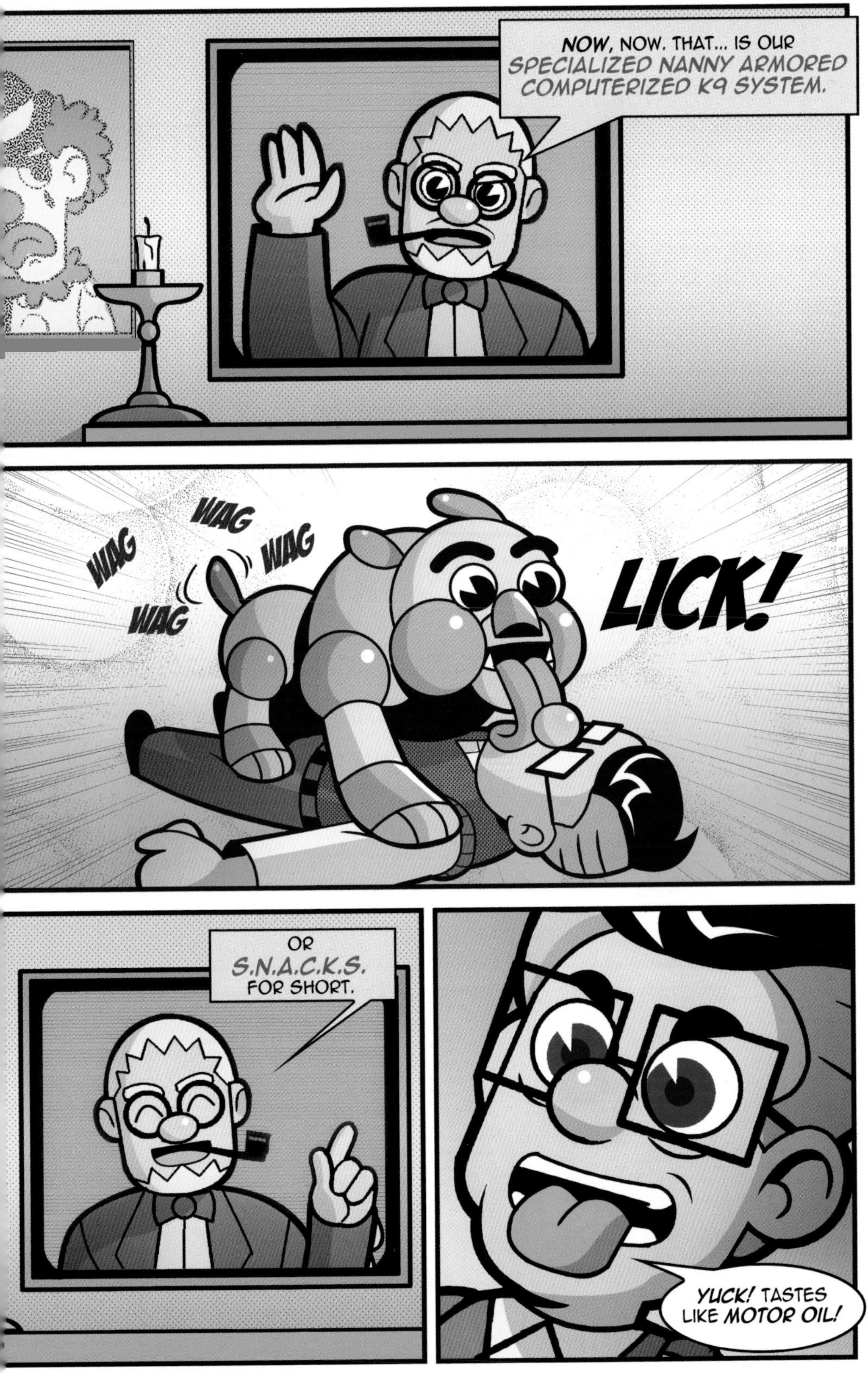
NOW, NOW. THAT... IS OUR SPECIALIZED NANNY ARMORED COMPUTERIZED K9 SYSTEM.
WAG
WAG
WAG
WAG
LICK!
OR S.N.A.C.K.S. FOR SHORT.
YUCK! TASTES LIKE MOTOR OIL!

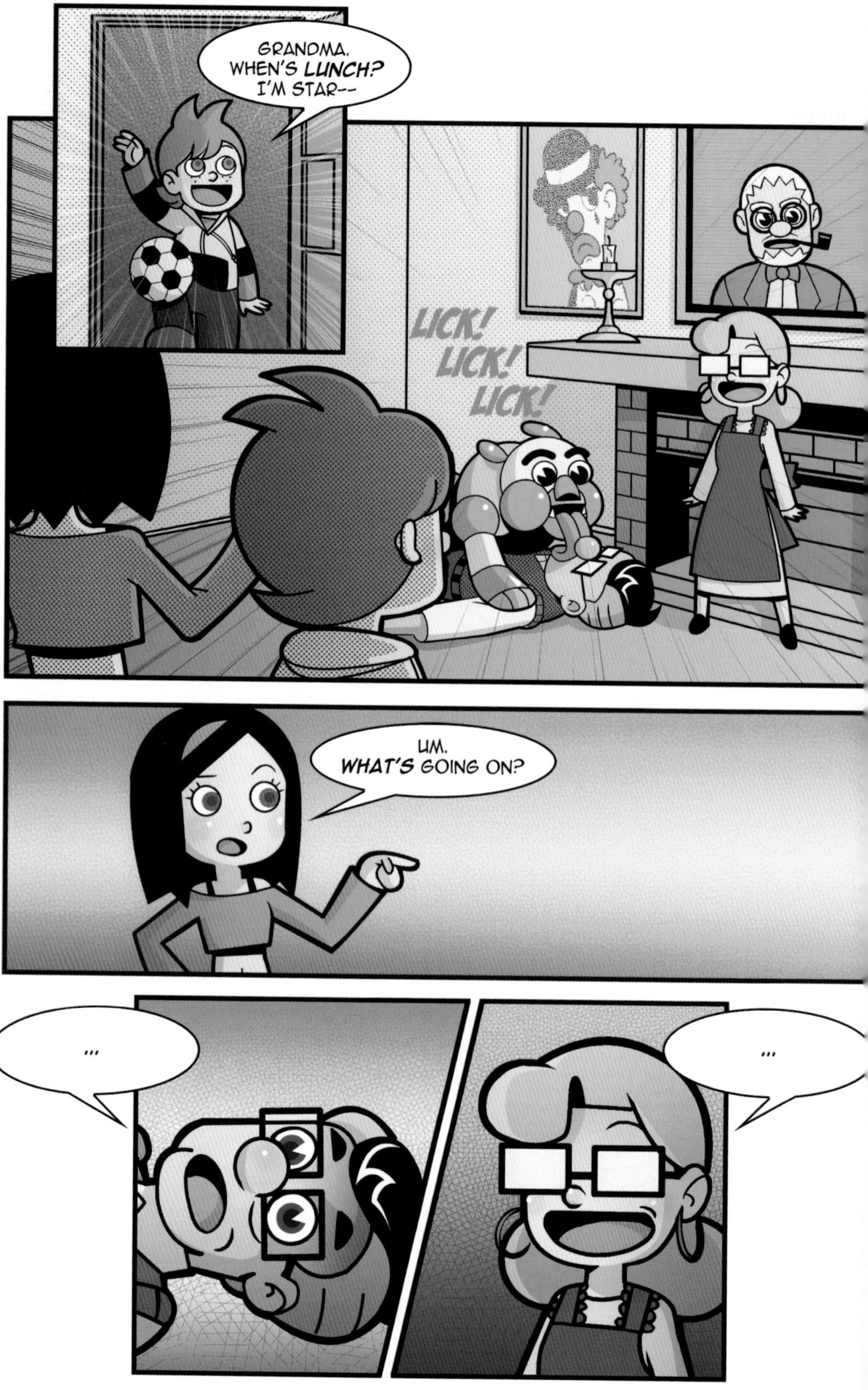
GRANDMA. WHEN'S LUNCH? I'M STAR--
LICK! LICK! LICK!
UM. WHAT'S GOING ON?
...
...

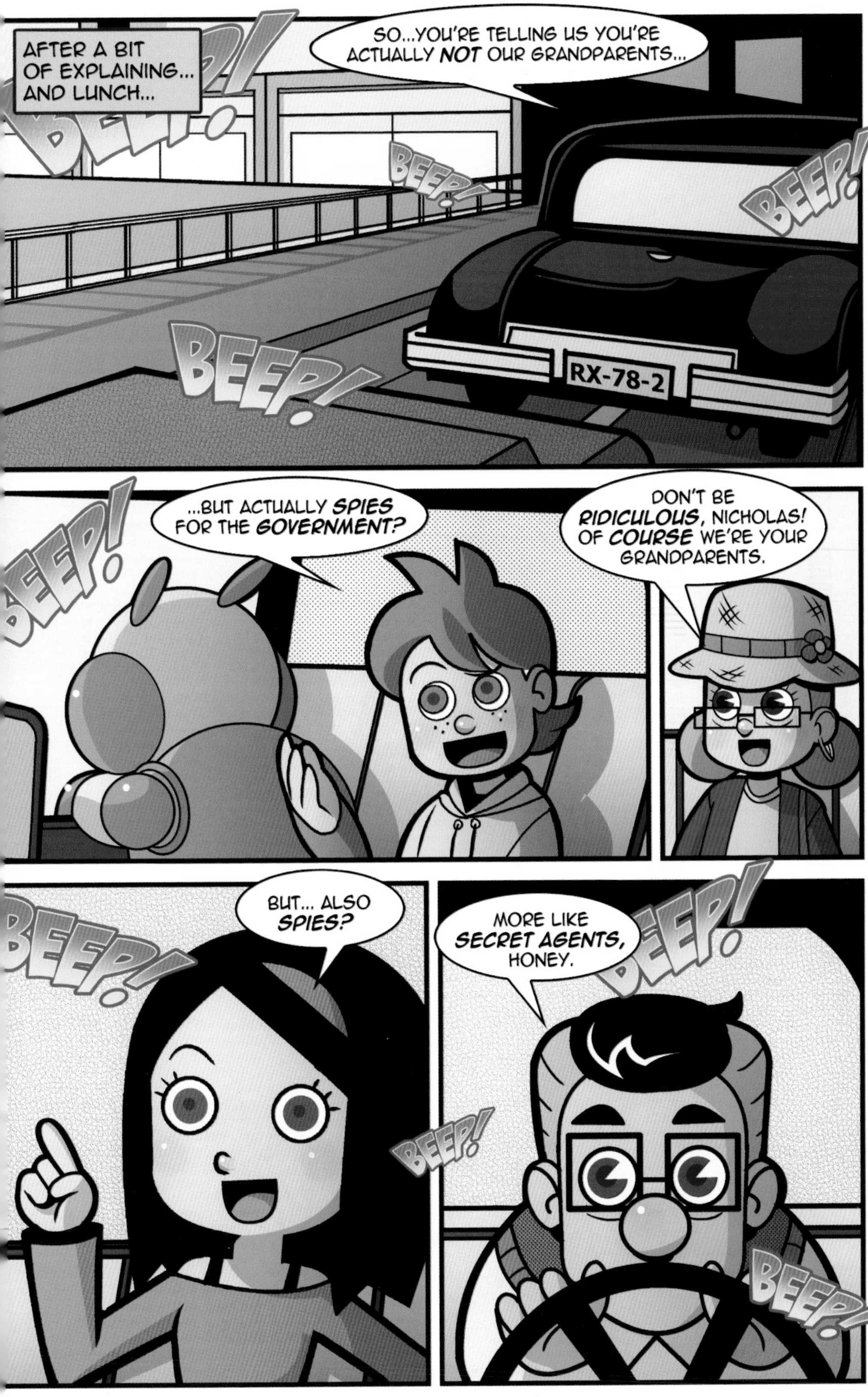
AFTER A BIT OF EXPLAINING... AND LUNCH...
SO...YOU'RE TELLING US YOU'RE ACTUALLY NOT OUR GRANDPARENTS...
BEEP!
BEEP!
BEEP!
RX-78-2
...BUT ACTUALLY SPIES FOR THE GOVERNMENT?
DON'T BE RIDICULOUS, NICHOLAS! OF COURSE WE'RE YOUR GRANDPARENTS.
BEEP!
BUT... ALSO SPIES?
MORE LIKE SECRET AGENTS, HONEY.
BEEP!
BEEP!
BEEP!
BEEP!

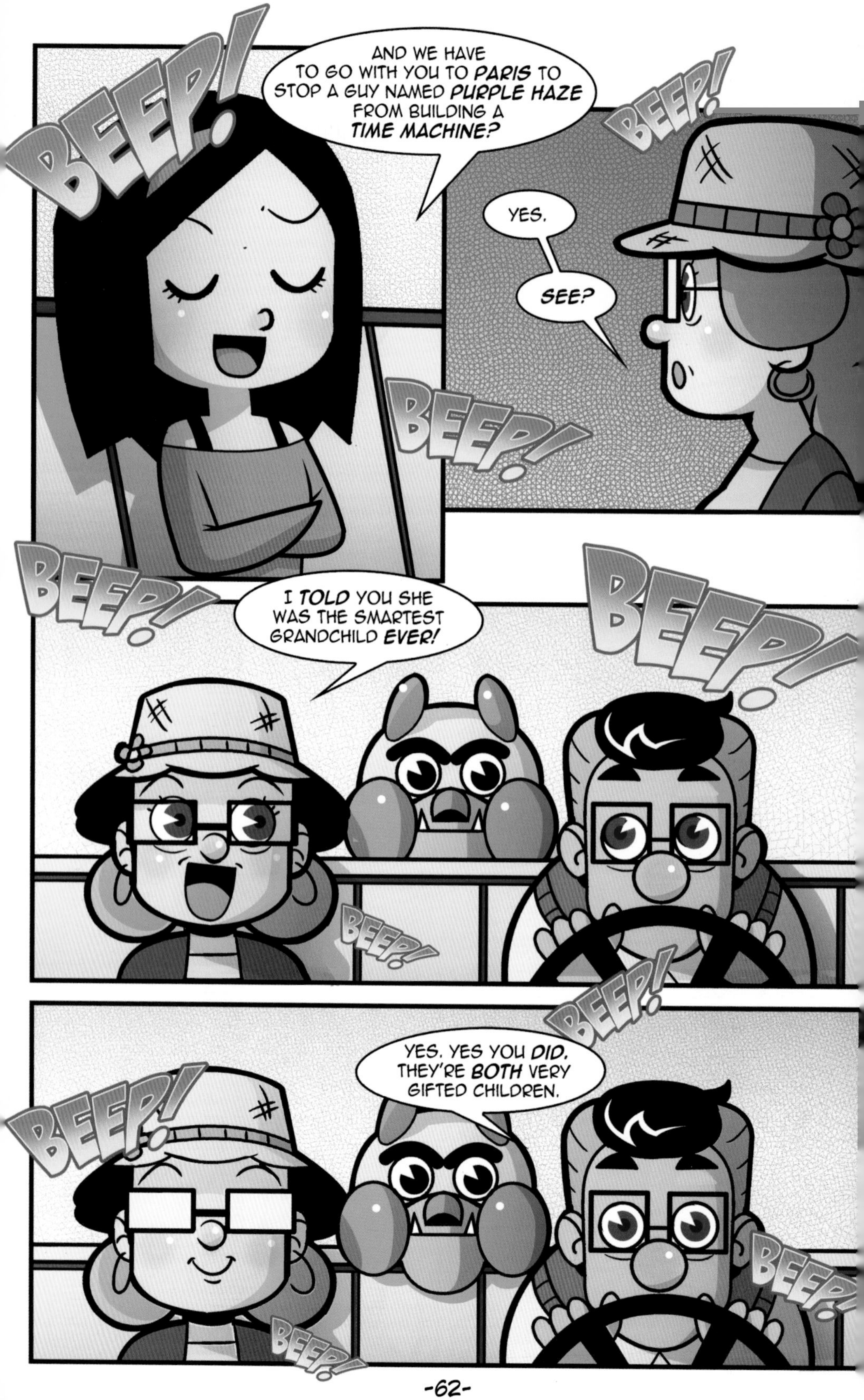
BEEP!
AND WE HAVE TO GO WITH YOU TO PARIS TO STOP A GUY NAMED PURPLE HAZE FROM BUILDING A TIME MACHINE?
BEEP!
YES.
SEE?
BEEP!
BEEP!
I TOLD YOU SHE WAS THE SMARTEST GRANDCHILD EVER!
BEEP!
BEEP!
BEEP!
BEEP!
YES. YES YOU DID. THEY'RE BOTH VERY GIFTED CHILDREN.
BEEP!
BEEP!
BEEP!

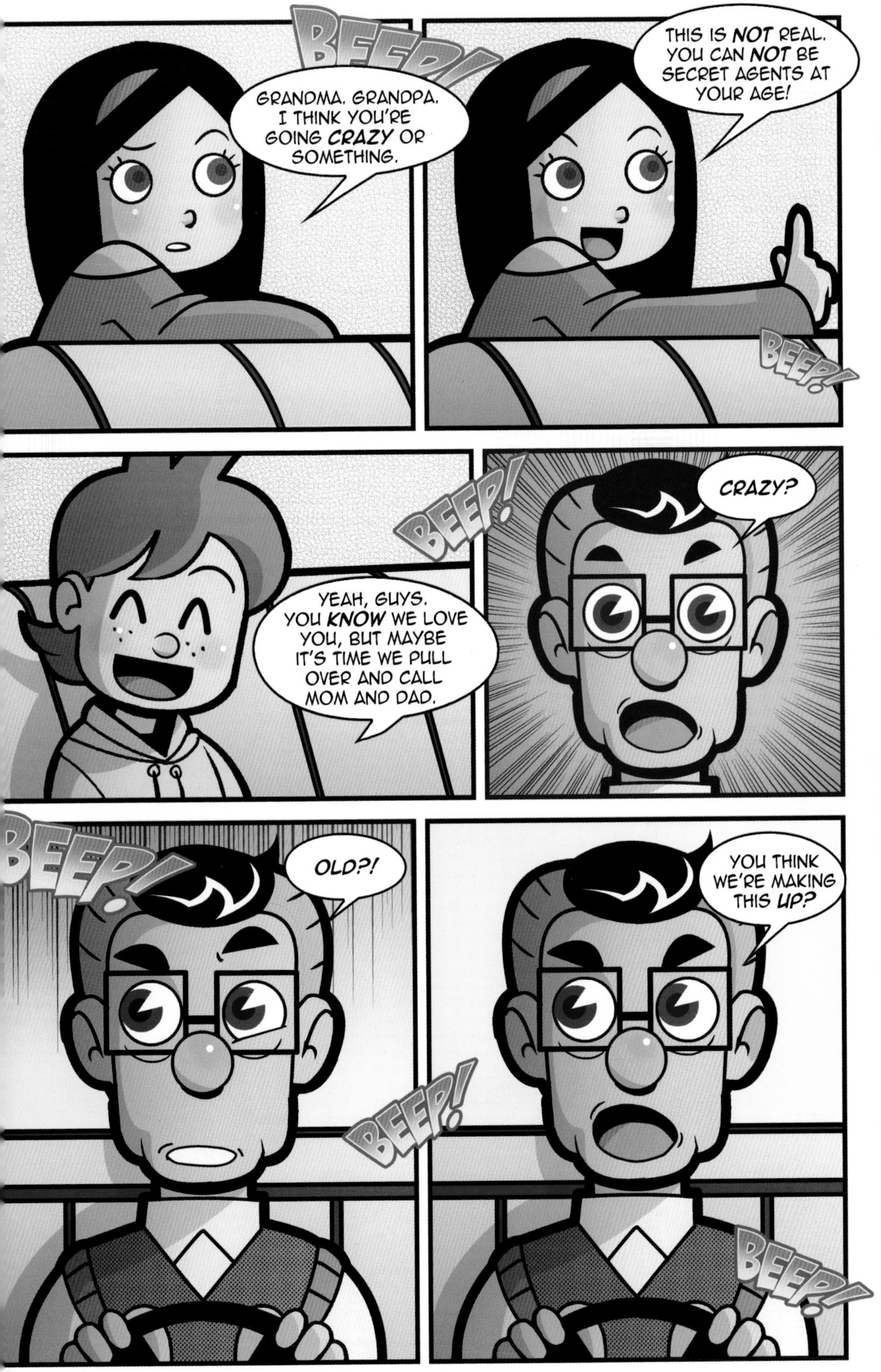
BEEP!
GRANDMA, GRANDPA, I THINK YOU'RE GOING CRAZY OR SOMETHING.
THIS IS NOT REAL. YOU CAN NOT BE SECRET AGENTS AT YOUR AGE!
BEEP!
BEEP!
YEAH, GUYS. YOU KNOW WE LOVE YOU, BUT MAYBE IT'S TIME WE PULL OVER AND CALL MOM AND DAD.
CRAZY?
BEEP!
OLD?!
BEEP!
YOU THINK WE'RE MAKING THIS UP?
BEEP!

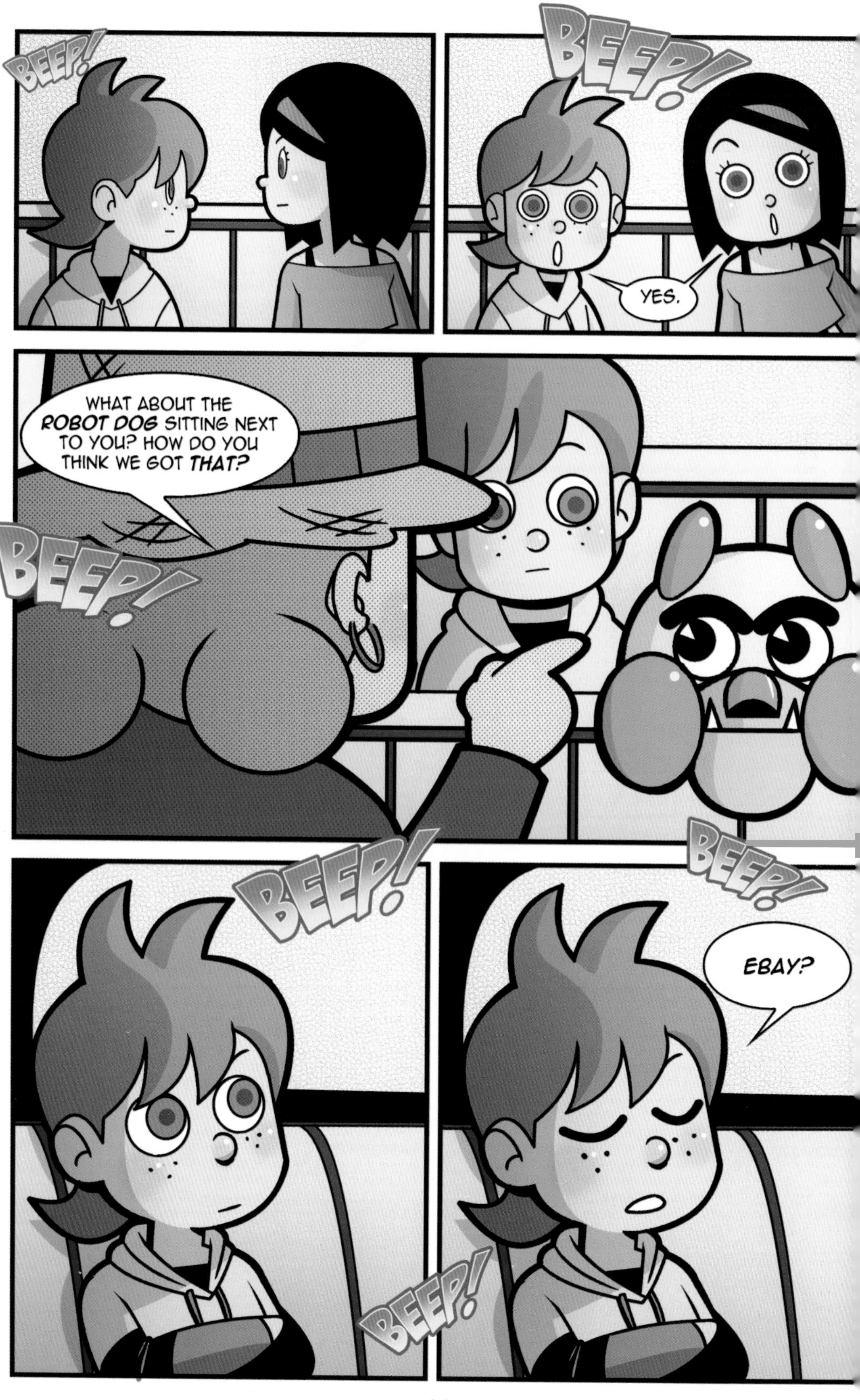
BEEP!
BEEP!
YES.
WHAT ABOUT THE ROBOT DOG SITTING NEXT TO YOU? HOW DO YOU THINK WE GOT THAT?
BEEP!
BEEP!
BEEP!
BEEP!
EBAY?

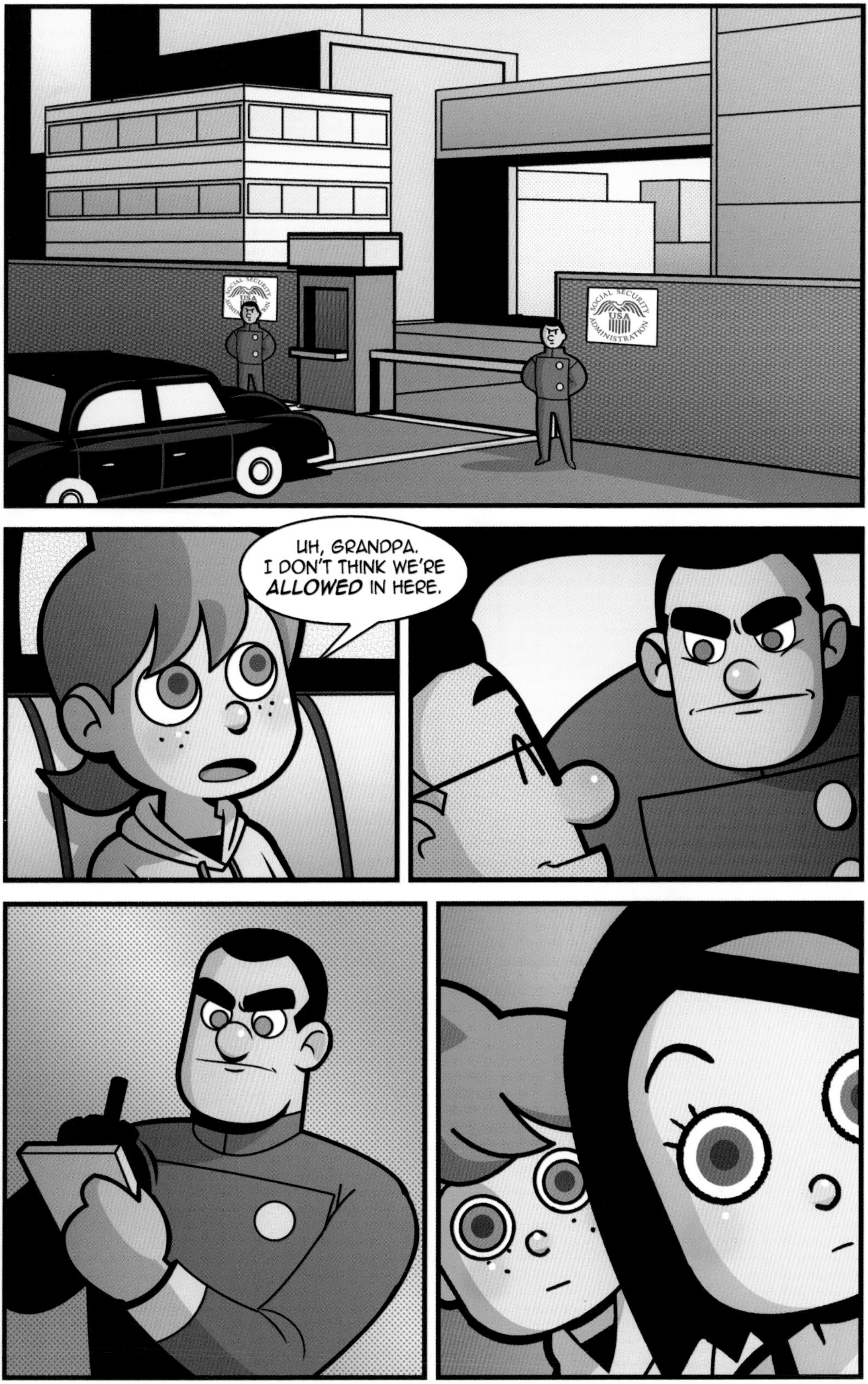
SOCIAL SECURITY
USA
ADMINISTRATION
UH, GRANDPA. I DON'T THINK WE'RE *ALLOWED* IN HERE.

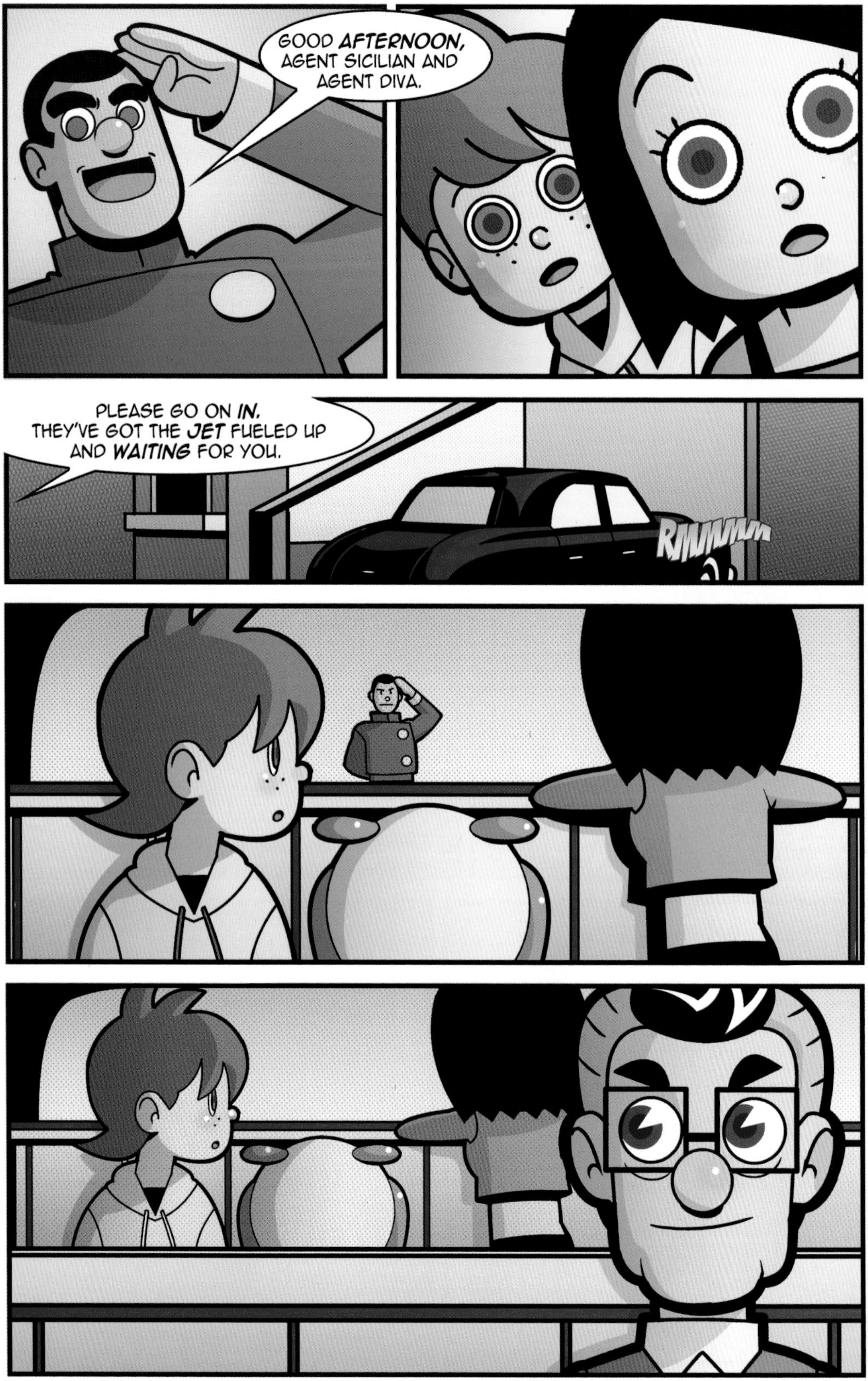
GOOD **AFTERNOON,** AGENT SICILIAN AND AGENT DIVA.
PLEASE GO ON **IN.** THEY'VE GOT THE **JET** FUELED UP AND **WAITING** FOR YOU.
RMMMM

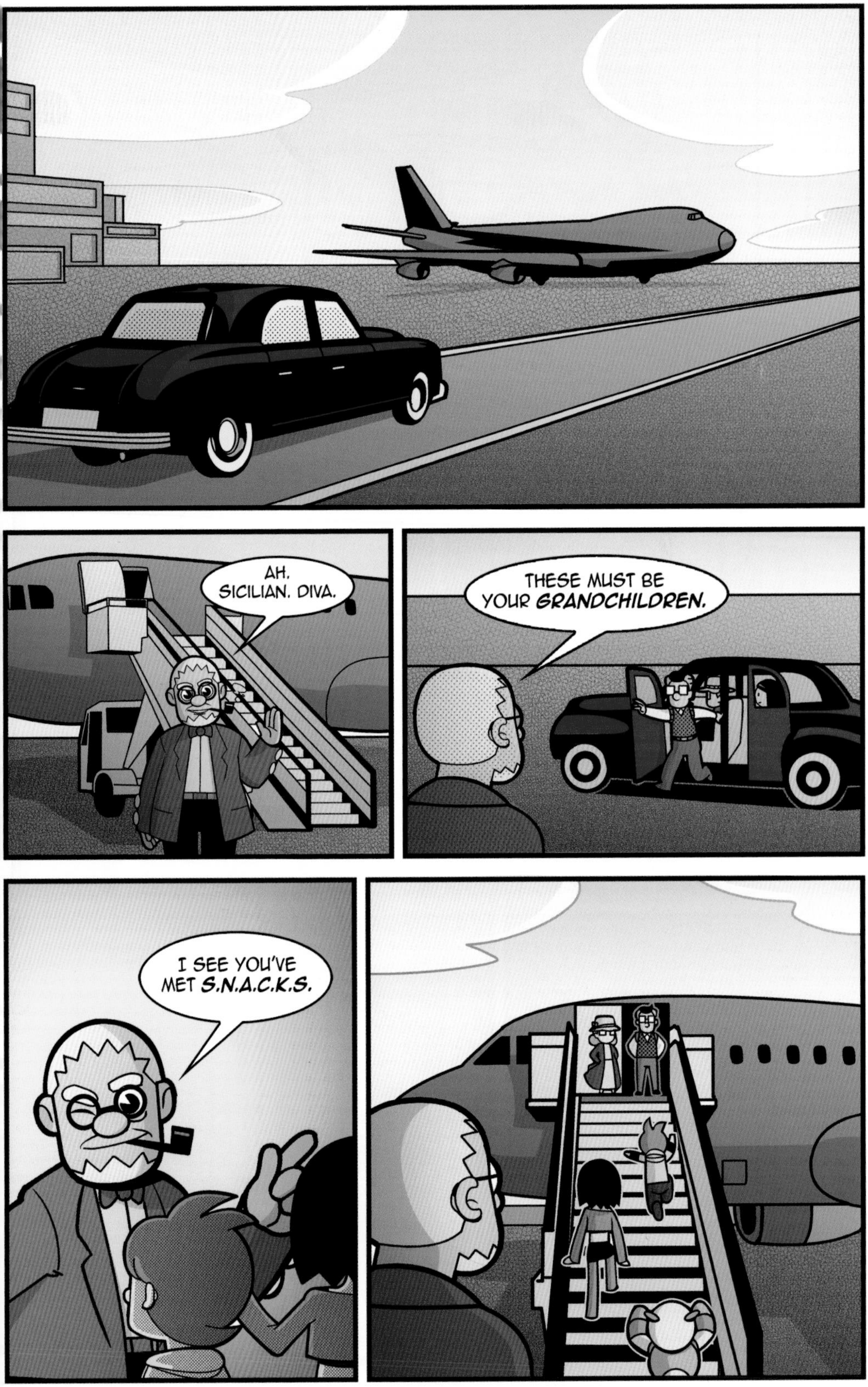
AH. SICILIAN. DIVA.
THESE MUST BE YOUR GRANDCHILDREN.
I SEE YOU'VE MET S.N.A.C.K.S.

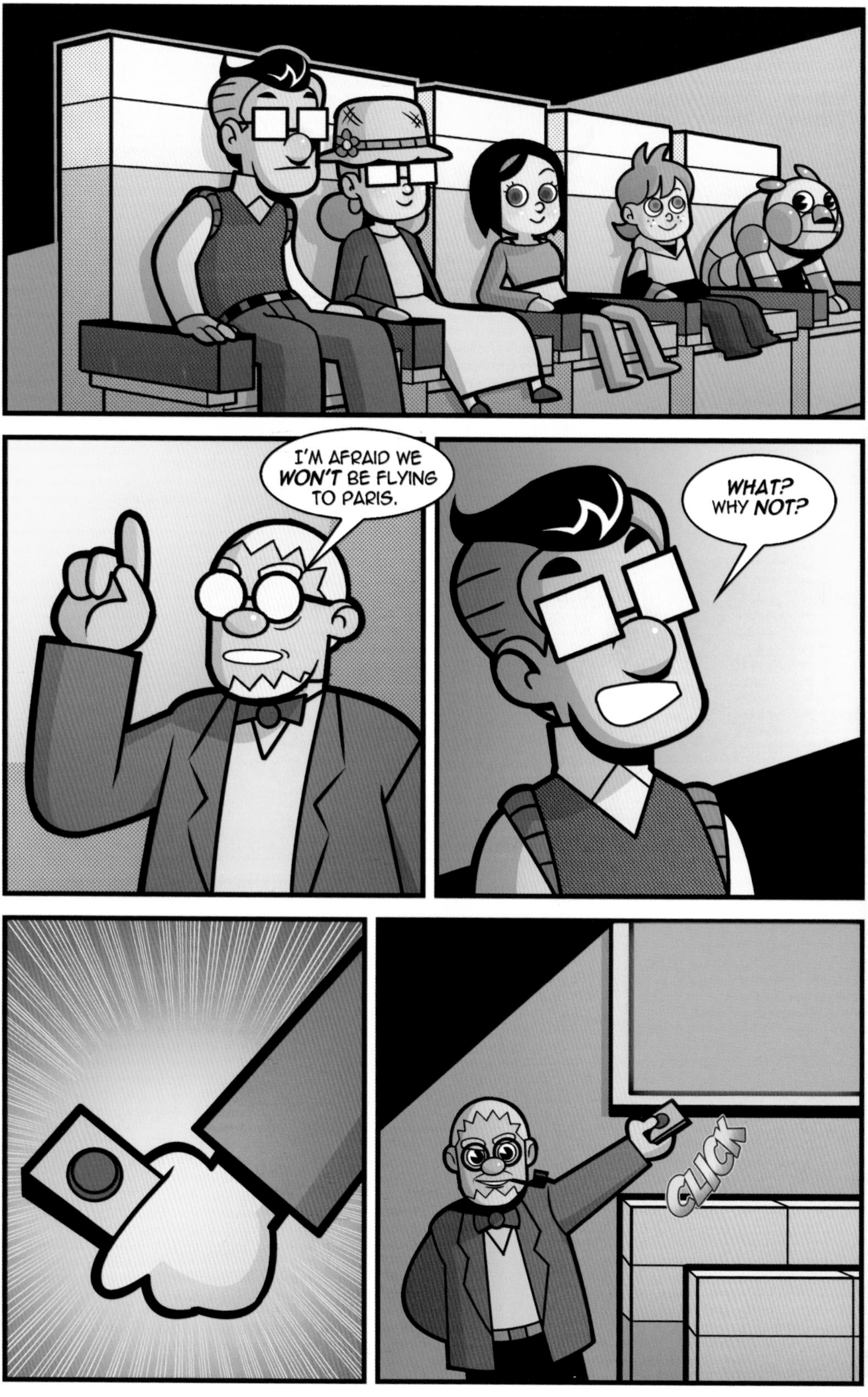
I'M AFRAID WE WON'T BE FLYING TO PARIS.
WHAT? WHY NOT?
CLICK

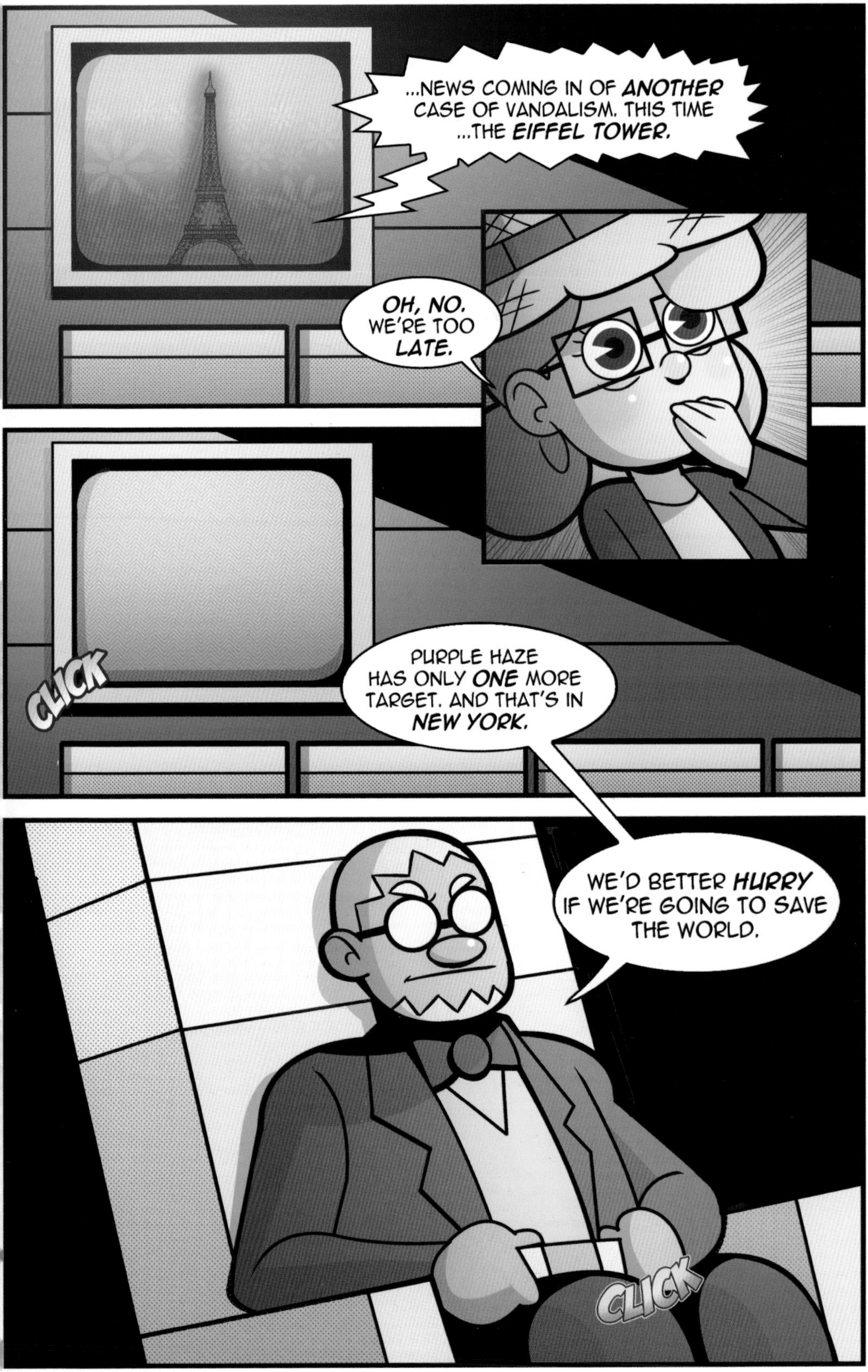
...NEWS COMING IN OF ANOTHER CASE OF VANDALISM. THIS TIME ...THE EIFFEL TOWER.
OH, NO. WE'RE TOO LATE.
CLICK
PURPLE HAZE HAS ONLY ONE MORE TARGET. AND THAT'S IN NEW YORK.
WE'D BETTER HURRY IF WE'RE GOING TO SAVE THE WORLD.
CLICK

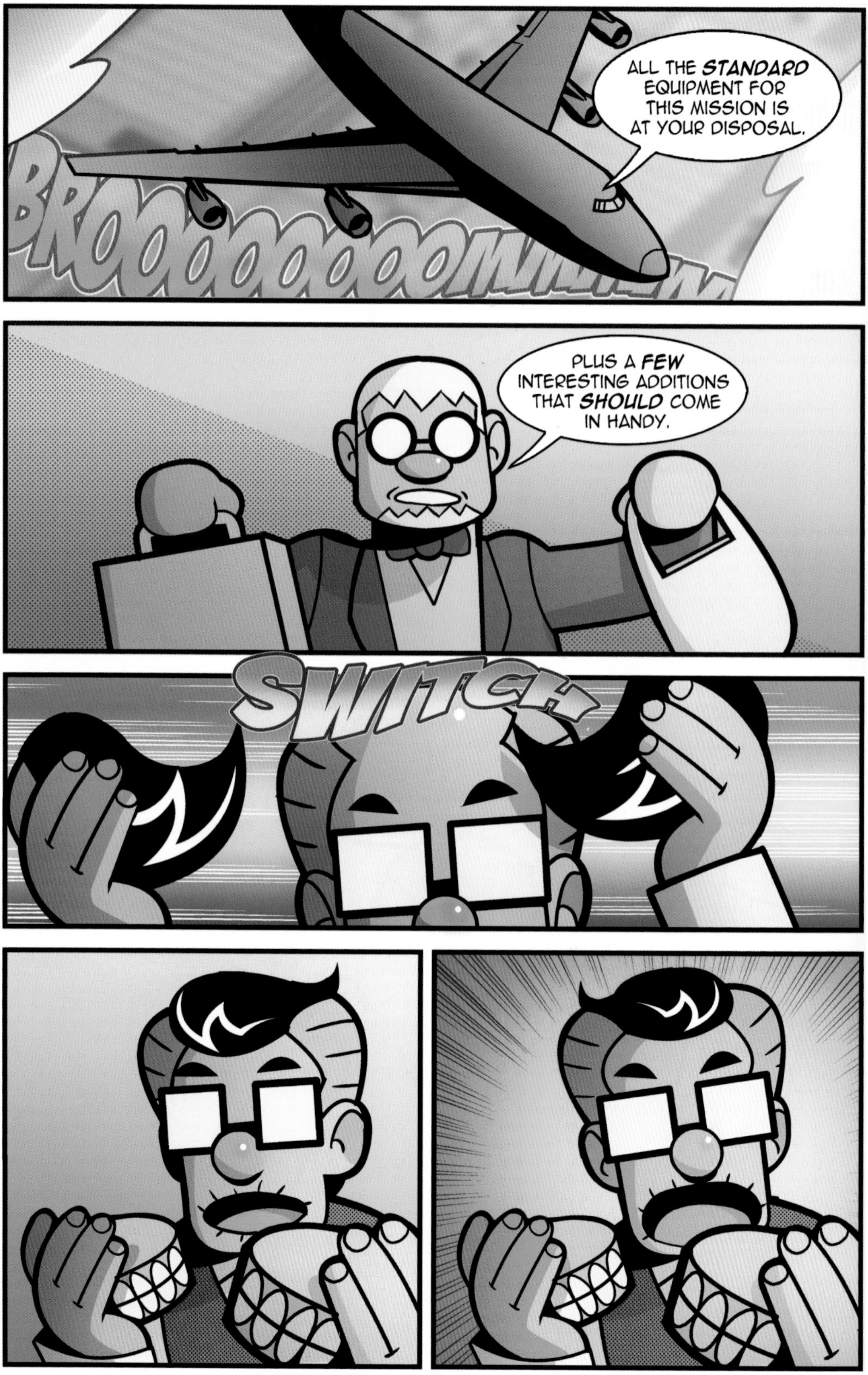
ALL THE STANDARD EQUIPMENT FOR THIS MISSION IS AT YOUR DISPOSAL.
BROOOOOOOOOMMMMM
PLUS A FEW INTERESTING ADDITIONS THAT SHOULD COME IN HANDY.
SWITCH

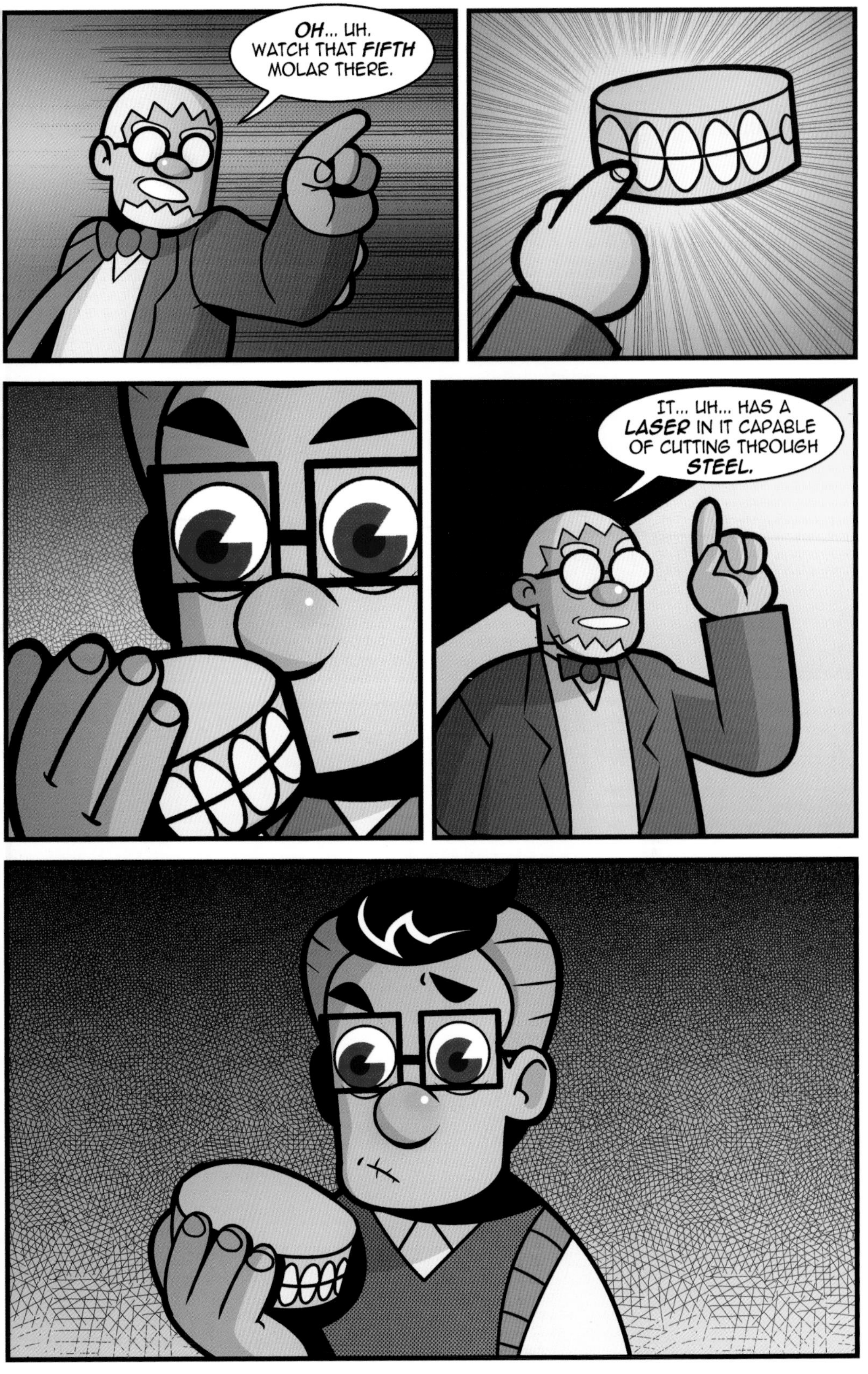
OH... UH. WATCH THAT FIFTH MOLAR THERE.
IT... UH... HAS A LASER IN IT CAPABLE OF CUTTING THROUGH STEEL.

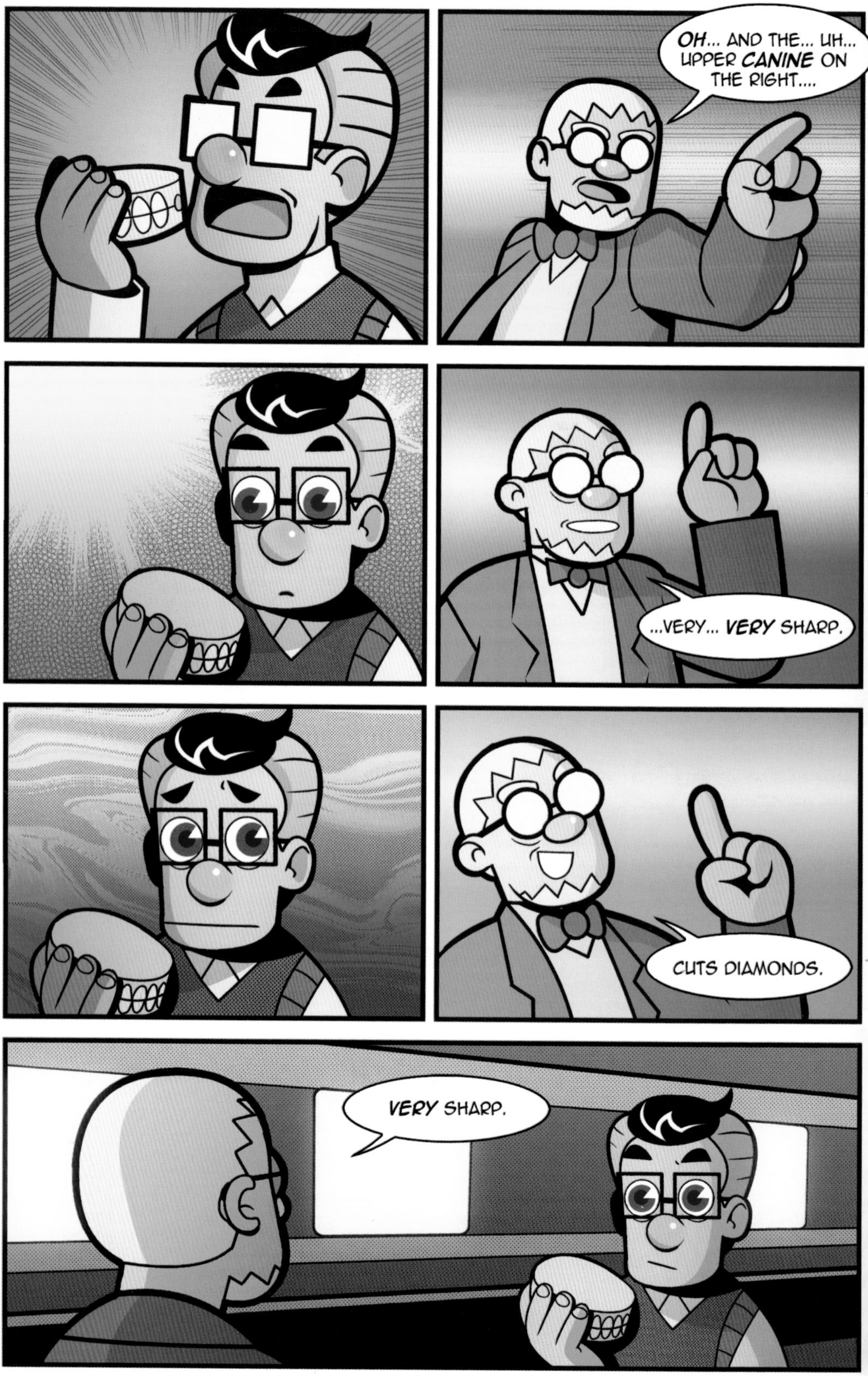
OH... AND THE... UH... UPPER CANINE ON THE RIGHT....
...VERY... VERY SHARP.
CUTS DIAMONDS.
VERY SHARP.

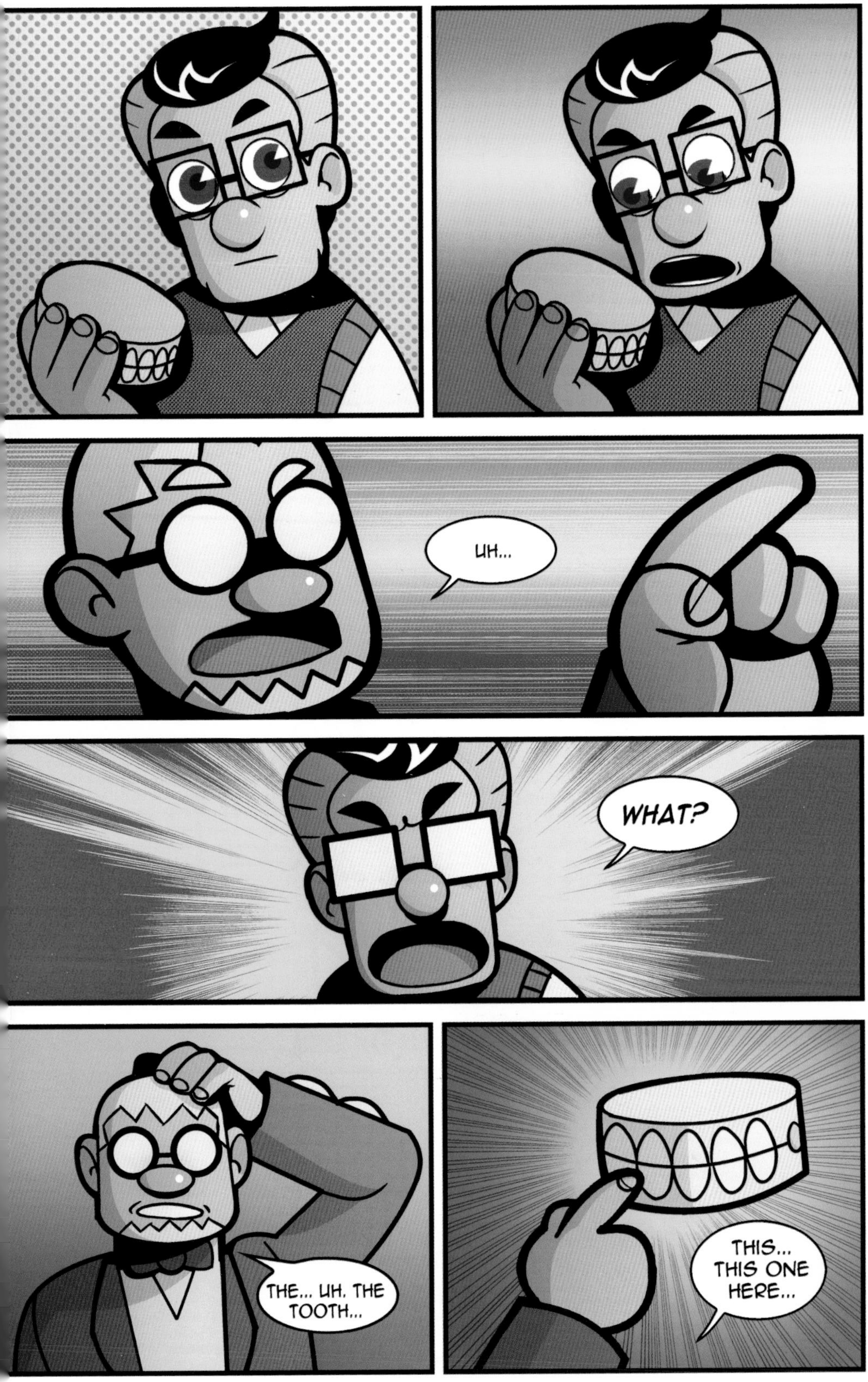
UH...
WHAT?
THE... UH, THE TOOTH...
THIS... THIS ONE HERE...

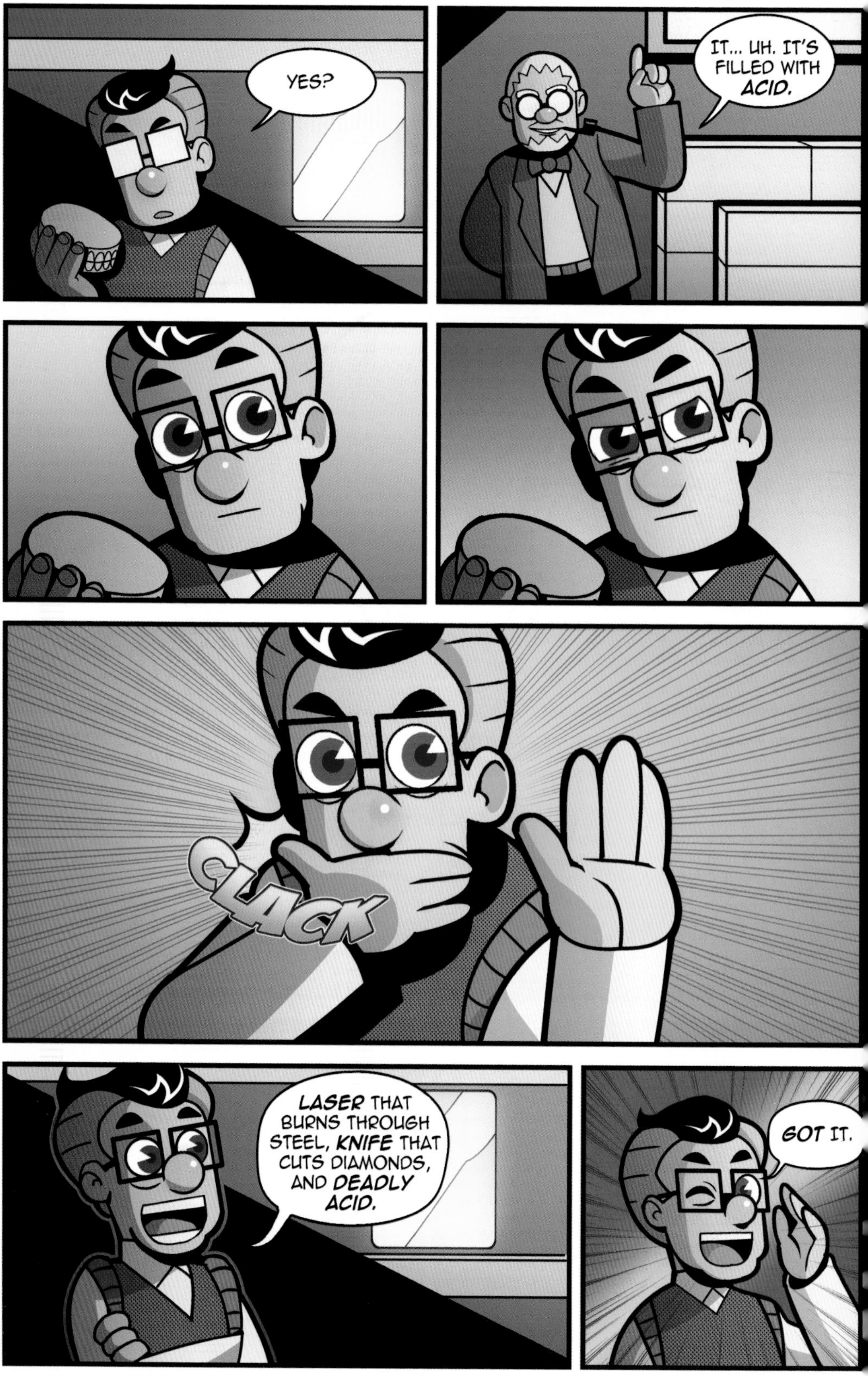
YES?
IT... UH. IT'S FILLED WITH ACID.
CLACK
LASER THAT BURNS THROUGH STEEL, KNIFE THAT CUTS DIAMONDS, AND DEADLY ACID.
GOT IT.

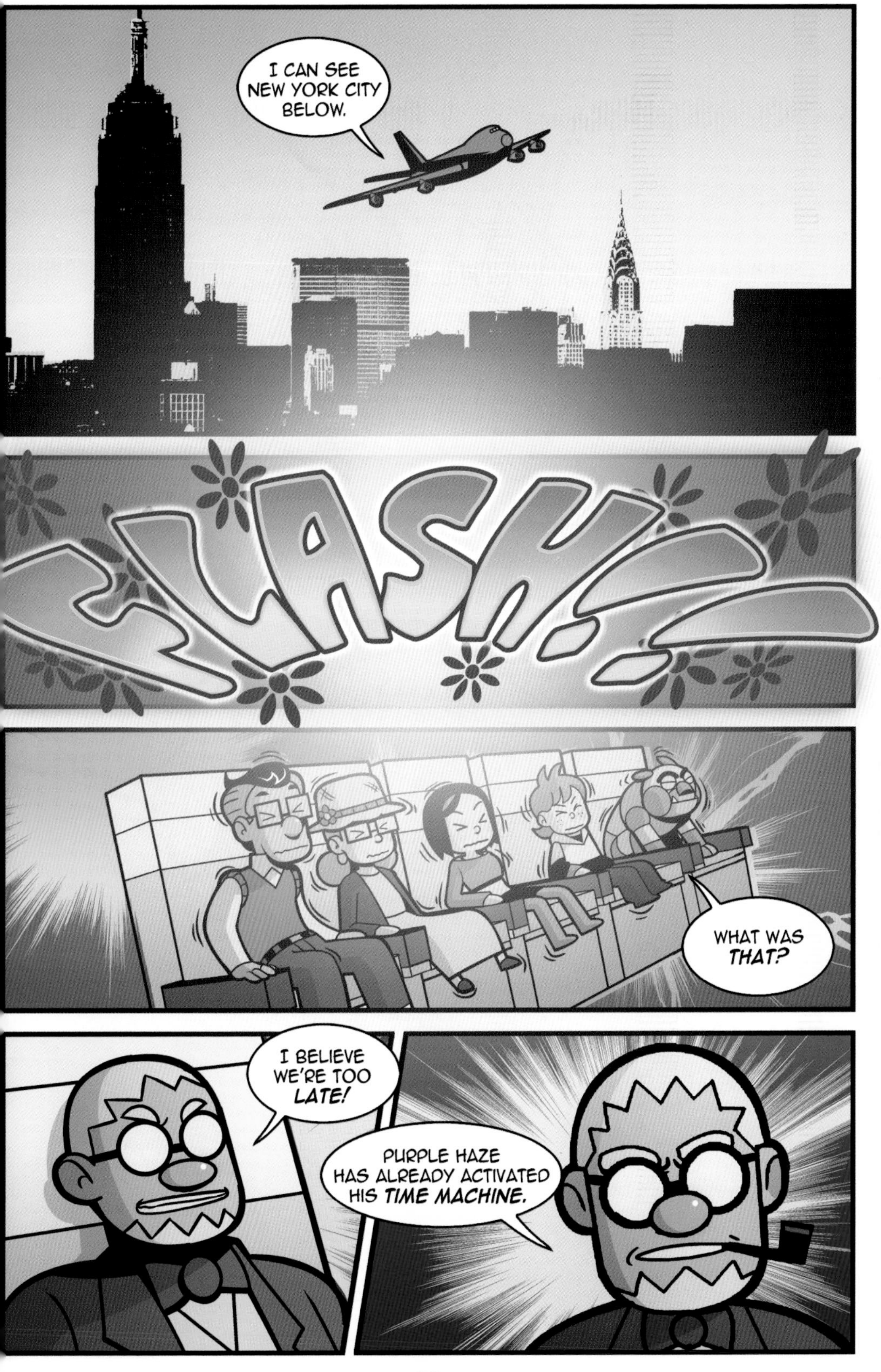
I CAN SEE NEW YORK CITY BELOW.
FLASH!
WHAT WAS THAT?
I BELIEVE WE'RE TOO LATE!
PURPLE HAZE HAS ALREADY ACTIVATED HIS TIME MACHINE.

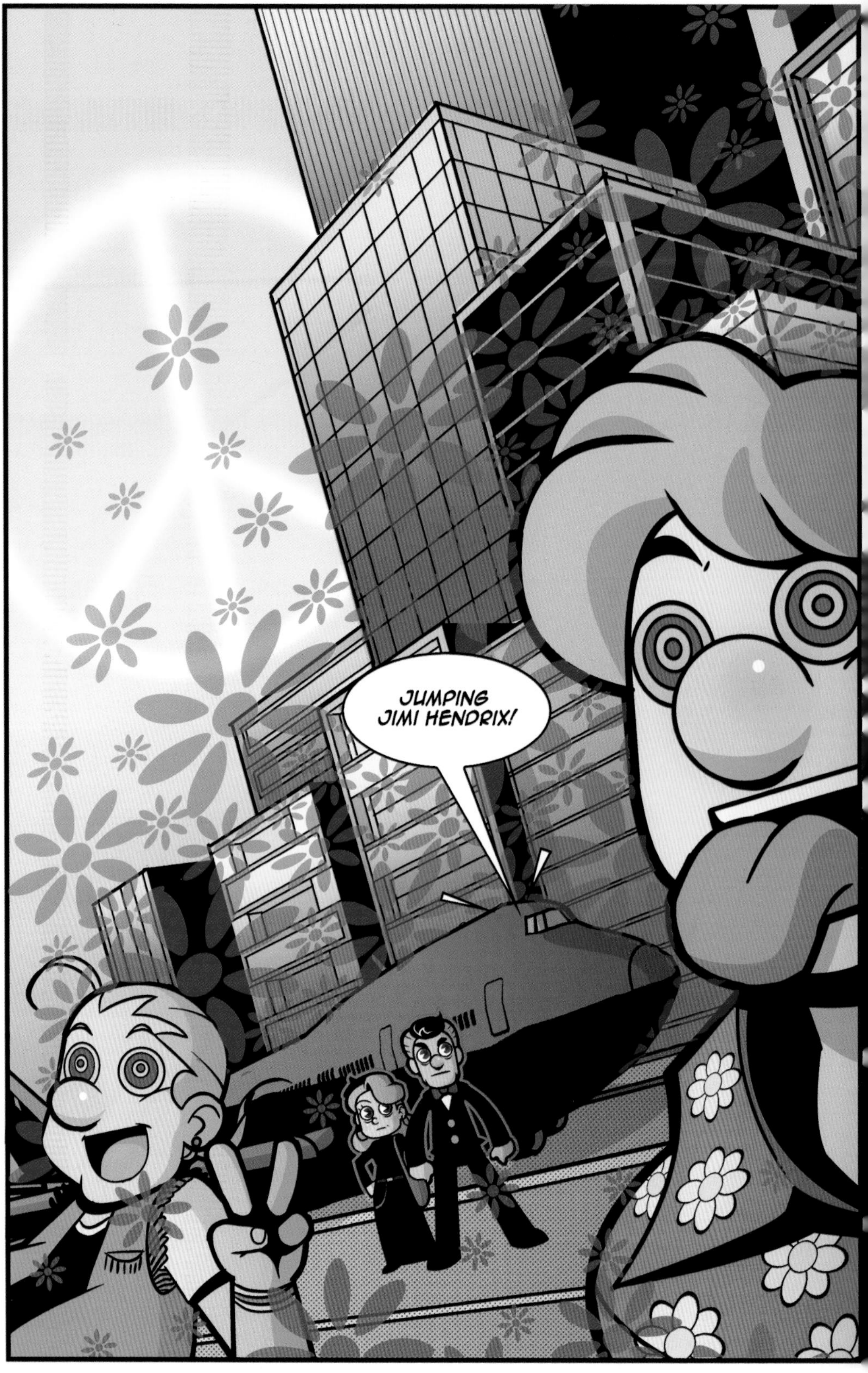
JUMPING
JIMI HENDRIX!

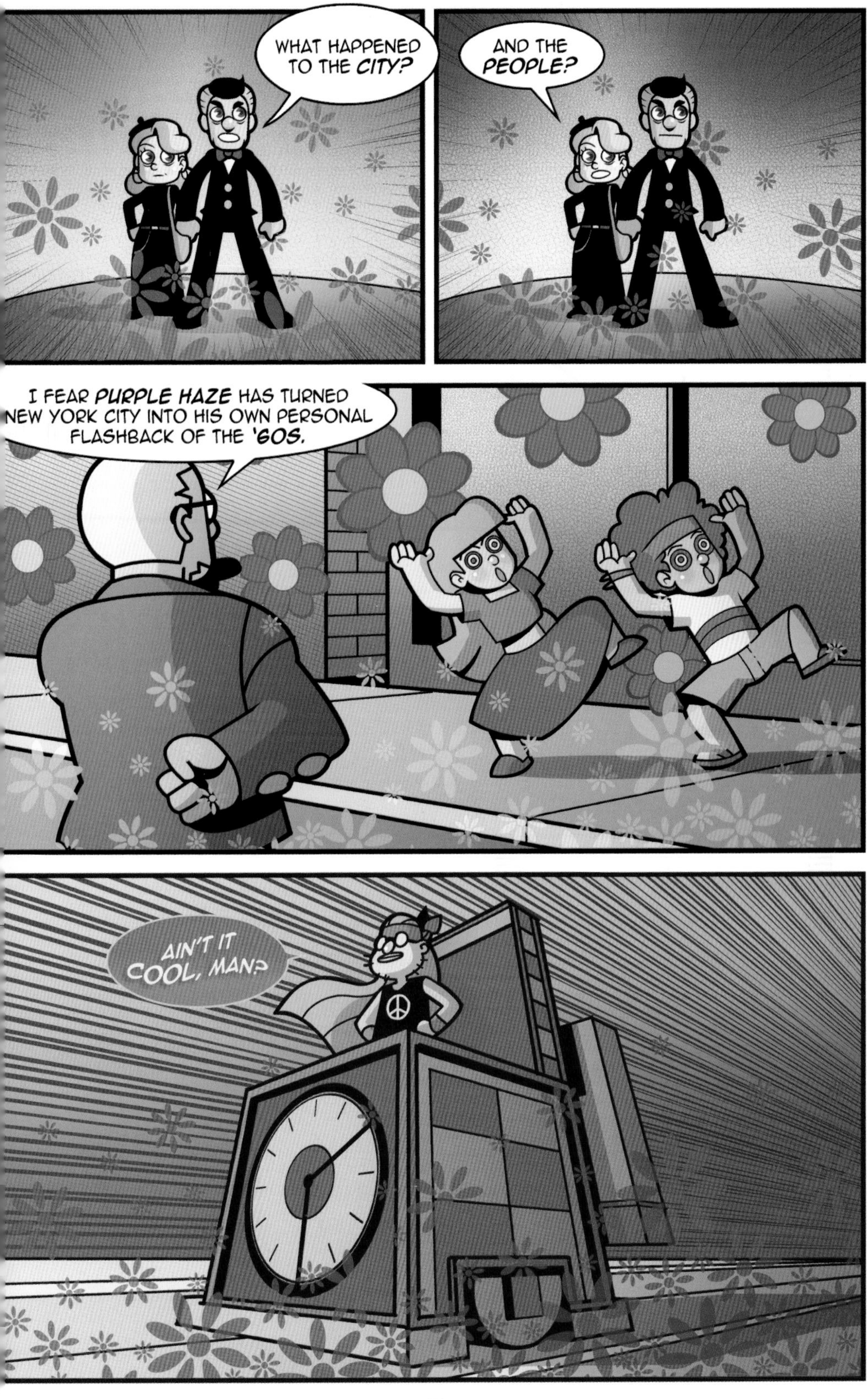
WHAT HAPPENED TO THE *CITY?*
AND THE *PEOPLE?*
I FEAR ***PURPLE HAZE*** HAS TURNED NEW YORK CITY INTO HIS OWN PERSONAL FLASHBACK OF THE ***'60S.***
AIN'T IT COOL, MAN?

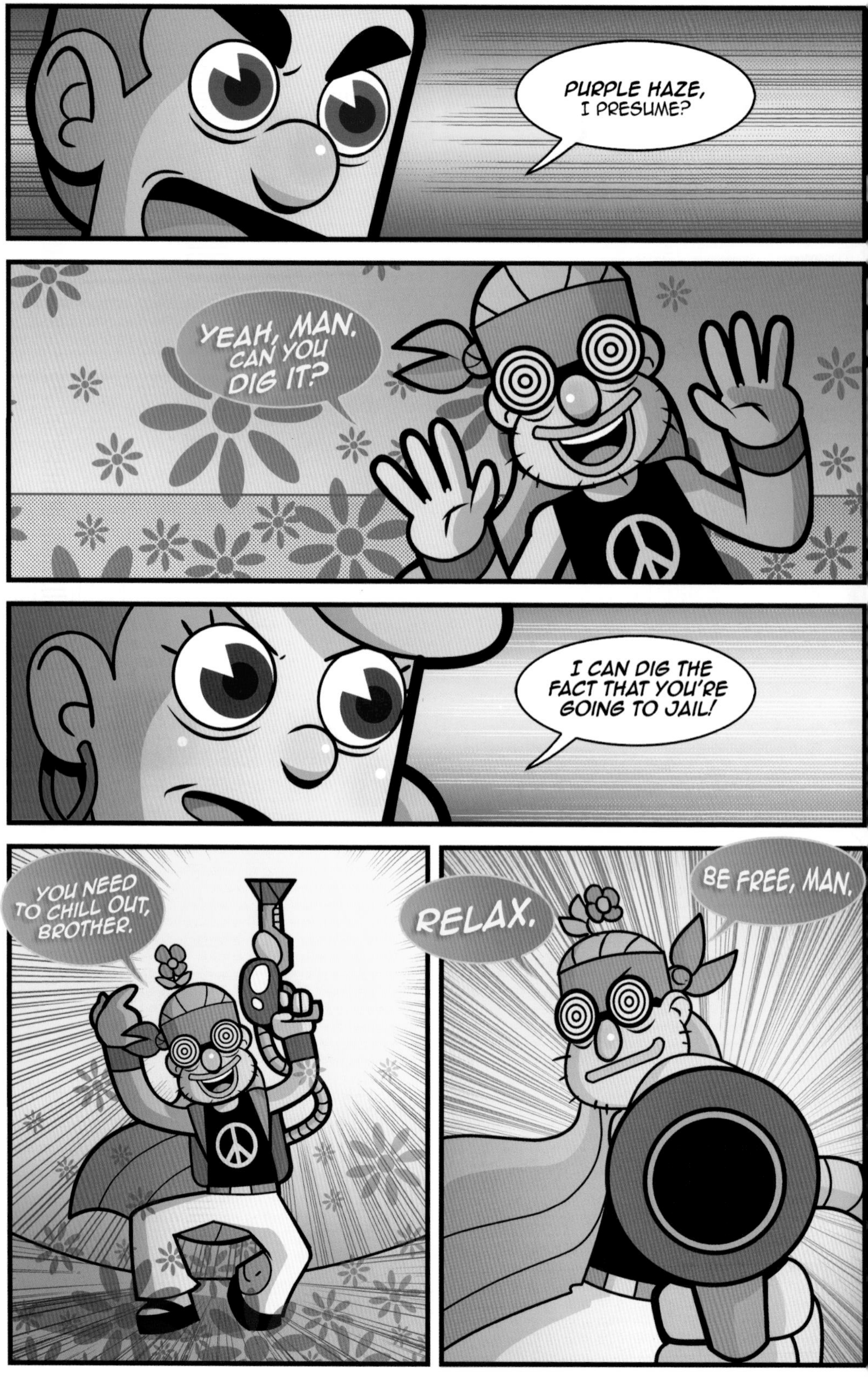
PURPLE HAZE,
I PRESUME?
YEAH, MAN.
CAN YOU
DIG IT?
I CAN DIG THE
FACT THAT YOU'RE
GOING TO JAIL!
YOU NEED
TO CHILL OUT,
BROTHER.
RELAX.
BE FREE, MAN.

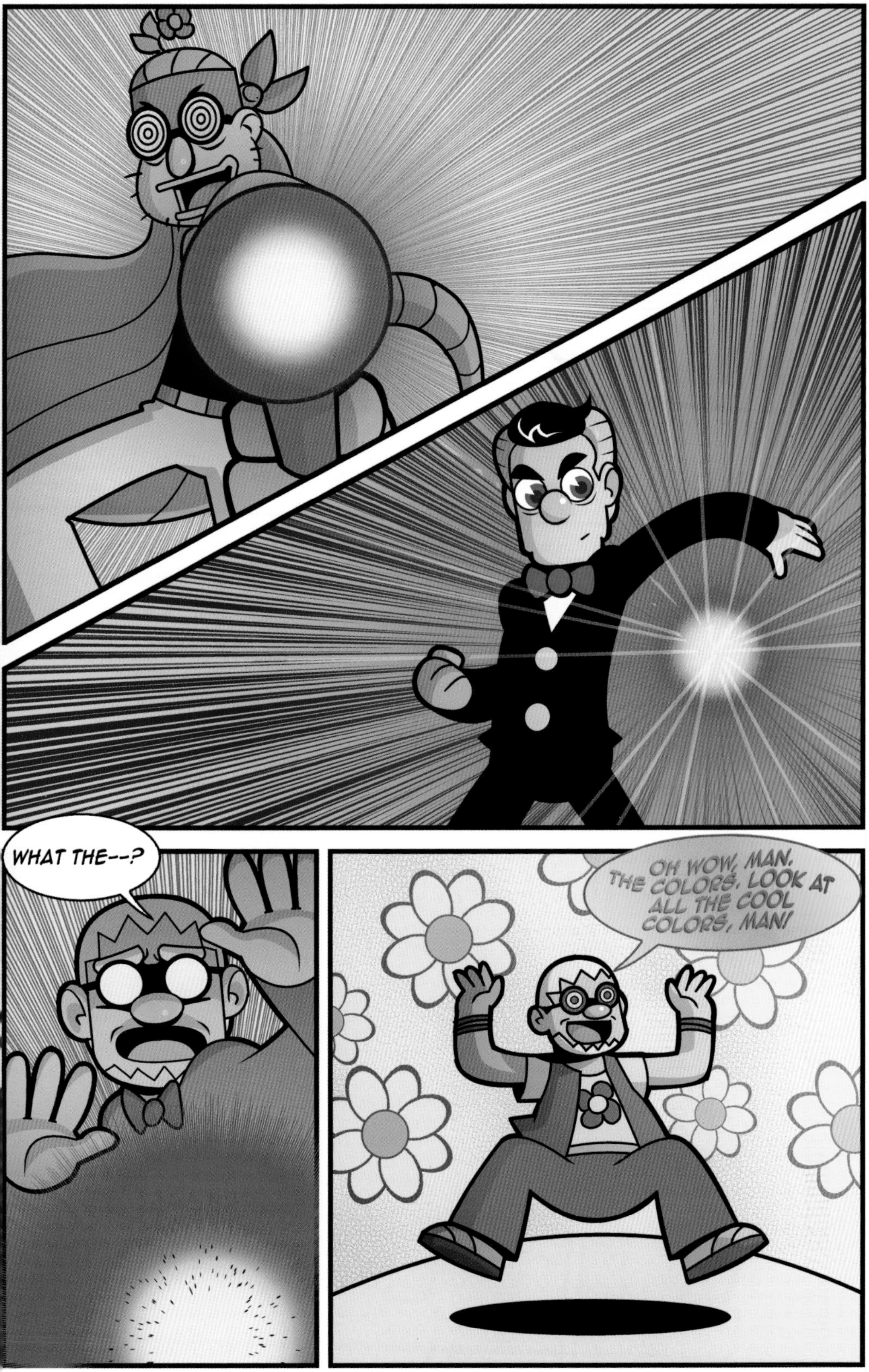
WHAT THE--?
OH WOW, MAN, THE COLORS, LOOK AT ALL THE COOL COLORS, MAN!

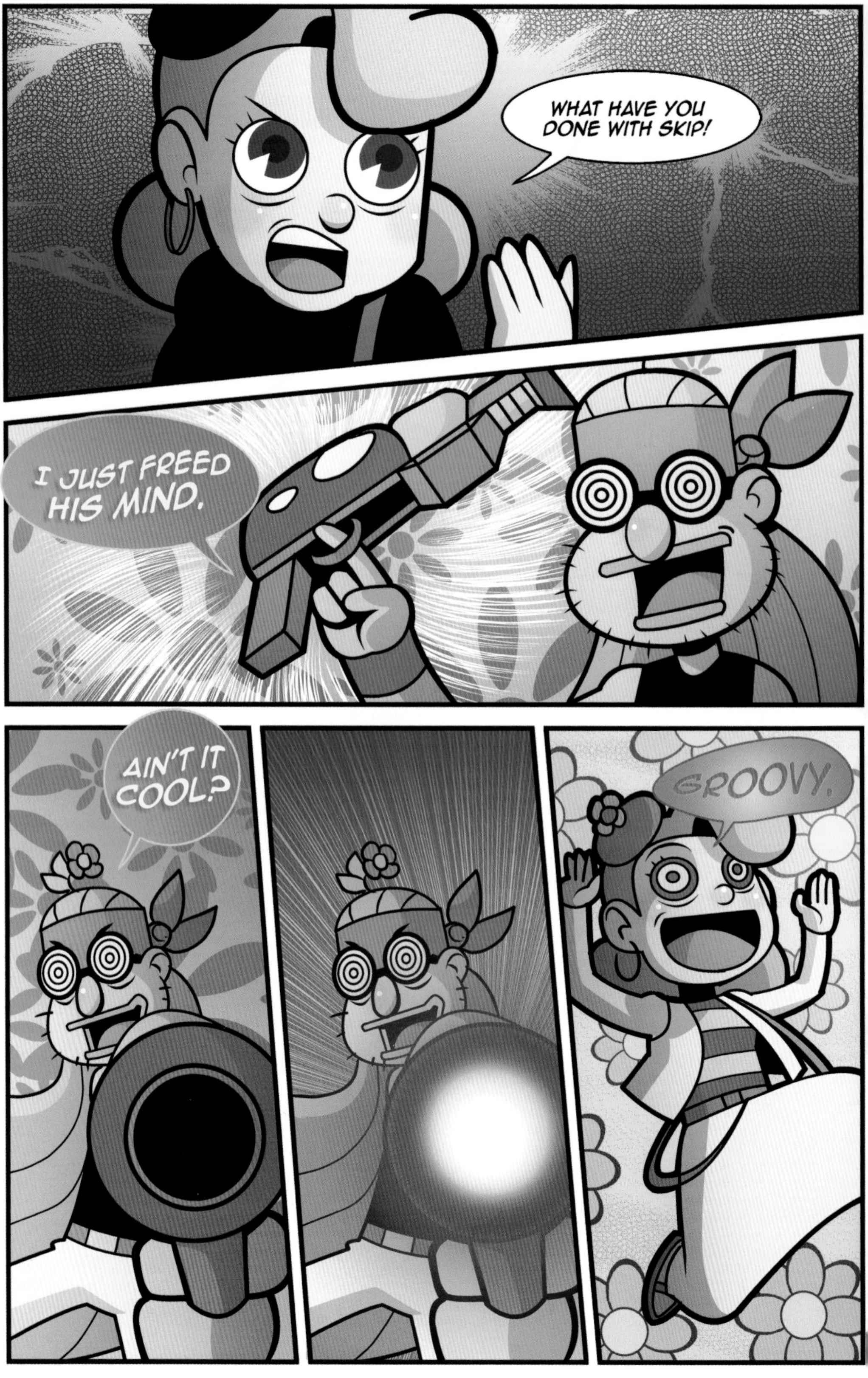
WHAT HAVE YOU DONE WITH SKIP!
I JUST FREED HIS MIND.
AIN'T IT COOL?
GROOVY.

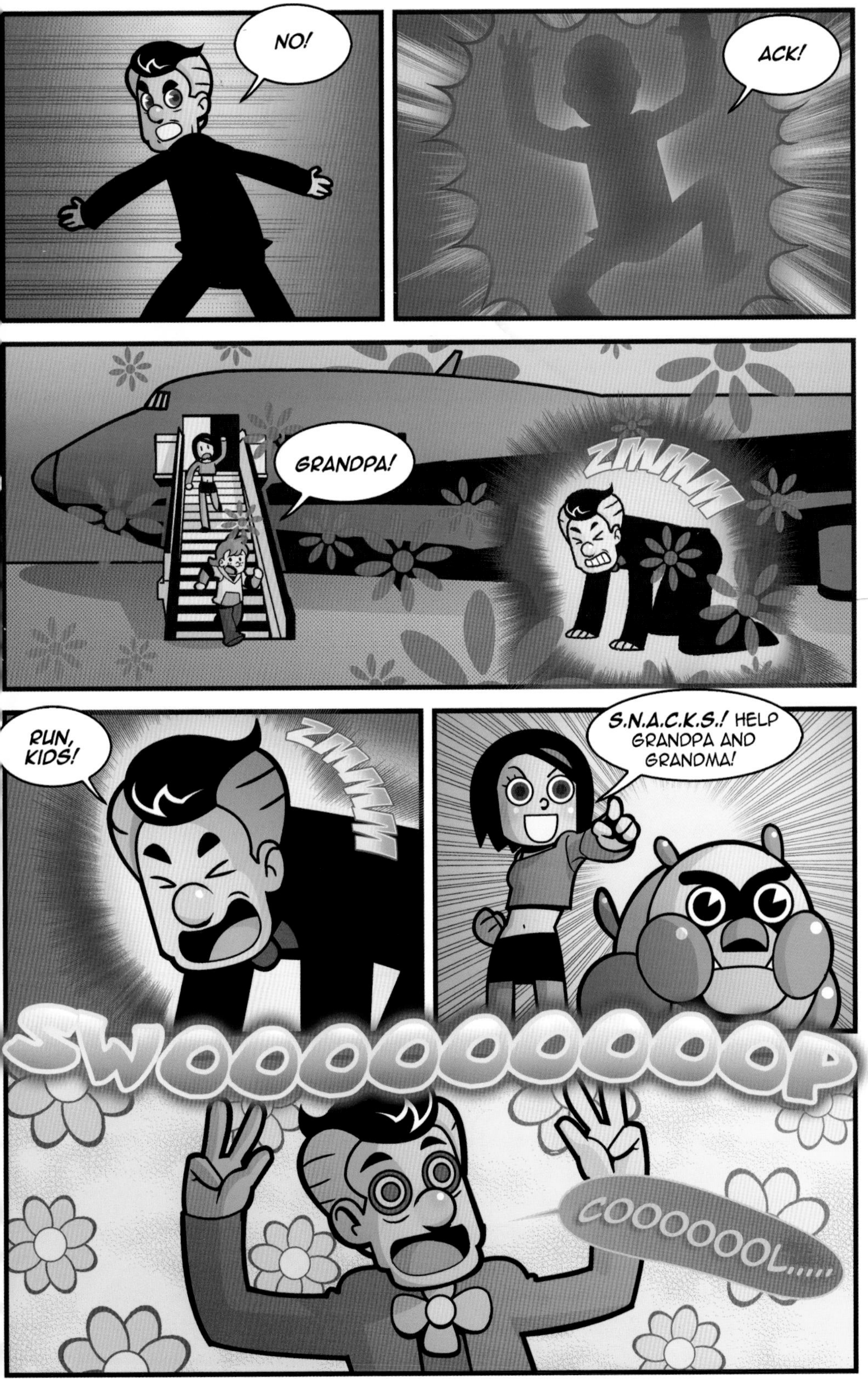
NO!
ACK!
GRANDPA!
ZMMM
RUN, KIDS!
ZMMMM
S.N.A.C.K.S.! HELP GRANDPA AND GRANDMA!
SWOOOOOOOOOOP
COOOOOOL.....

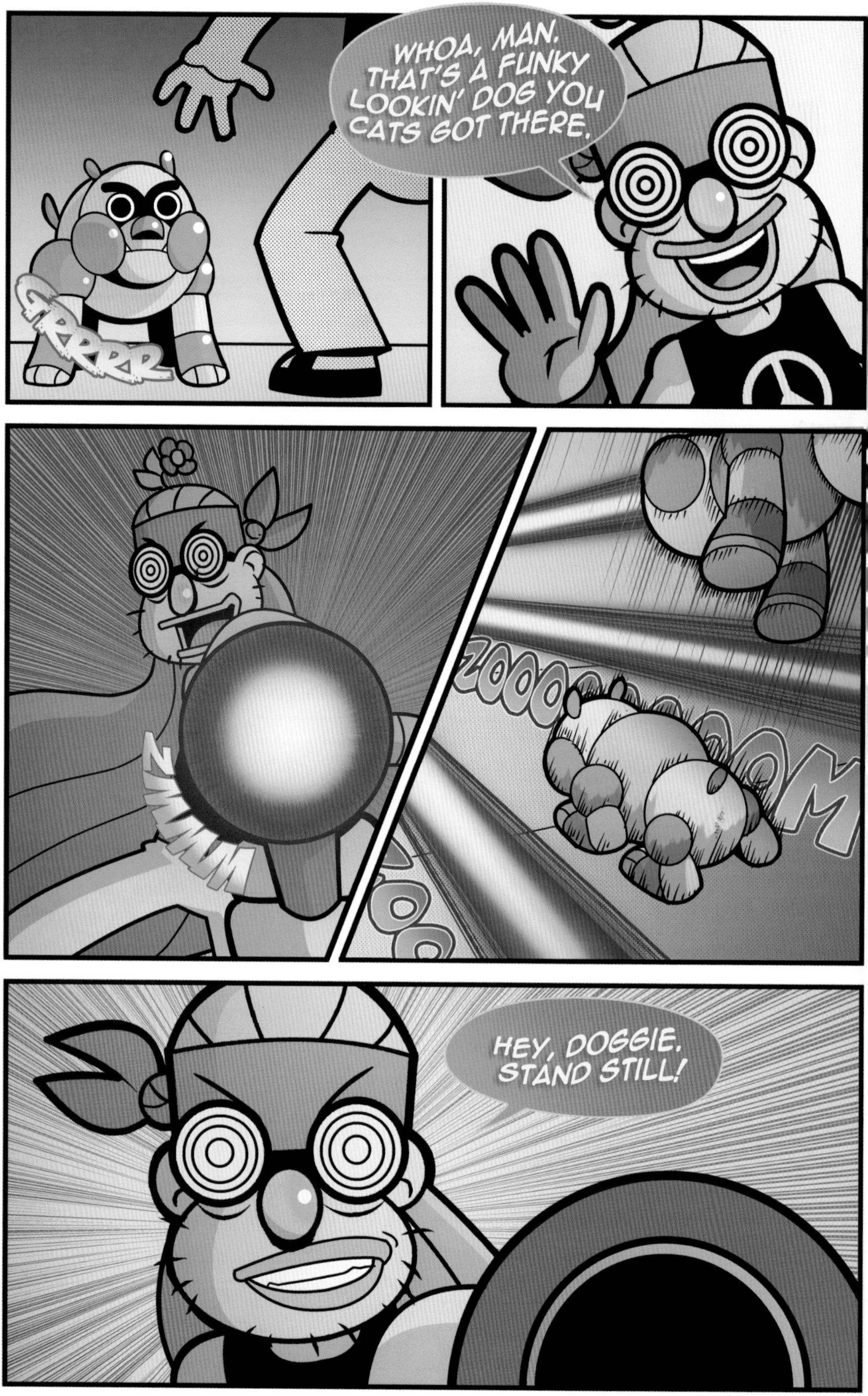
WHOA, MAN. THAT'S A FUNKY LOOKIN' DOG YOU CATS GOT THERE.
HEY, DOGGIE, STAND STILL!

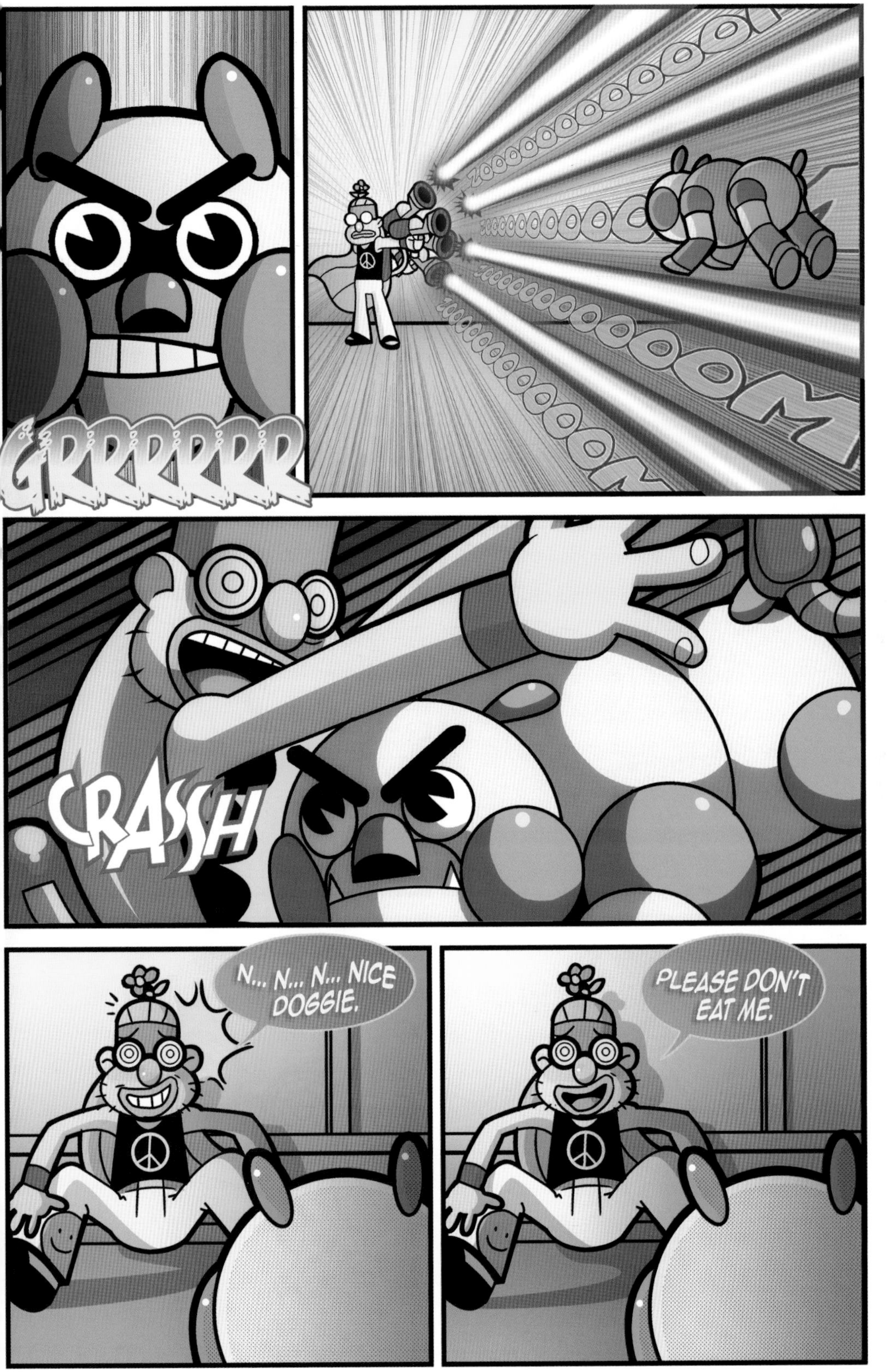
GRRRRRR
CRASSH
N... N... N... NICE DOGGIE.
PLEASE DON'T EAT ME.

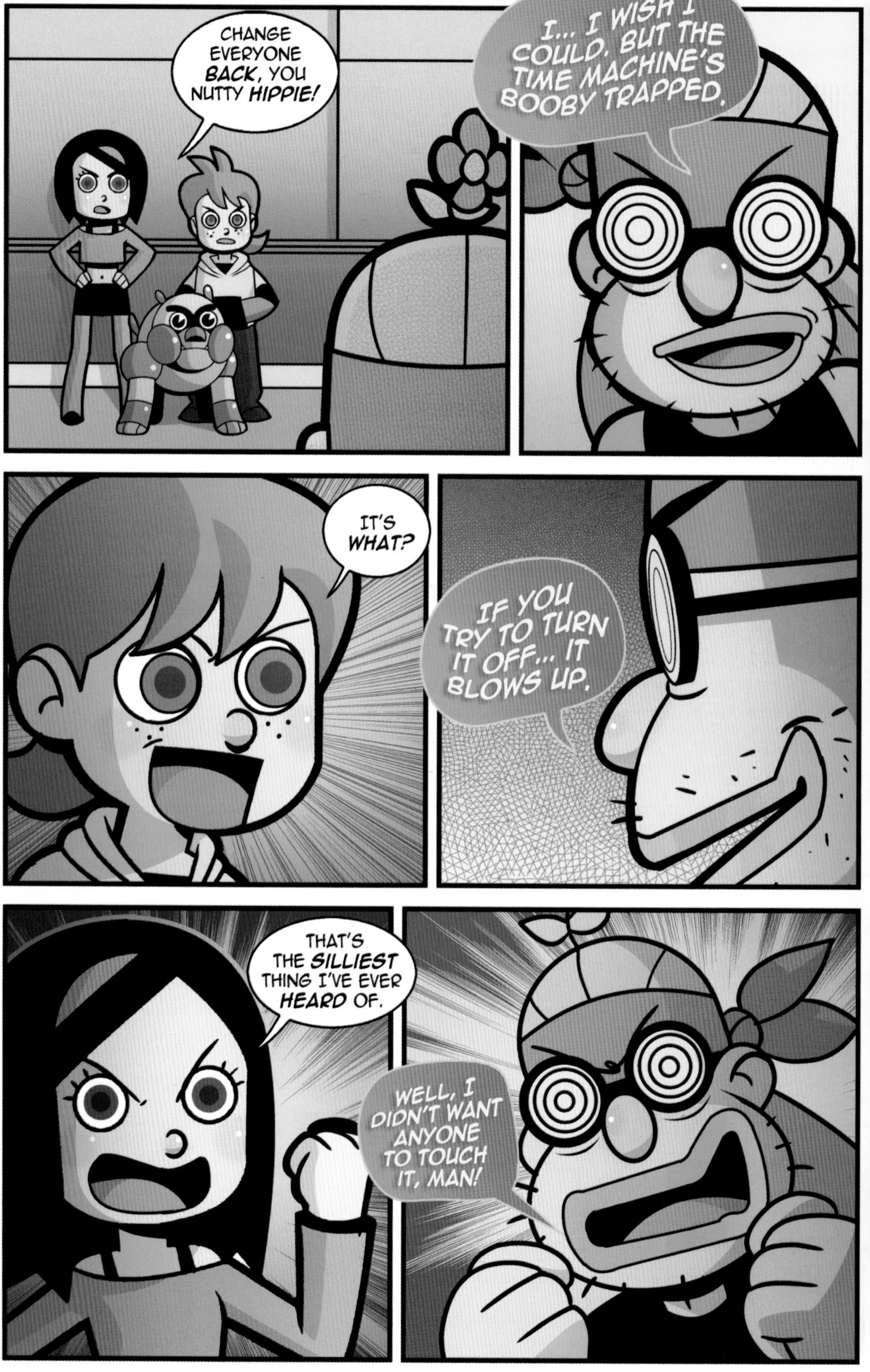
CHANGE EVERYONE BACK, YOU NUTTY HIPPIE!
I... I WISH I COULD, BUT THE TIME MACHINE'S BOOBY TRAPPED.
IT'S WHAT?
IF YOU TRY TO TURN IT OFF... IT BLOWS UP.
THAT'S THE SILLIEST THING I'VE EVER HEARD OF.
WELL, I DIDN'T WANT ANYONE TO TOUCH IT, MAN!

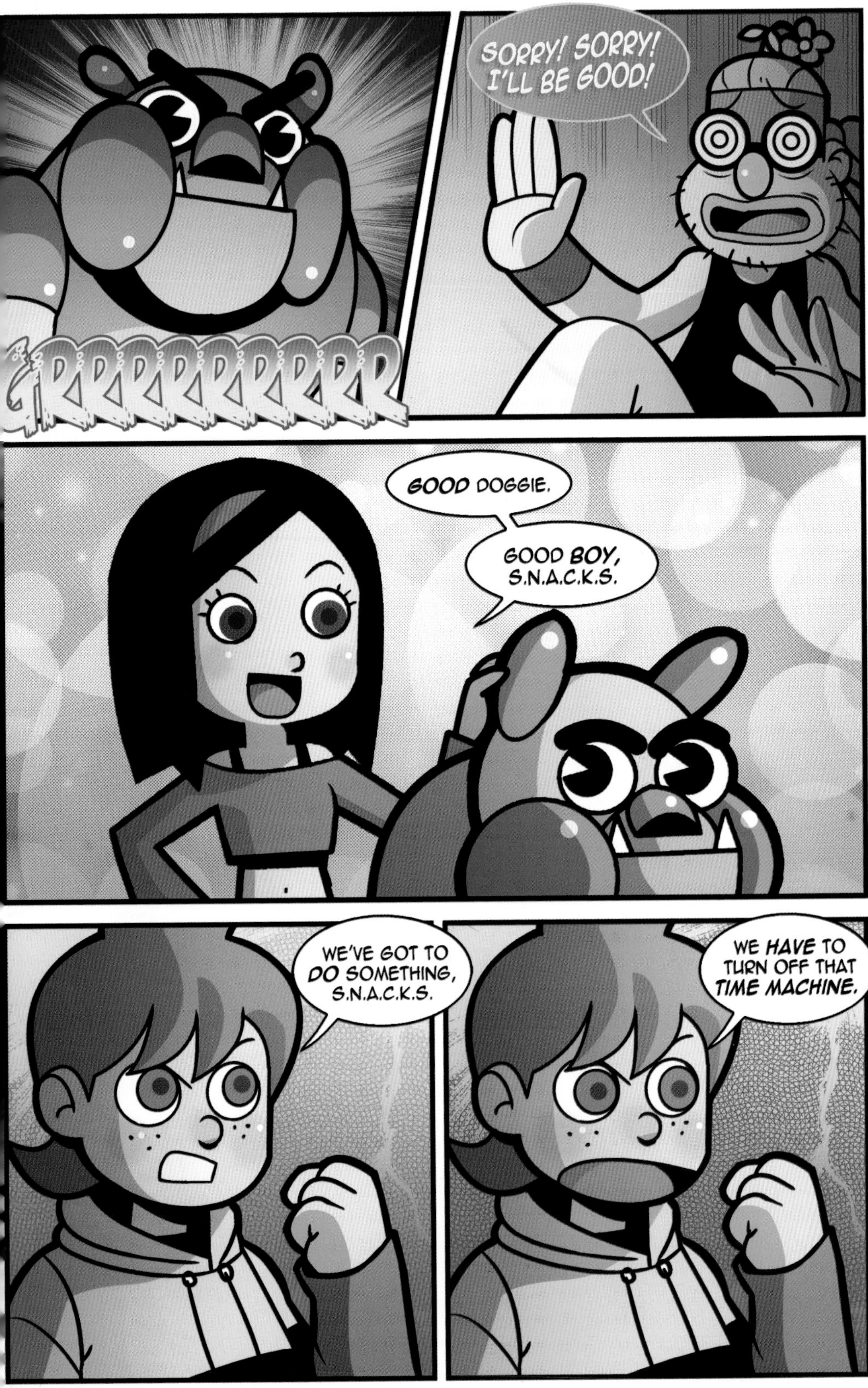
GRRRRRRRRRRR
SORRY! SORRY! I'LL BE GOOD!
GOOD DOGGIE.
GOOD BOY, S.N.A.C.K.S.
WE'VE GOT TO DO SOMETHING, S.N.A.C.K.S.
WE HAVE TO TURN OFF THAT TIME MACHINE.

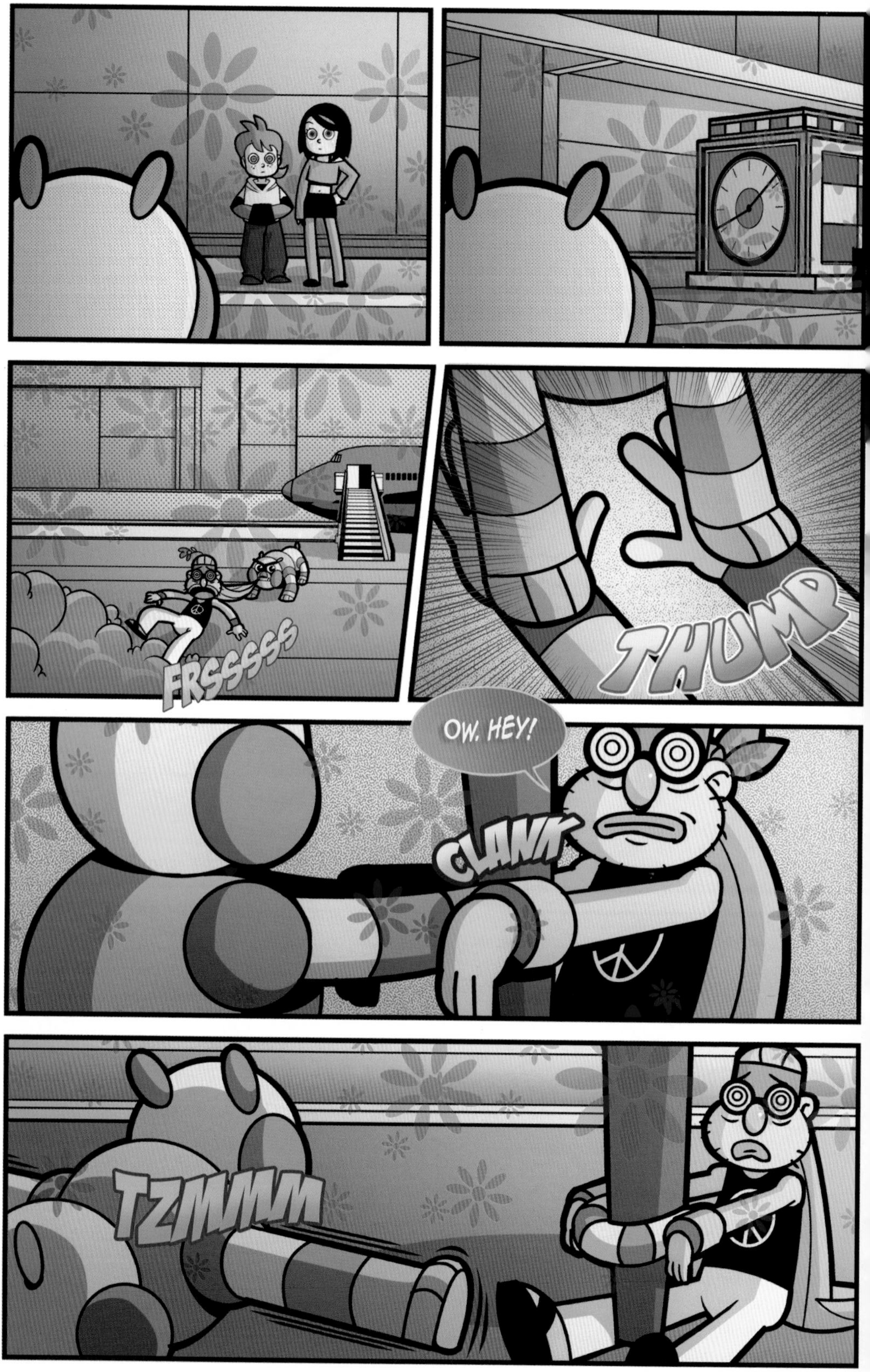
FRSSSSS
THUMP
OW. HEY!
CLANK
TZMMM

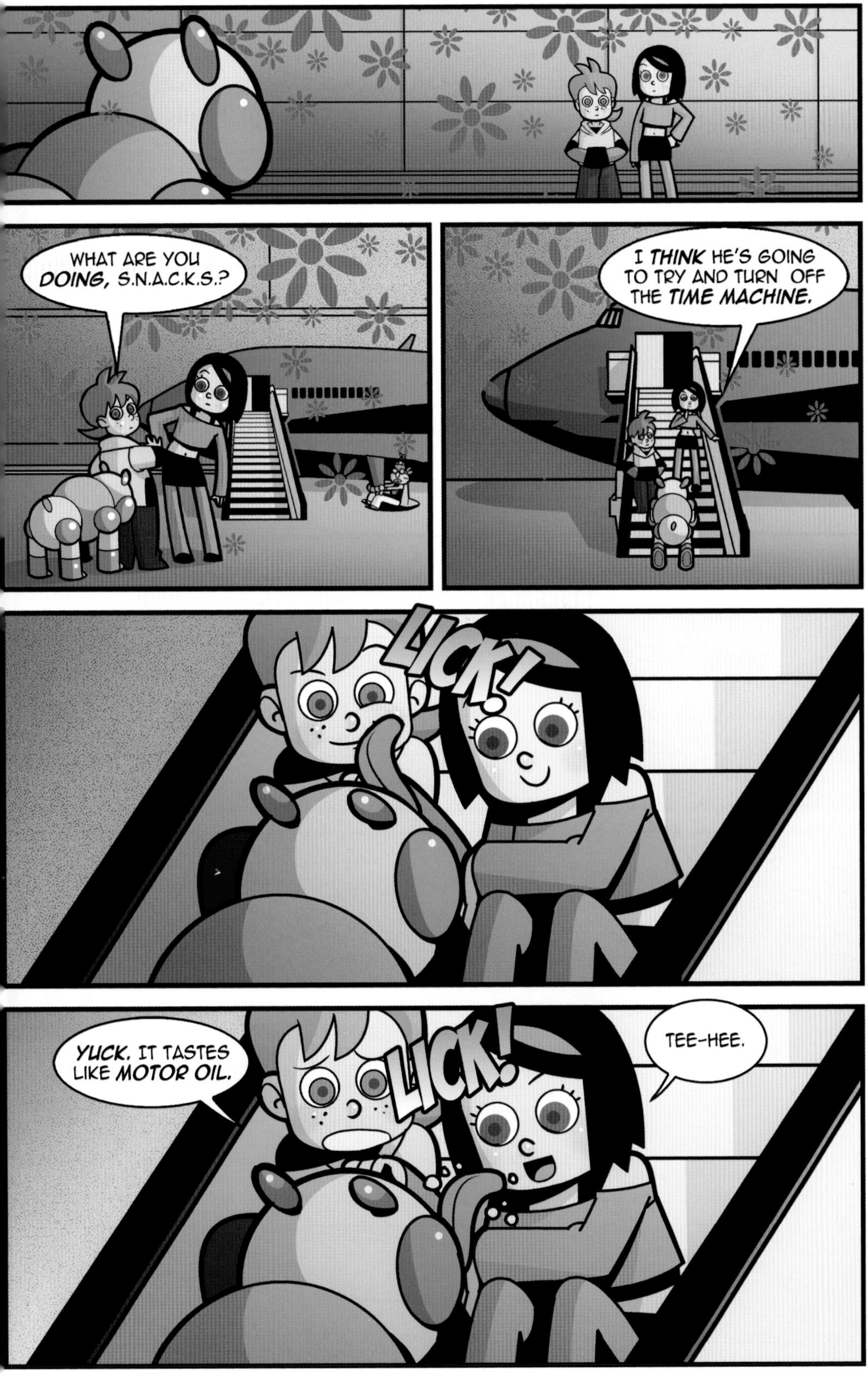
WHAT ARE YOU DOING, S.N.A.C.K.S.?
I THINK HE'S GOING TO TRY AND TURN OFF THE TIME MACHINE.
LICK!
YUCK. IT TASTES LIKE MOTOR OIL.
LICK!
TEE-HEE.

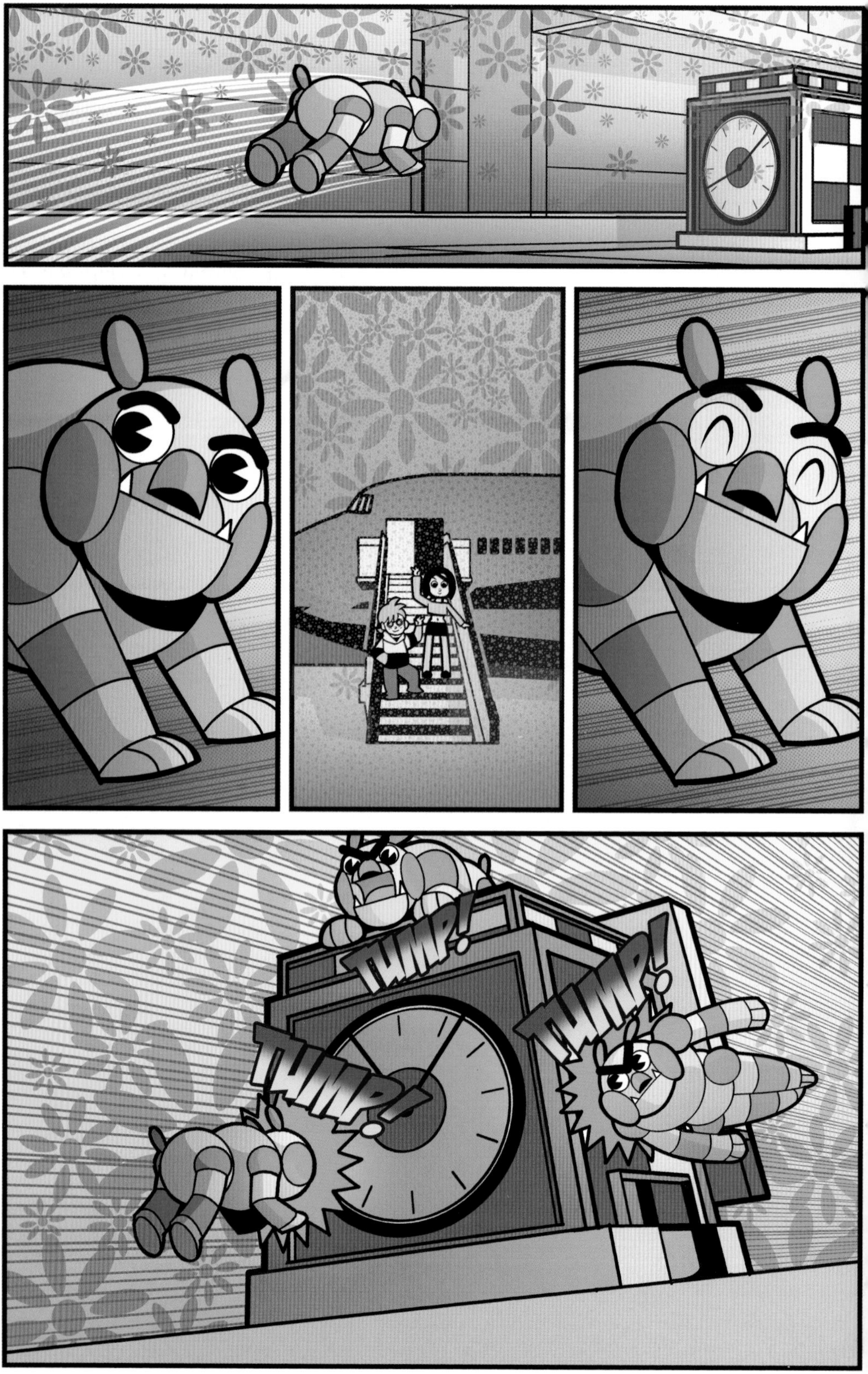

THUMP!
THUMP!
THUMP!

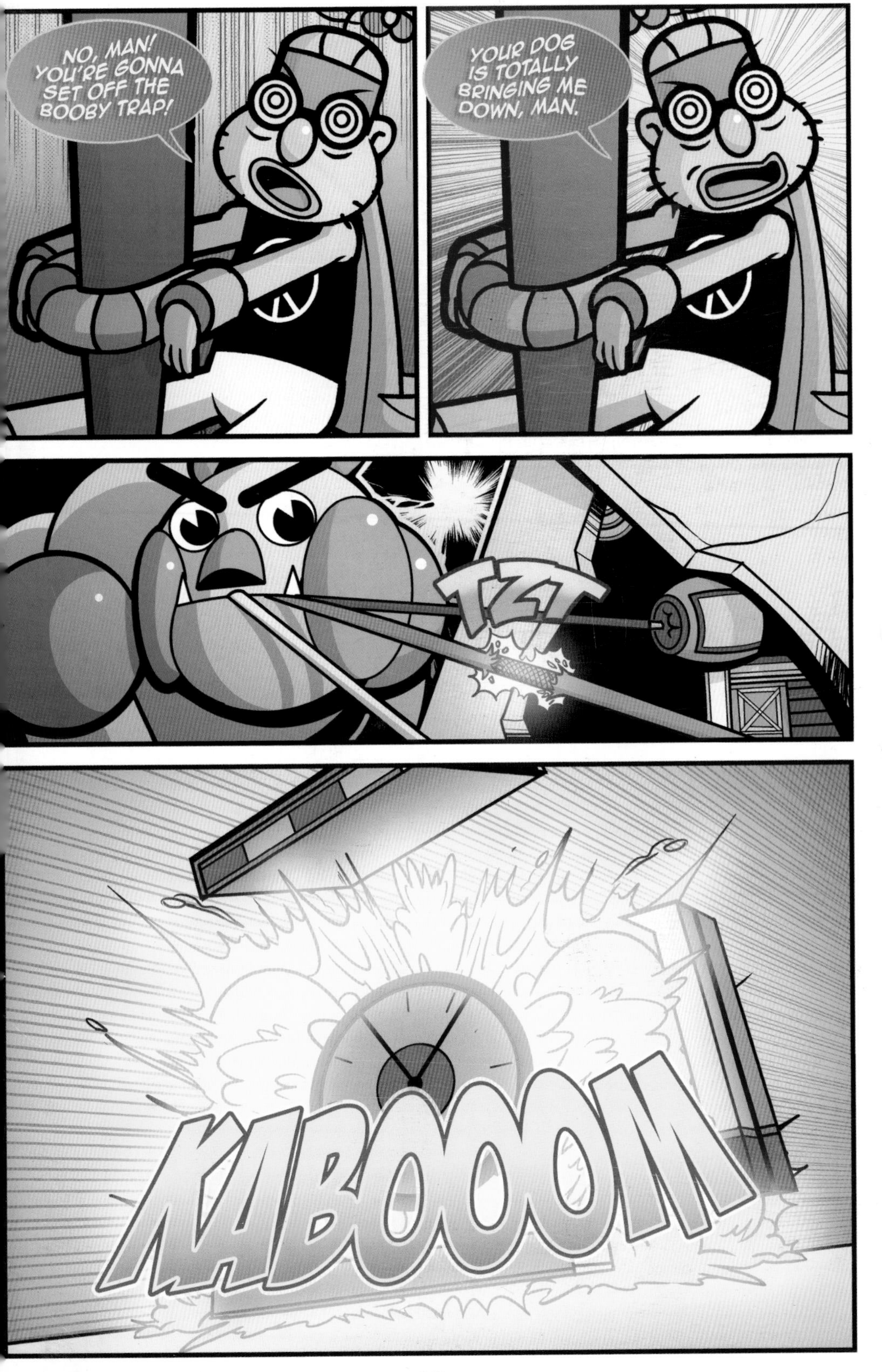
NO, MAN! YOU'RE GONNA SET OFF THE BOOBY TRAP!
YOUR DOG IS TOTALLY BRINGING ME DOWN, MAN.
TZZT
KABOOOM

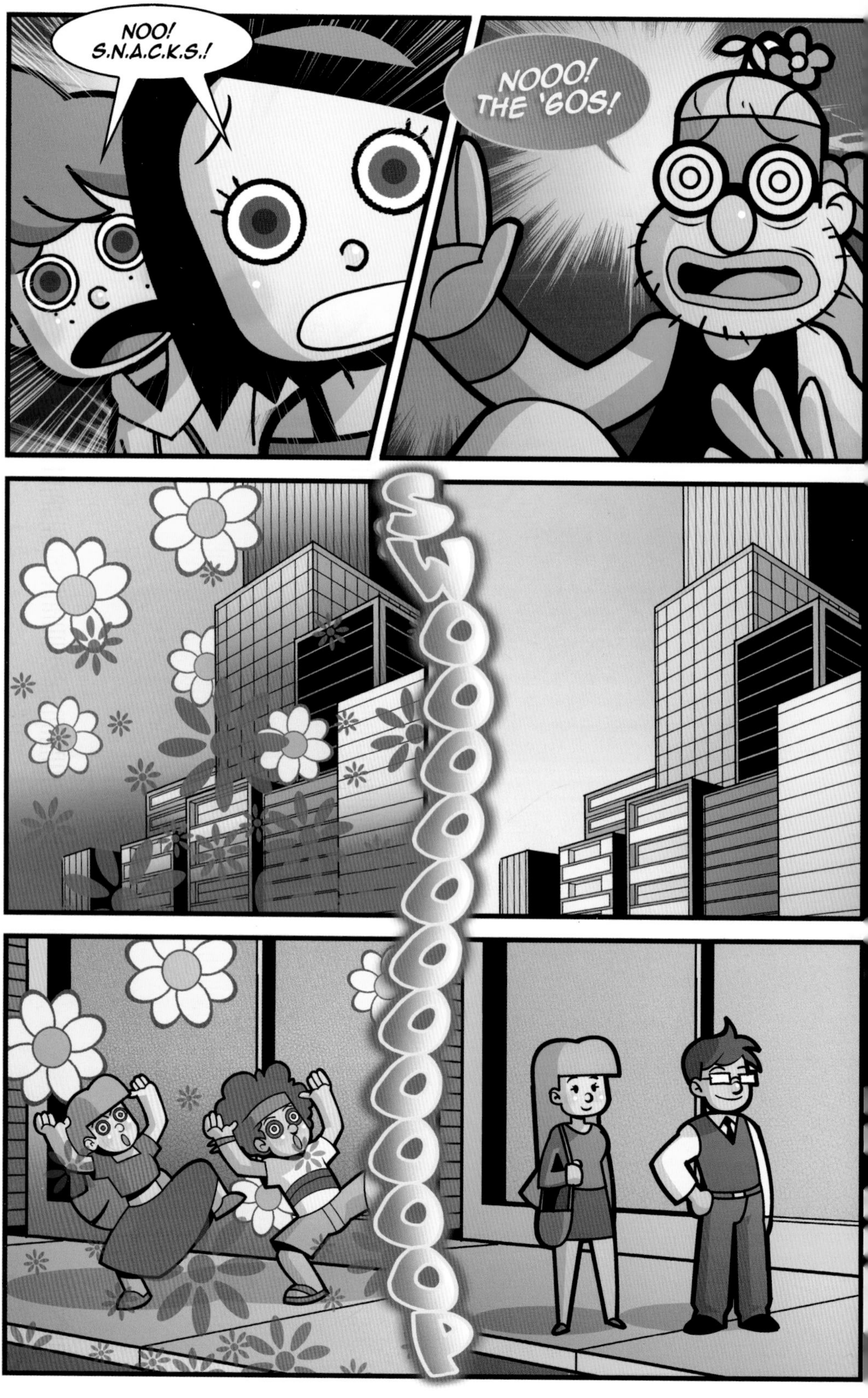
NOO! S.N.A.C.K.S.!
NOOO! THE '60S!
SWOOOOOOOOOOOOOP

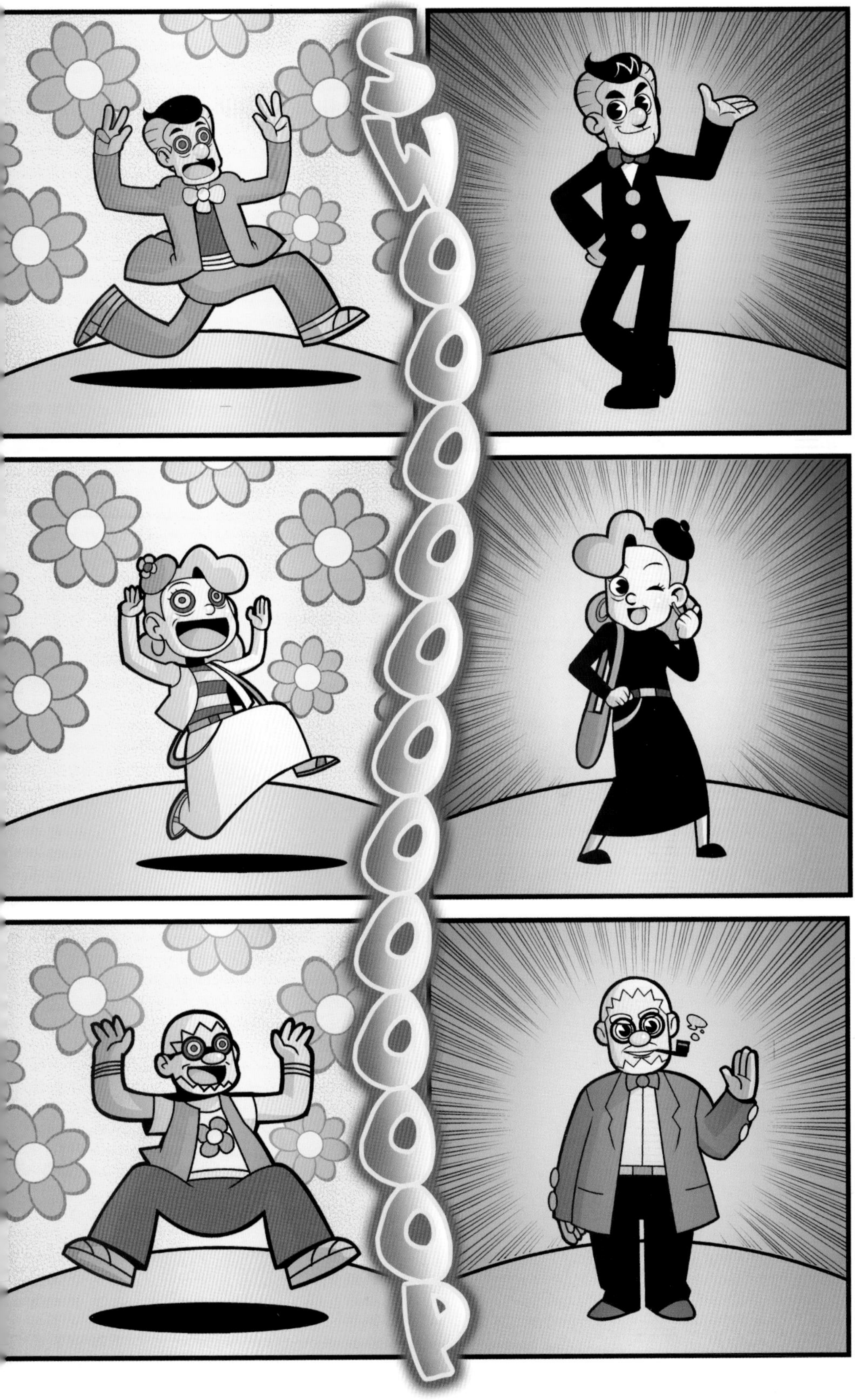
SWOOOOOOOOOOOOOP

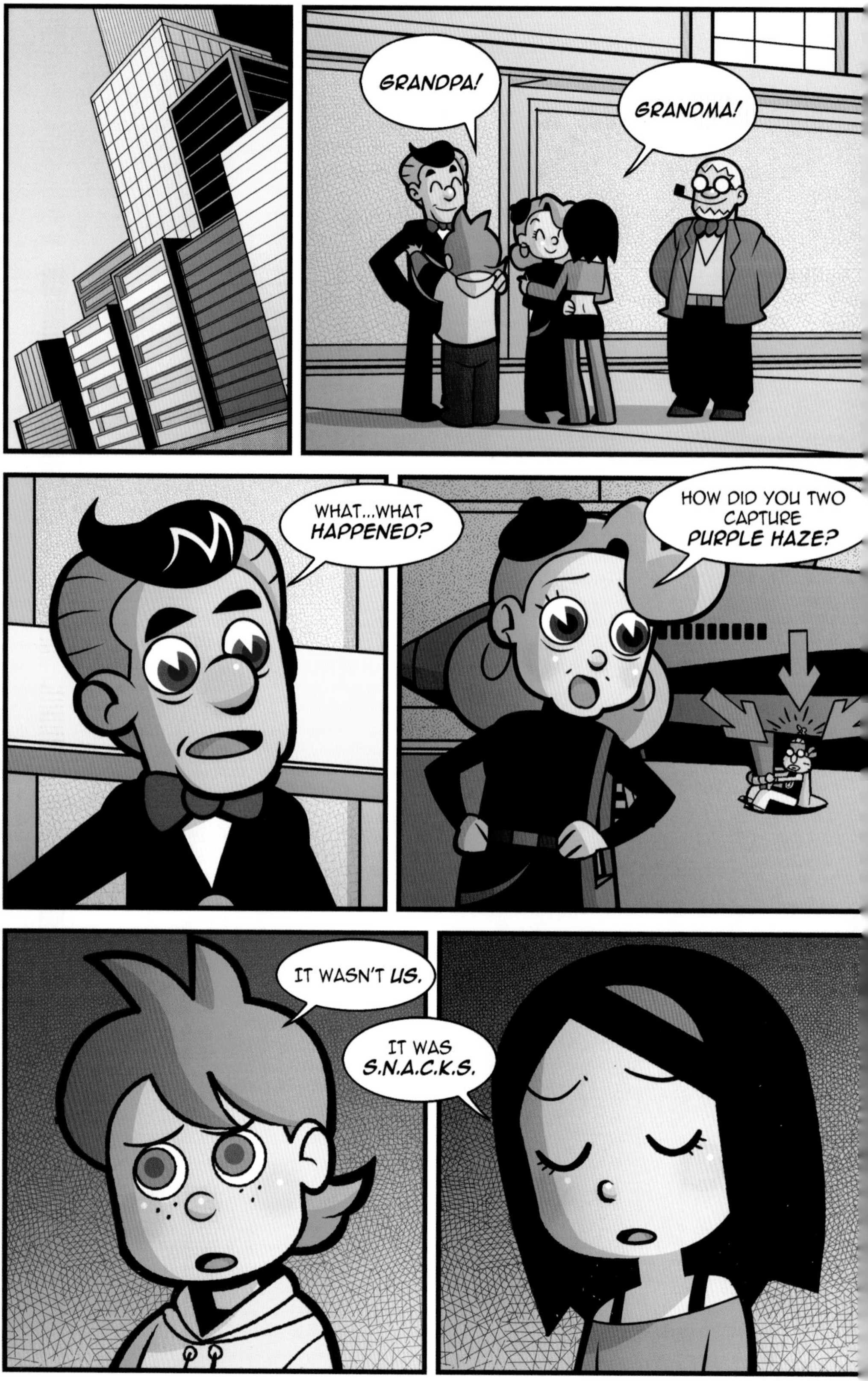
GRANDPA!
GRANDMA!
WHAT...WHAT HAPPENED?
HOW DID YOU TWO CAPTURE PURPLE HAZE?
IT WASN'T US.
IT WAS S.N.A.C.K.S.

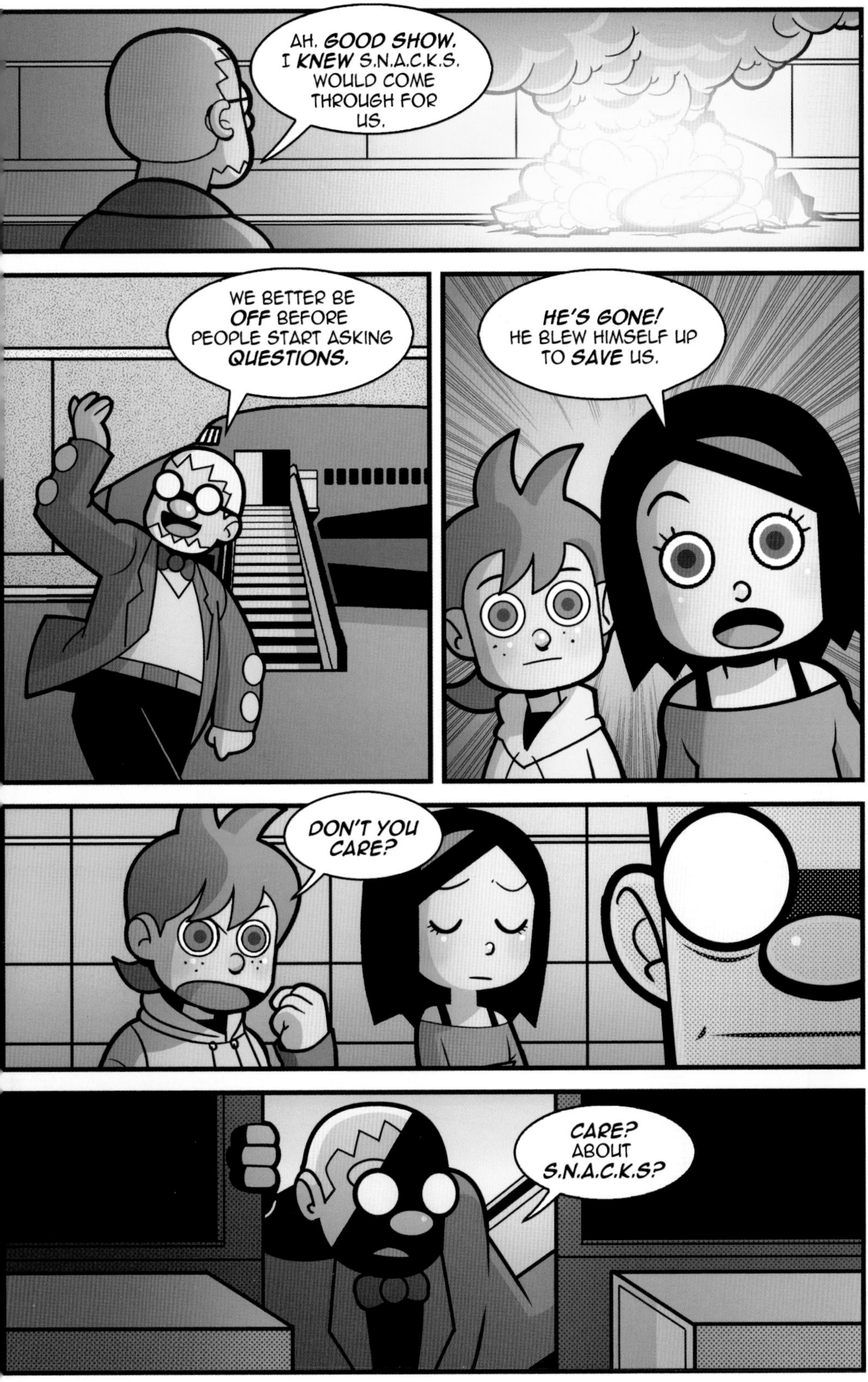
AH. GOOD SHOW. I KNEW S.N.A.C.K.S. WOULD COME THROUGH FOR US.
WE BETTER BE OFF BEFORE PEOPLE START ASKING QUESTIONS.
HE'S GONE! HE BLEW HIMSELF UP TO SAVE US.
DON'T YOU CARE?
CARE? ABOUT S.N.A.C.K.S?

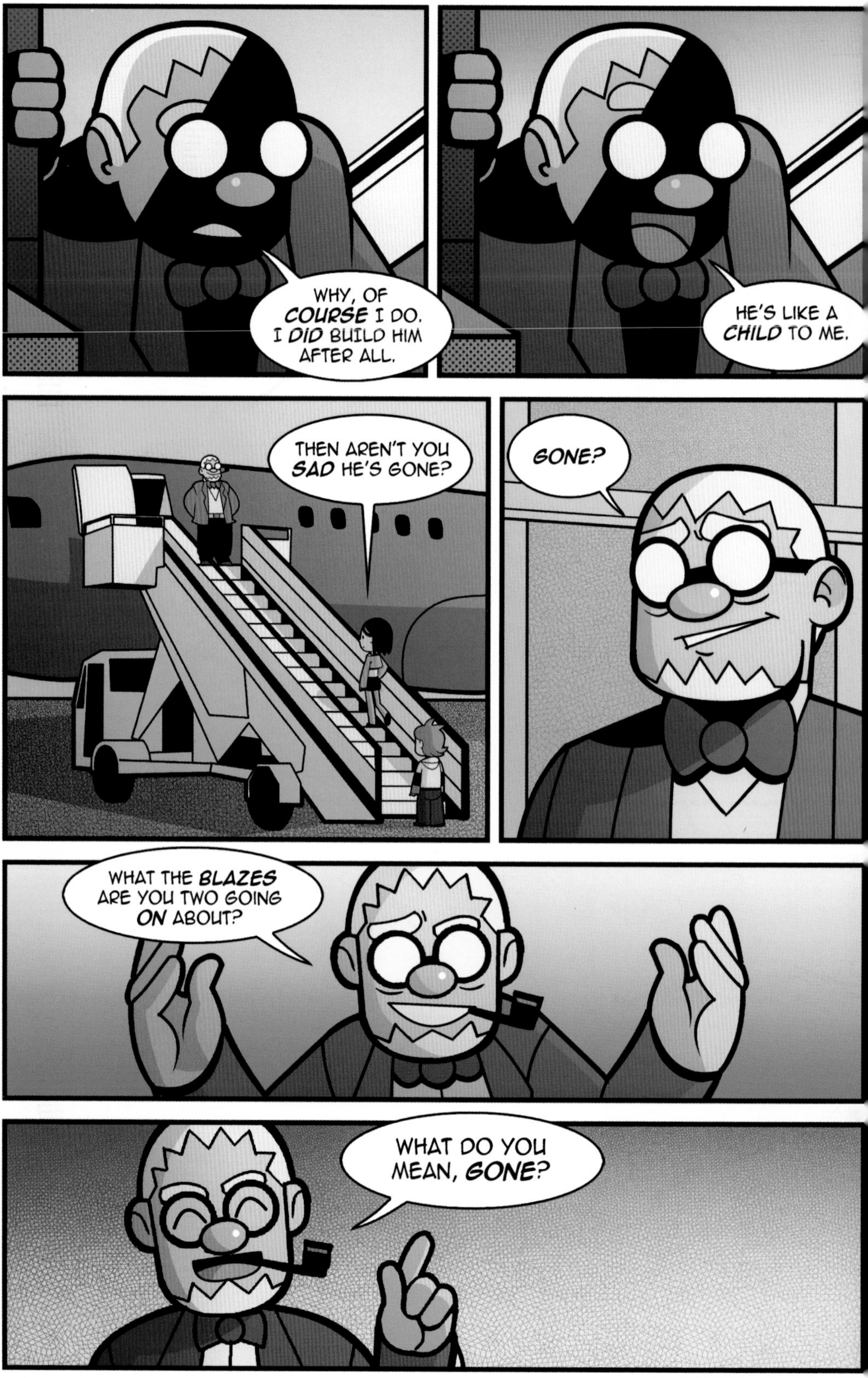
WHY, OF COURSE I DO. I DID BUILD HIM AFTER ALL.
HE'S LIKE A CHILD TO ME.
THEN AREN'T YOU SAD HE'S GONE?
GONE?
WHAT THE BLAZES ARE YOU TWO GOING ON ABOUT?
WHAT DO YOU MEAN, GONE?

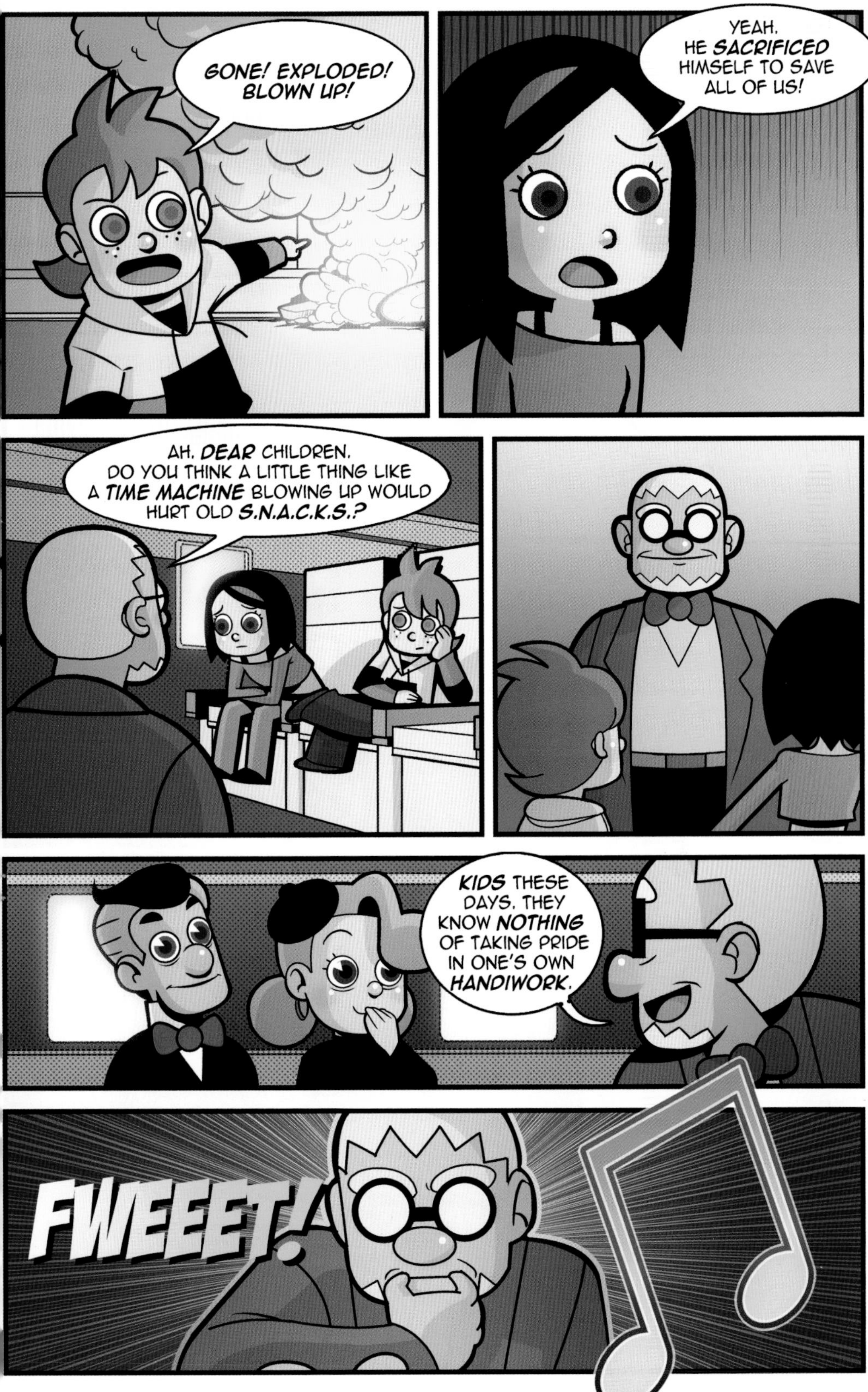
GONE! EXPLODED! BLOWN UP!
YEAH. HE SACRIFICED HIMSELF TO SAVE ALL OF US!
AH. DEAR CHILDREN. DO YOU THINK A LITTLE THING LIKE A TIME MACHINE BLOWING UP WOULD HURT OLD S.N.A.C.K.S.?
KIDS THESE DAYS. THEY KNOW NOTHING OF TAKING PRIDE IN ONE'S OWN HANDIWORK.
FWEEET!

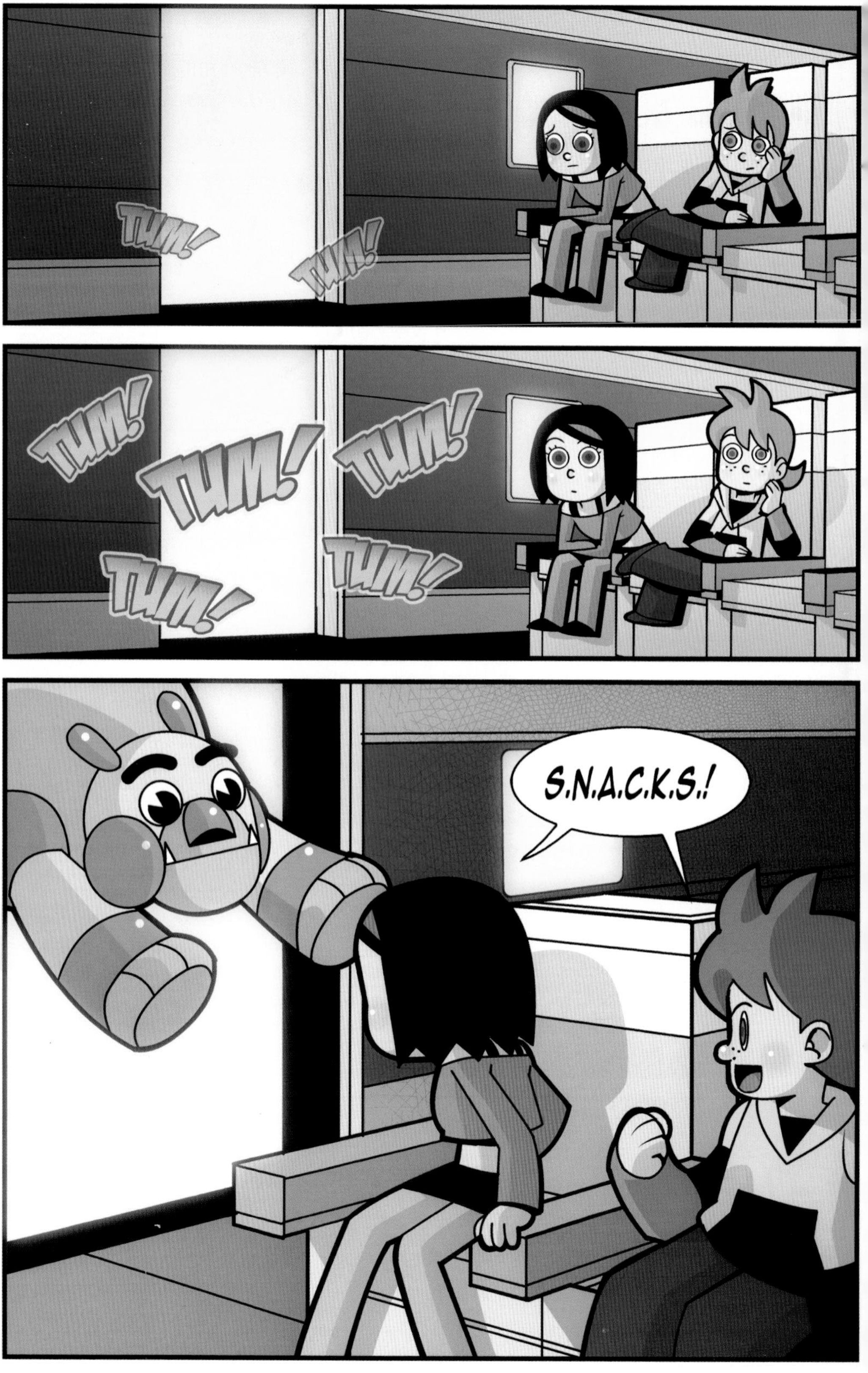
TUM!
TUM!
TUM!
TUM!
TUM!
TUM!
TUM!
S.N.A.C.K.S.!

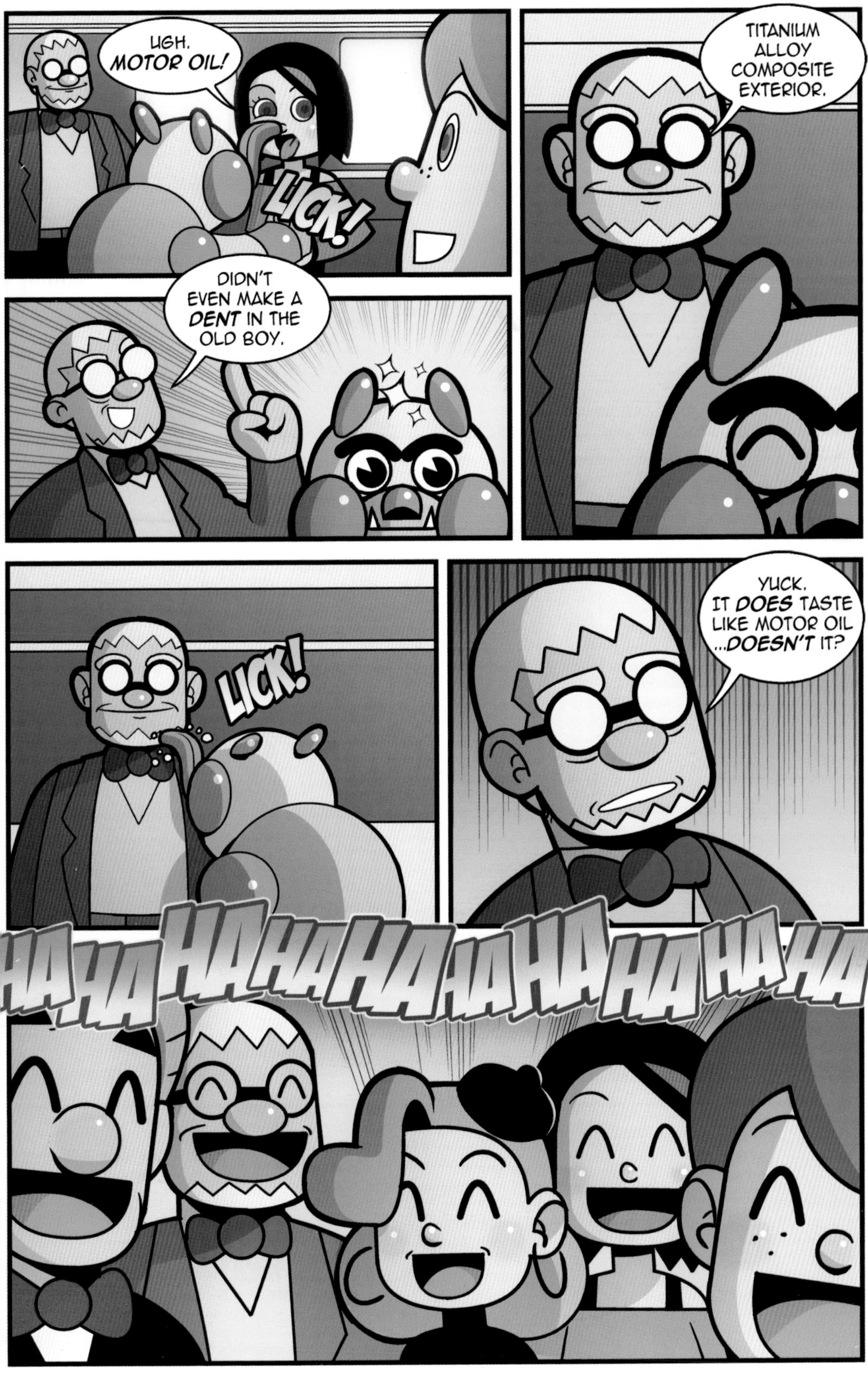
UGH. MOTOR OIL!
LICK!
TITANIUM ALLOY COMPOSITE EXTERIOR.
DIDN'T EVEN MAKE A DENT IN THE OLD BOY.
LICK!
YUCK. IT DOES TASTE LIKE MOTOR OIL ...DOESN'T IT?
HA HA HA HA HA HA HA HA HA HA HA HA

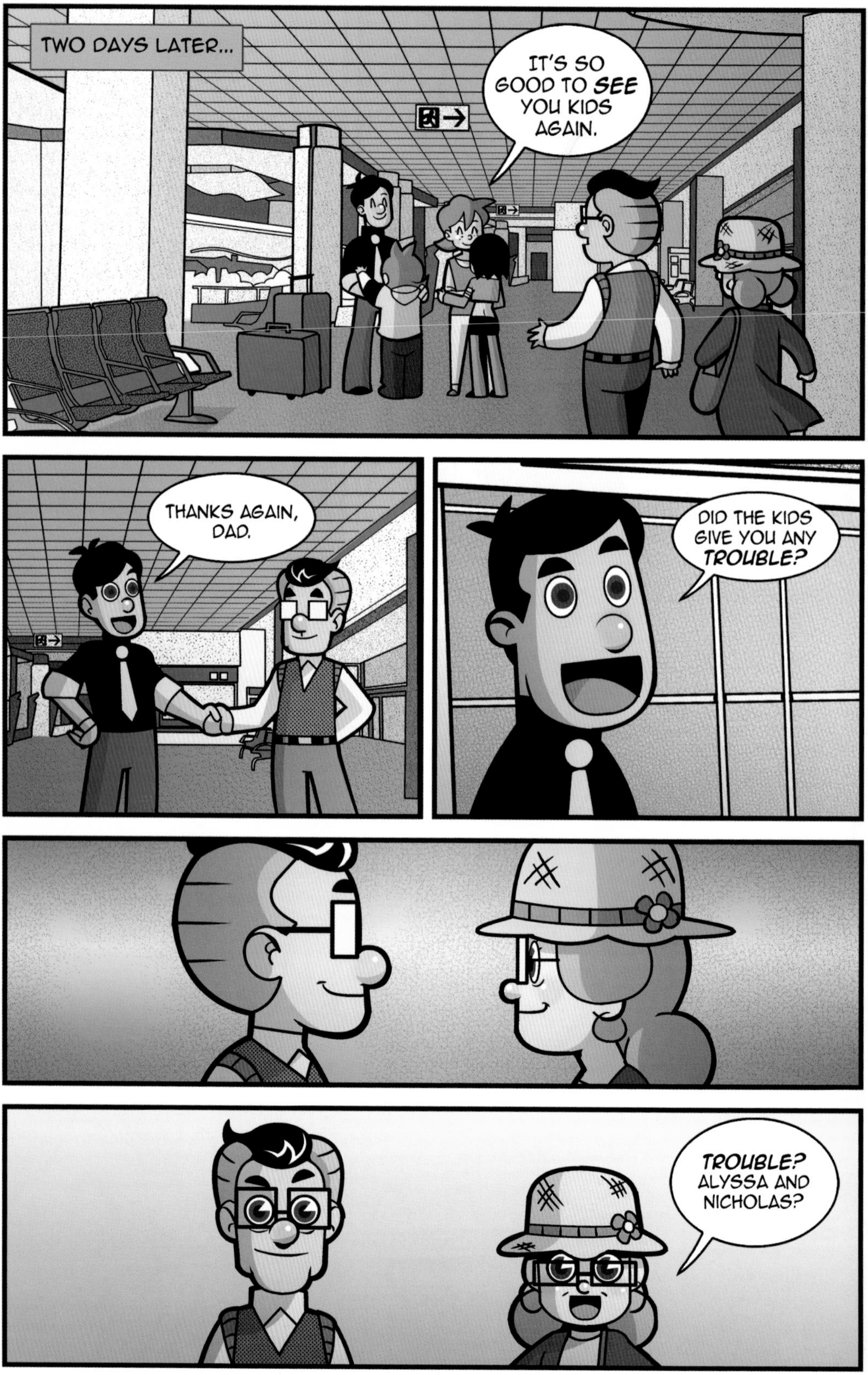
TWO DAYS LATER...
IT'S SO GOOD TO SEE YOU KIDS AGAIN.
THANKS AGAIN, DAD.
DID THE KIDS GIVE YOU ANY TROUBLE?
TROUBLE? ALYSSA AND NICHOLAS?

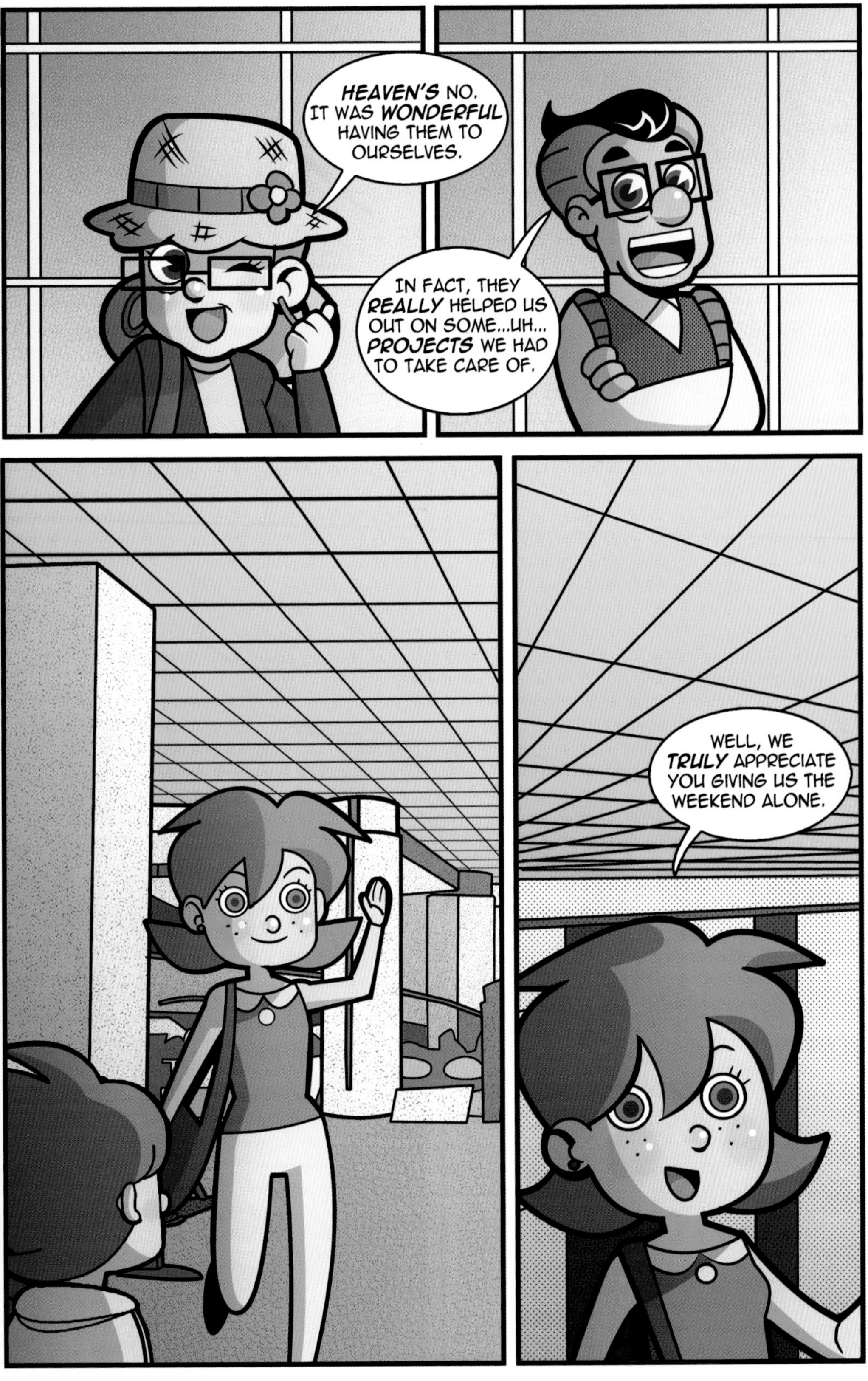
HEAVEN'S NO. IT WAS WONDERFUL HAVING THEM TO OURSELVES.
IN FACT, THEY REALLY HELPED US OUT ON SOME...UH... PROJECTS WE HAD TO TAKE CARE OF.
WELL, WE TRULY APPRECIATE YOU GIVING US THE WEEKEND ALONE.

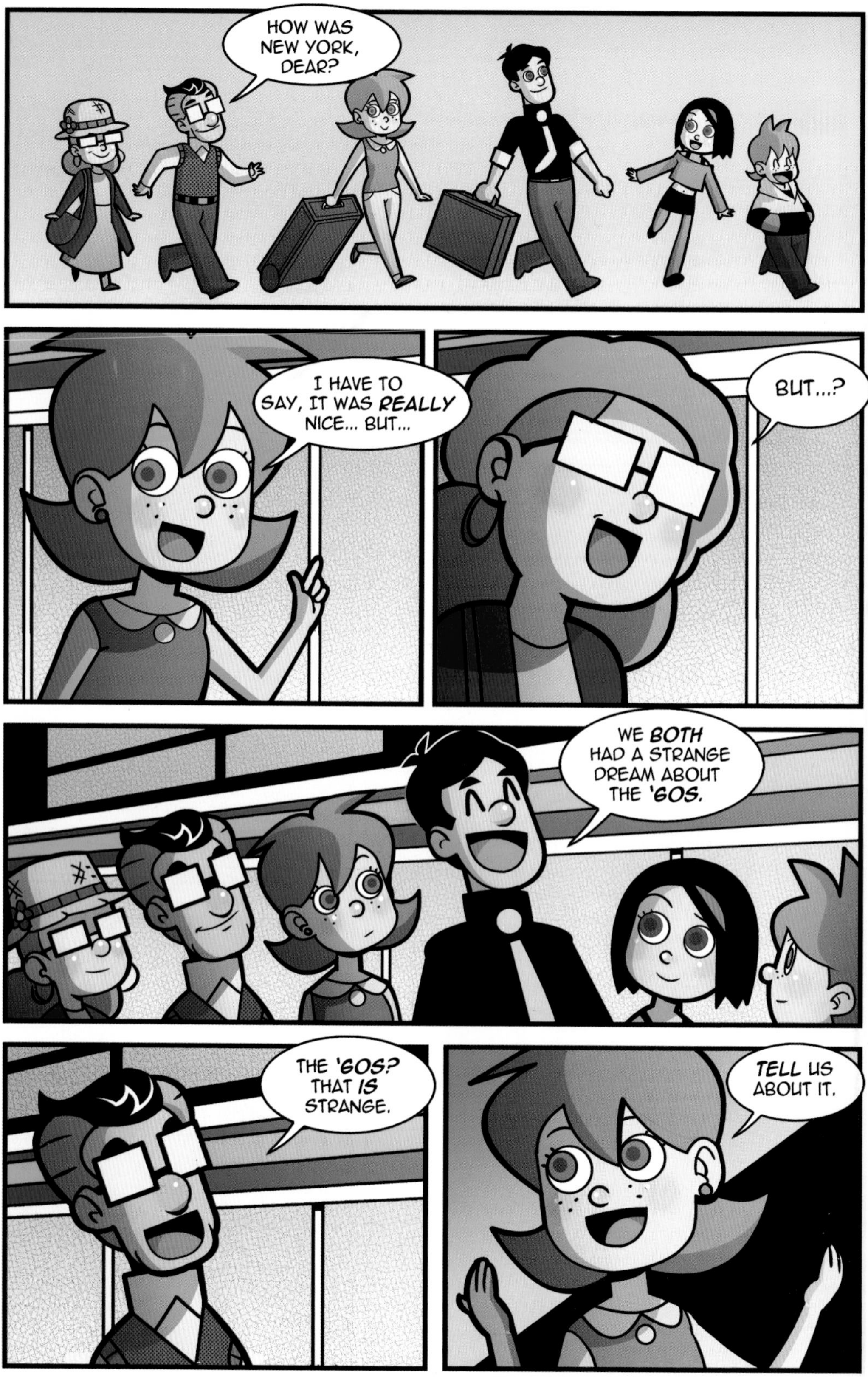
HOW WAS NEW YORK, DEAR?
I HAVE TO SAY, IT WAS REALLY NICE... BUT...
BUT...?
WE BOTH HAD A STRANGE DREAM ABOUT THE '60S.
THE '60S? THAT IS STRANGE.
TELL US ABOUT IT.

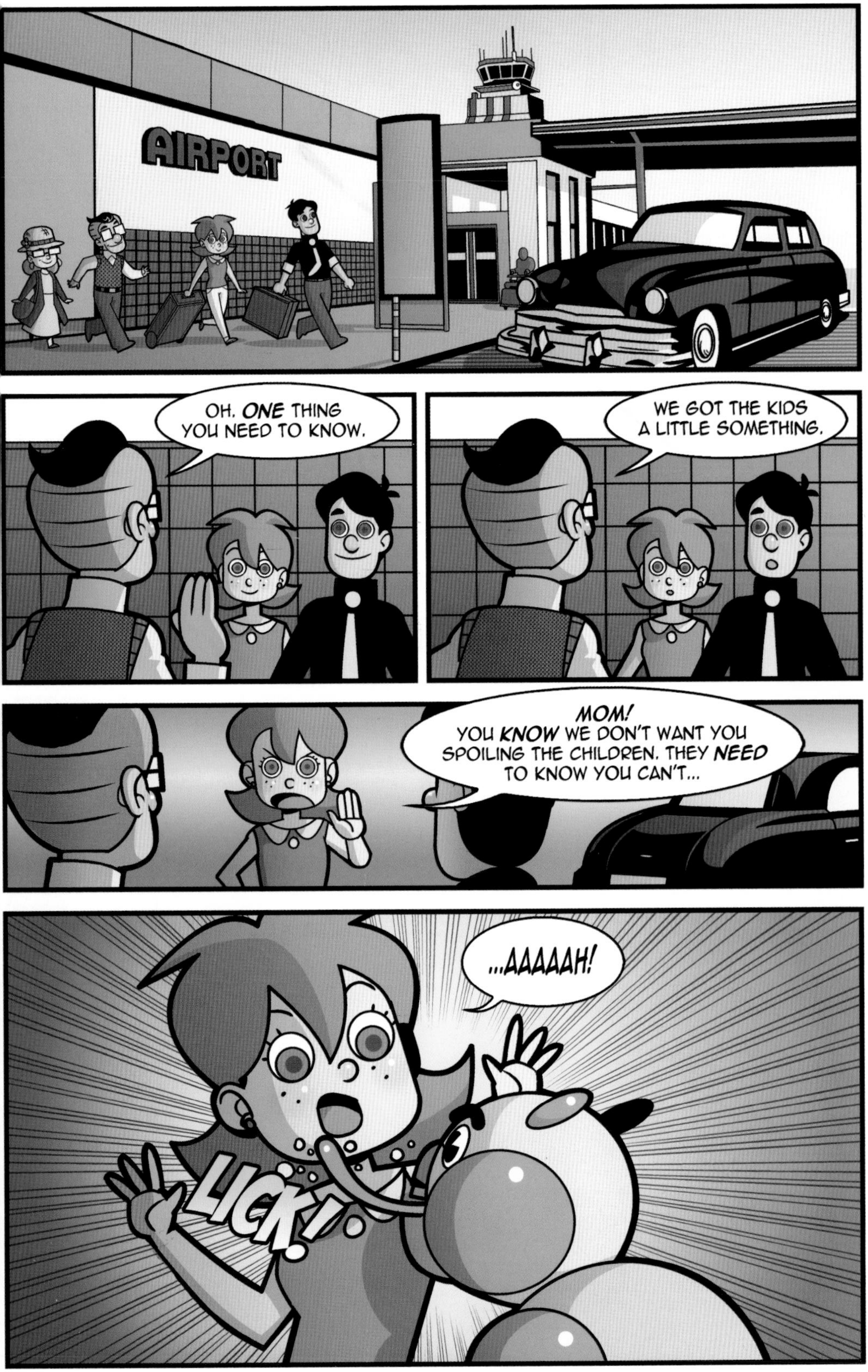
AIRPORT
OH. ONE THING YOU NEED TO KNOW.
WE GOT THE KIDS A LITTLE SOMETHING.
MOM! YOU KNOW WE DON'T WANT YOU SPOILING THE CHILDREN. THEY NEED TO KNOW YOU CAN'T...
...AAAAAH!
LICK!

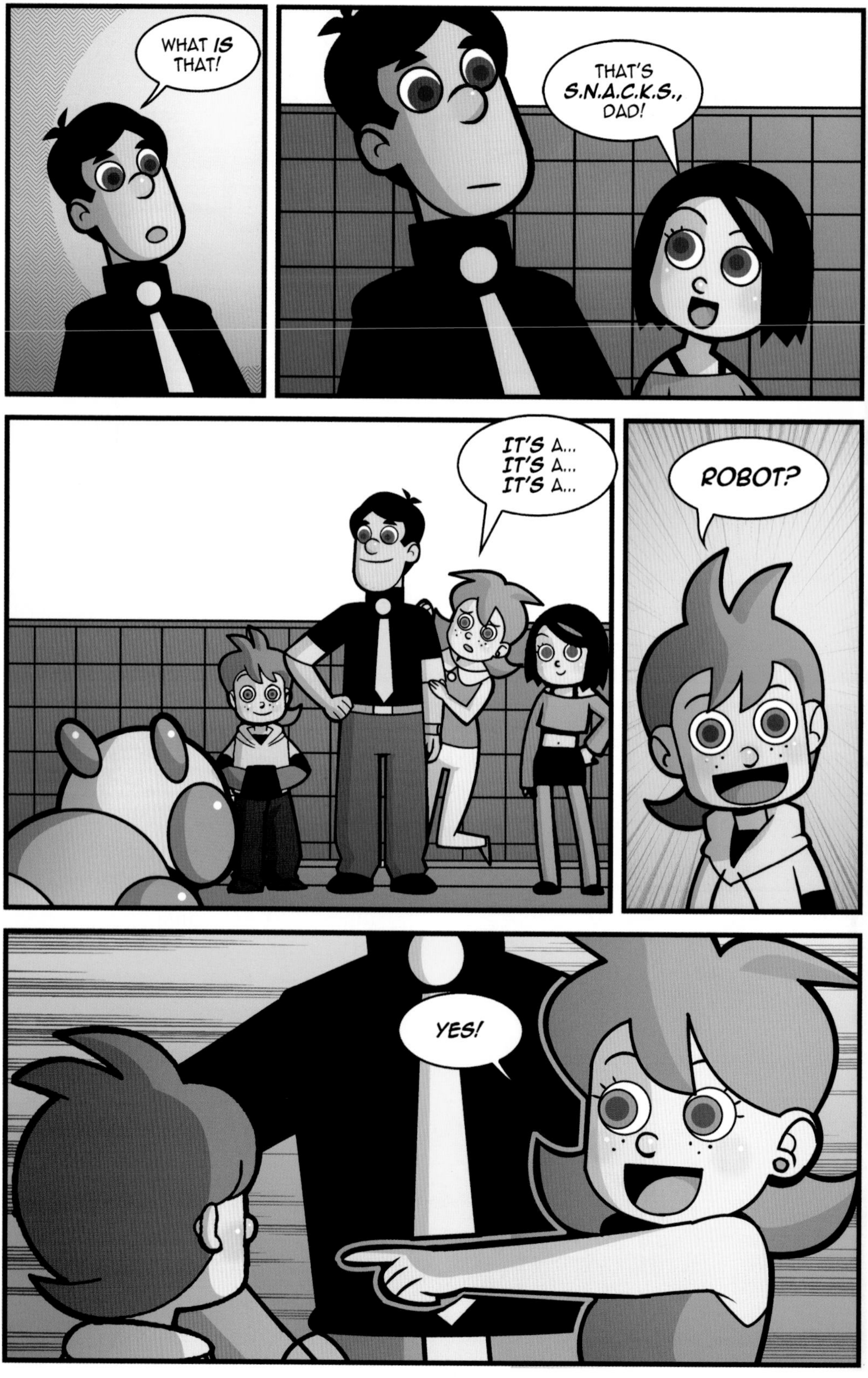
WHAT IS THAT!
THAT'S S.N.A.C.K.S., DAD!
IT'S A... IT'S A... IT'S A...
ROBOT?
YES!

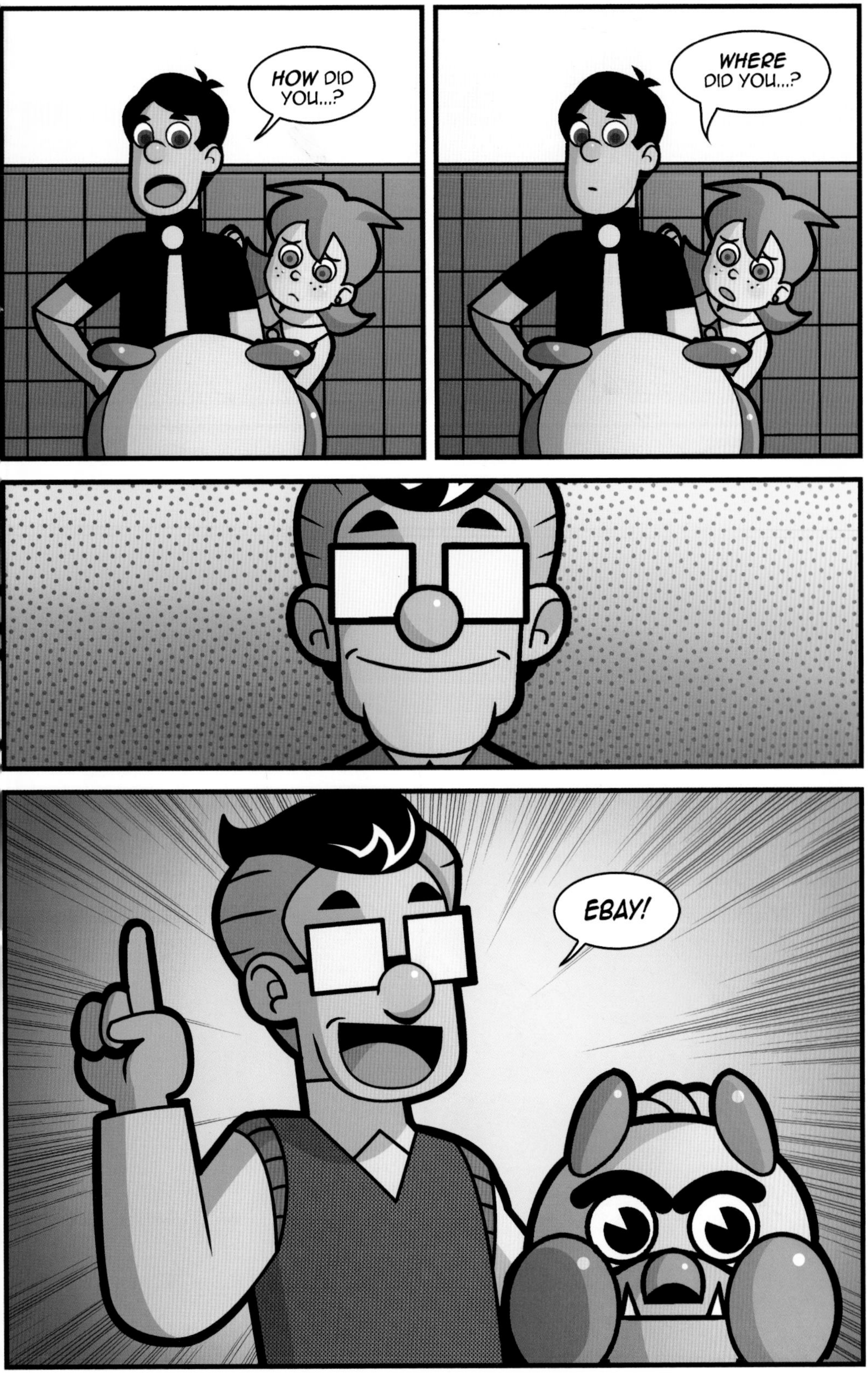
HOW DID YOU...?
WHERE DID YOU...?
EBAY!

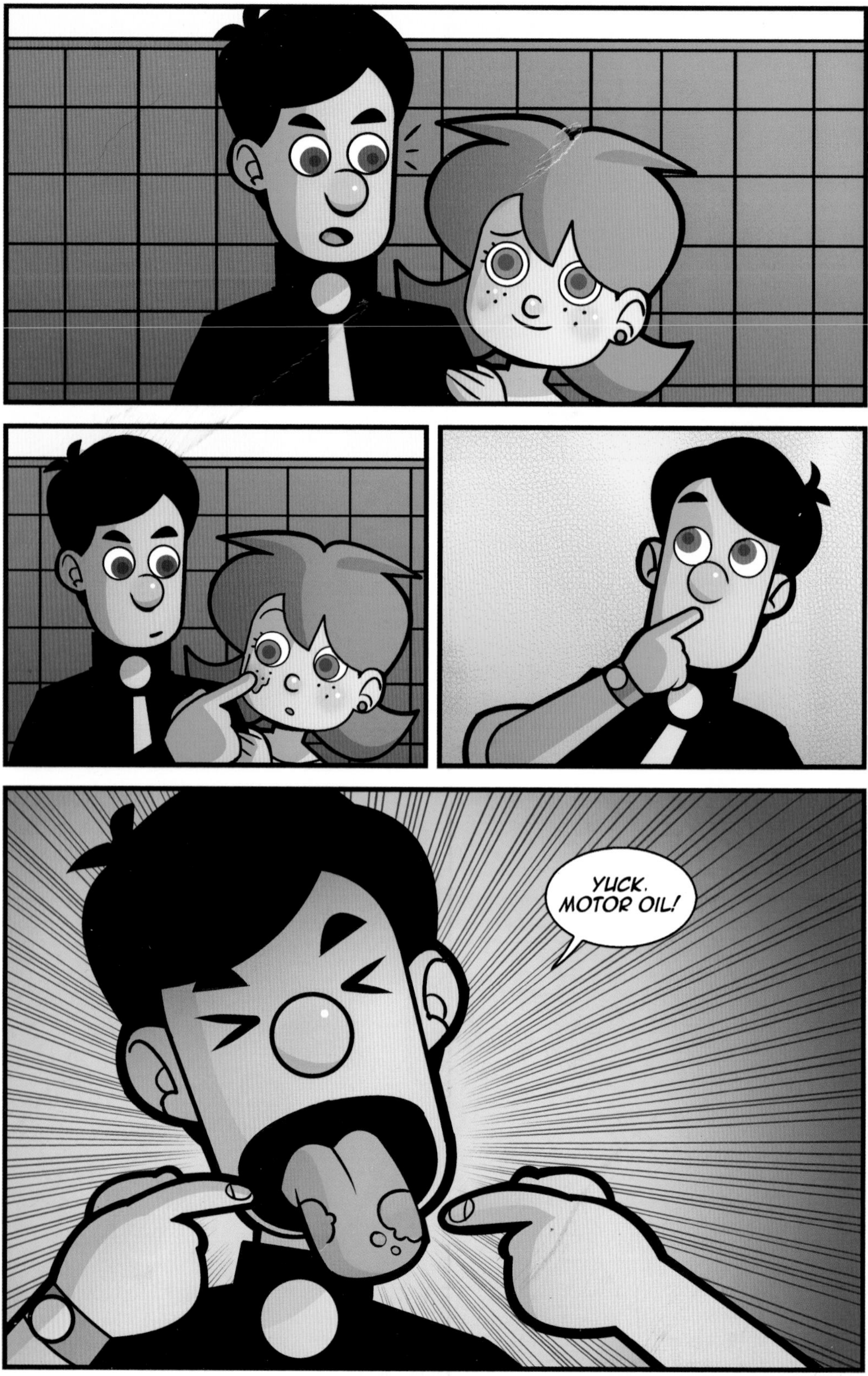
YUCK.
MOTOR OIL!